Riptide

Crime Stories
by
New England Writers

Edited by

Skye Alexander
Kate Flora
Susan Oleksiw

LEVEL BEST BOOKS
PRIDES CROSSING, MASSACHUSETTS 01965

Level Best Books
P.O. Box 161
Prides Crossing, Massachusetts 01965
www.levelbestbooks.com

text composition/design by Susan Oleksiw
cover design by Skye Alexander
Printed in the USA

ISBN 0-9700984-1-3

Library of Congress Catalog Card data available.

First Edition
10 9 8 7 6 5 4 3 2 1

Contents

Introduction

It's been an exciting and educational year since we birthed our first anthology of crime stories by New England writers in 2003. As those of you who know us may recall, Level Best Books began as a one-time effort to publish an anthology of crime fiction before going on to other works. It has turned into much more.

We spent a year working on *Undertow: Crime Stories by New England Writers*, and another year promoting it. In the process, we fell in love with our writers, with our collaboration, with the booksellers and libraries who supported our endeavor, and with the idea of mingling old voices and new voices to produce a snapshot of the New England crime scene. When we introduced *Undertow* at the second annual New England Crime Bake, we got to watch the pleasure on the faces of our first-time authors as they signed their published work for the first time. We got to take pride in a job well done. And we knew we wanted to do it again.

Riptide: Crime Stories by New England Writers is the result of that decision—our second annual anthology, with a much bigger collection of stories, a wider range of voices. Once again, we have an opportunity to treat mystery readers to great fiction by established talents and introduce rising new stars.

The best part of this business sometimes, oftentimes, is being part of a community of writers. The beginners remind us of the day our agents called and said, "Are you sitting down? Are you ready?" and then gave us the good news about that first book contract. The more established writers show us how grace and generosity can go hand in hand with success. Many authors remain good friends after years of sharing advice and support.

Writers work in isolation. No one sits beside us to say, "Pay no attention to that evil little voice that is telling you to rub a red magic marker over that blank page. No, you don't have to throw your beloved computer out the window just because that paragraph is awful. Yes, you will write a better one." But mystery writers always have someone they can call for help and encouragement, someone who'll answer questions, who won't smirk at another's difficulties, who won't show off or brag about a recent success.

Perhaps mystery writers are so down to earth, so decent to our peers, because we deal with death and violence on a regular basis (at least in our imaginations). But whatever the reason, the community of writers we know and belong to is a special reward for the hard work of telling a story well, then finding someone to put money behind that story so others can read it, too.

So, read these stories, enjoy the different visions each writer presents of New England and the world. Scan the biographies and gasp a little at the diverse experiences in these lives. Then think about them all as a group, men and women who find something redeeming in writing about crime and in sharing their vision, their gifts, and their passion with readers. If you're someone who wants to write mysteries, or already does, these are your neighbors. And if you're one of those wonderful, special people who love stories and read them again and again, you are part of our community, too. May you find here life-long friends.

Skye Alexander
Kate Flora
Susan Oleksiw

October 2004

By Design

Janice Law

Le Corbusier said houses were "machines for living." Not so. Houses are shells for the soul. More, they are instruments of the soul like violins. They suggest, they shape, they insinuate. Great artists all know this. Would Poe's Montresor have conceived revenge against his victim without those vast palazzo cellars? Would Stoker's Dracula have managed in some suburban villa? Give Kafka's Josef K rooms full of light and air, top the court with a classical rotunda, and *The Trial* evaporates.

But those, you say, are literary creations, the airy stuff of writers' brains. True, true, but consider the effort put into homes, into décor; remember the industries supported by home improvement, DIY fanatics, decorators, arrangers, and renovators of all sorts. Please don't pretend it's all for comfort or status or, worst yet, for that lowliest of aspirations, convenience.

My case will be instructive. I was not seriously looking for a new apartment when I visited the converted hotel at the behest of my friend Nate Cohen. He owns five floors of vintage Back Bay charm and nostalgia, a brownstone pile with high ceilings, fine architectural detail, and a semi-scandalous history. Good stuff, but I had a valuable condo apartment in the South End.

Nate had called me in on some design questions, since historic interiors of the nineteenth and early twentieth centuries are my specialty. Our consultation finished, he invited me to see the newly built penthouse. Not my thing, normally, completely new or really old being my preference every time, but he insisted.

A clever bit of engineering, he said. They'd constructed the addition right over the shallow hip roof of the original, then recreated the profile in the roof over the penthouse. "A fabulous space. You have to see it."

"Over the original roof? You didn't tear out the old structure?"

"Preserved for posterity. And keeps the former attic for some of the services."

We took the newly installed elevator up to the penthouse, which I could see was a fine job, modern and clean, but with tasteful stylistic echoes of the original building beneath. Lovely views, too, with glimpses of Trinity Church. The bathroom was particularly fine, limestone and glistening white tile set in a running bond, not as ostentatious as marble, but appropriate and luxurious. There was an authentic nineteenth-century sink and tub, plus a modern shower tucked into one corner.

"Very nice, but the plumbing must have been a nightmare, what with that extra roof underneath." Hear that? Pay attention! When have I ever been interested in plumbing? In my estimation, one pays other people to worry about the details of plumbing.

"You can bet that was a major issue. See this?" He lifted the mat that lay in front of the sink. A square, outlined in brass, was set into the floor. "The trap," Nate said.

"Really?"

"Have to lock it if you have children, but it's convenient for workmen," Nate said, and as if I would be interested, he grasped the neat brass ring and lifted the square. I saw pipes disappearing into a vast darkness.

"So you—or a repairman—could actually go down there?"

"Oh, sure. You can stand on the roof. Slopes, of course, but there's a ton of space. A ton. Too bad it's not saleable. We've got hundreds of square feet of prime Boston real estate down there."

"A little short on light and air," I said, but already I was infected with the spirit of the place. Two days later I made an offer, and in three months, having worked out the financing and sold my former apartment, I moved into the penthouse.

I like to be on site when I'm working on a design project. Of course, the apartment was move-in condition, as they say in the trade, but I had ideas for improvements, cosmetic changes, and other, only dimly realized plans. I chose William Morris's Willow pattern for the dining room. Maybe a tad familiar, but a personal favorite and right for the period of the hotel. I like the arabesques made by the thin, narrow willow leaves and the overall effect of a net.

More Morris for the master bedroom; there's a company out West that does ravishing reproductions. I'd decided on a theme, arabesques and thickets and interwoven branches, a bow to the tastes of the turn-of-the-century hotel, on the one hand, and to the whole new "green" mood of today, on the other. "So clever," my friends said. "So characteristic."

I'd gotten rid of most of my old furniture in the move. I like to do that now and then, clear out, start with a new palette, a clean slate. It refreshes the eye. Besides, I like to live in a place for a while, catch the vibrations, find out what the space wants for décor, for furnishings. You'd be surprised how clearly certain rooms communicate.

Bentwood, this one said, bentwood and craftsman and a few classic pieces, modern and French. I like the more austere periods of French furniture. And a dark tonality. Yes, yes, lovely light from the big windows, but the woodwork wanted to be dark, the walls rich-toned with the subtle patterns of the Morris wallpapers.

During this time of improvements and decoration, I never opened the trap to the roof below. Are you surprised at my self-discipline? My patience? Remember, I owned the penthouse, and I had lots of time. It was only when the decorations were almost complete, when the absorbing work of choosing and shopping and overseeing was finished, that I sat one night in my living room—rose and aubergine with velvet drapes and parquet floor—and knew between one drink and the next that the time had come.

After changing into a pair of jeans and a sweatshirt, I went to the kitchen closet for the caver's lamp I'd acquired and for the stout length of yellow nylon rope which, like Ariadne, I intended to use as a guide. I went into the bathroom to move the mat and had, just at that moment, a little fear that it had all been an illusion, that there was no trap, that my friend Nate had in some way deceived me.

But there it was, a darkly shadowed rectangle opening to the underworld. People aren't educated classically these days, more's the pity. Hadean openings like Lake Avernus were a feature of the ancient world. Dante stumbled on his entrance that night in the trackless wood, and a grieving Orpheus found the steps to Tartarus. We don't believe such things any more, so we are not forewarned about dangerous spaces.

I tied my rope to the sturdy leg of the fine antique sink and dropped the coil down into the darkness. Have I mentioned that I have an absolute horror of dark and enclosed spaces, and, at the same time, an equally strong compulsion to explore them? The very thought of caves and crypts fills me with terror and excitement and a wonderfully heightened alertness.

These sensations began when I was a mere infant, creeping toward the bottom of my crib beneath the blankets and shrieking with fear at the difficulty of turning around under Mother's neatly tucked sheets. I graduated to caves and tunnels and labyrinthine cellars.

Here I had my very own hidden space. I switched on my lamp

and slipped through the opening. All the rooms with plumbing were in the center of the apartment, just above the peak of the roof, and my feet touched old metal before my head had quite dropped below the surface of the limestone bathroom floor.

I crouched and looked around. In front of me, the peak of the roof rose almost to the penthouse joists and beams, long horizontals broken only by the shaft for the elevator. Behind me, a long shallow slope extended to the outer walls, where I discovered that one could walk comfortably along the old gutter behind the parapet, now replaced by the outer walls of the addition.

I traced the circumference of the roof, my rope in hand, just in case I stepped onto some rotting fabric, or some depredations of the plumbers, who had, indeed, hacked out a chase for the pipes that disappeared through the roof and down into the original building. The air was close, with an agreeable smell of new wood and metal, and another, disagreeable, odor of old soot, mold, and city dirt. I hadn't gone far before I kicked something and jumped, startled by a dead pigeon. A random avian corpse left untidy? Or an unfortunate inhabitant of the original attic, walled up and forgotten?

Although it was a hip roof, what would have been the gable ends were quite steep, and the new walls being close to the original fabric, I had to slide crab-wise across the face of the old tin and asphalt. Halfway around, I could no longer see the light from my apartment, just a faint glow over the top of the ridge; the whole far side was in darkness. If one should trip, fall, step through the surface, which, yes, was dry and crumbling—what then? Especially if the light upstairs was out, and the trap closed.

I wondered if either the roof or the attic floor underneath were insulated. How well would sound travel in that space, and would noise reach the apartments below? These were the questions that insinuated themselves before I scrambled out from the dark side. Ahead, I saw the opening of the trap with the white tiles and flooring of the bathroom above reflected and amplified, the glittering halogen lights like lesser suns.

I clambered to the plumbing chase and reached the exit. Pulling myself up was the only real effort, and I thought that a small ladder might be useful. Should I have Nate put one in, using future plumbing work as an excuse? But even as I had this thought, I rejected it. I would do it myself. Whatever was in the space above the roof—now or later—would be my secret.

The next day I purchased a ladder, a rope contraption designed for exiting burning suburban split-levels. I screwed it onto the joists that boxed the trap in the bathroom, securing an easy descent to the roof cavity, my secret space. With this amenity, trips to the underworld became a routine indulgence, and I became familiar enough with my hidden kingdom to know that it was destined to be filled in some special way. Truly, nature abhors a vacuum—and not just in the realm of physics.

I suppose you'll allow, just for purposes of illustration now, that everyone has a person, persons, a list of persons, whose removal would benefit the world. Yes? Dictators, torturers, demented politicians, mad scientists. We can agree on that, I think, and also that there are people we could cheerfully delete from our daily lives. I've got a little list, not one of them'd be missed, as the Lord High Executioner puts it so succinctly. I'm very fond of Gilbert and Sullivan and also of Monty Python.

The only difficulty with little lists is that we rarely have the opportunity to erase a name. We are like a Montresor without an ample palazzo, forced to swallow our pride or risk life and freedom to secure revenge. Sitting in my little paneled study furnished with a chintz-covered sofa, a leather bérgère and a French Empire desk, I realized I was in a unique and enviable position.

There surely were some people I disliked, given that unpleasantness with the condo board at my previous address. Numero uno was Lamont Matthews, who forced me off the condo board and out of the building. He had only himself to blame if he reaped the consequences.

I made my plans, all theoretical, of course. I really did believe this was just an exercise, a little displaced aggression. Just the same, I was careful and thorough. I acquired a few samples of a potent animal tranquilizer from one of my decorating clients. The taste for nineteenth-century artifacts is more widespread than you'd imagine among people on the cultural (and pharmaceutical) cutting edge.

I also bought, at a variety of stores, heavy-duty garment bags, duct tape, and extra large garbage bags, which shows, I suppose, how theory tips over into action.

And then I waited, understanding that the keys to success were planning and spontaneity. Planning, so that nothing would go wrong when the moment presented itself, and spontaneity so that there would be no trail, no appointment in the planner, no one to say, Lamont mentioned he was having dinner with . . . Or, I know for a fact they were meeting at . . . None of that.

I was content to wait indefinitely, but still, with my plans in place, with the space yawning under my feet, I found myself dropping into a bar I knew Lamont frequented and which, in happier times, had been a favorite of mine. Two weeks passed, three, then there he was in the crush of the young and striving, his smooth face bearing all the marks of youthful success and indulgence.

I greeted him cheerfully, bought him a drink, discussed my new apartment, a much better fit for my temperament. Lamont thought he'd defeated me completely, and in his triumph, he was quite willing to hoist a glass or two, even to accompany me to another bar and then downtown to my new residence.

Everything worked like a charm. I had worried about my rugs, about stains and damage, but it was easier than I'd thought. The human animal is a fragile creature. The actual disposal was another, more difficult matter. I hadn't anticipated that, a little illustration of the fact that mostly we worry about the wrong things.

I got the deceased Lamont trussed up nicely in plastic and duct tape, then into the first of a series of zip-closed garment bags, which I planned to reinforce with tape. So far, so good.

The problem came when I tried to put him down the trap. I hadn't realized Lamont was such a size. Self-discipline is so important; I really have no respect for people who let themselves go.

Out of the garment bag, then. Just the plastic, and down he went into the darkness and slid—I admit, I did not have the ropes quite right that first time—down the sloping roof to the remains of the parapet. This would never do. The perimeter of the roof was assuredly dark, but plumbers come with lights and suppose, just suppose, some curious type were to swing his flashlight away from the chase and the pipes? It was not to be thought of.

Besides, Lamont belonged on the dark side and I was determined to put him there. I packed him up again and began the struggle to get him over the hump, so to speak. I slipped several times going up the roof, raising nasty clouds of old dust and dirt and mold, and cut my right hand once and my left hand twice, before I reached the ridge.

His package wanted to stick between the ridge and the joists above. Had that extra garment bag been a mistake? Had I punctured some of the plastic and nylon? A desperate inspection, frantic last-minute repairs, then using all my strength and weight, I thrust Lamont over the peak and heard him roll down the other side.

I was gasping with the effort, but still I had to go down the slope to the parapet and scramble halfway around the roof to be sure that, yes, Lamont rested in peace, his shroud intact, right at the very edge of the old roof. We lie down in darkness, as the

Elizabethan essayist puts it. And where more appropriate for a weaselly condo politician than right there?

I climbed back up my ladder, dirty and exhausted. I took off my sweatshirt, jeans, and the heavy boots I've found invaluable for exploring, and put them away along with the duct tape and the caver's lamp. I closed the trap in the floor, replaced the mat. Everything is as before, I thought. I went all through the penthouse, just to check, but nothing was different. I ran a bath and lay in my large, antique, beautifully refinished tub and thought that I had satisfied both myself and the space, the cavernous space, which even with that thought seemed to expand in my mind. Something in the memory of its shadows whispered, There are others.

Oh, indeed, there were. But not right away. I don't want you to think I'd missed the enormity of what I'd done. I hadn't, not at all, especially not since a police detective visited me three weeks after Lamont's disappearance. I was gracious and helpful. I described how I'd run into Lamont in the bar, had a drink, hashed over old condo politics. I expressed my dismay, my ignorance, my regrets. Was crossed off the list.

But caution seemed advisable, and weeks passed, months, a year. It was only when Ari Cipri stiffed me over a big resort motel contract that I harkened to the whispers from the darkness and began, once again, to make plans.

I met Ari at a conference, pretended that bygones were bygones, dropped a pill in his drink and walked him out to my van, where I'd told him I had a particularly fine silk rug. Which I did, as a matter of fact, but poor Ari was unable to conclude what would truly have been a bargain. Amazing how greed and vice lead the unwary down the primrose path.

Ari's disappearance was second-page news; parasite that he was, he'd had a certain spurious glamour. I read the stories from end to end, but I made sure that every scrap went out for recycling with not so much as a clipping for a memento. The noise about his disappearance taught me caution. The yawning gulf between roof and floor would have to be satisfied with its "furnishings." I resolved to avoid temptation, to rise above the irritations of the design trade.

I stuck to this admirable resolution until I was sued by a disgruntled client, a true suburban monster, tasteless, ruthless, tactless. She lived in a gated community with every entrance electronically surveilled. Oh, she was cautious—but also acquisitive and greedy. My countersuit was proceeding nicely when, hoping to get me to settle on the cheap, she decided we should meet. I took that as a sign. Was it my fault that Mrs. Fennelley had no head for alcohol? That I had to help her to her car? That I loaded her, instead, into my van?

You can see how things went. Good resolutions were defeated time and again by the ghastly unreasonableness of the metropolitan population. Opportunity was not just put in my path but flung into my lap, and, really, I did my whole profession a favor when I sent Daphne Fennelley over the hump.

Still, she brought investigators closer to home than was really advisable. A missing ex-client, a missing *disgruntled* ex-client, presented more of a problem than a member of my former condo's board or a professional rival. Once again, I resolved to end the business.

I was in control, after all, and I had to admit that the distractions of "the underworld" had created professional difficulties. Without Ari and Lamont, I doubt Daphne Fennelley would ever have wound up at her lawyer's.

I resumed normal life. I resisted every stray impulse to open the trap in the bathroom floor. I stopped my weekly checks of the roof space, though I did continue my practice of dropping rat poison pellets down into the gulf. No point in encouraging vermin.

And if, sometimes, more than sometimes, frequently, as I

drifted off to sleep or lay soaking in my antique tub I heard that darkness whisper, I ignored it. Architecture is designed to enhance our lives not to elicit our darker impulses. I did very well, and though I began to think I might do ever better elsewhere, that it was about time for a new apartment, new furniture, a new look, a cleansing of the visual palette, I consoled myself with the thought that the penthouse had brought me a unique series of experiences.

For these, my continued residence did not seem too high a price to pay. Instead of a move, I decided on redecorating. On reflection, foliage and arabesques were too confining, and my rich, somber colors suggested secrets unplumbed. Presciently, I had decorated for the future, for what was yet to be when I first designed the apartment.

Now I wanted to suggest other things, light, air, an airy simplicity. Even the fine, vaguely Edwardian bathroom might have to go, although that might require work on the piping, which might lead to explorations of the chase and the roof cavity. Although I hate half measures and compromise in design, I thought that new paper, a new palette might suffice.

That plan was already in motion, my life dedicated to sweetness and light, when I got word that the building was to be cabled for high-speed Internet access. Nate called, apologetic, to say that they would need access to my apartment. "Not a problem," I said.

"Well, it might be a nuisance. Unavoidable, though."

I asked what he meant and got the answer. They were going to drop the cable down through the old roof for the lower floors, and run a single wire up to mine. "No drop off," Nate said. "You'll have the best reception in the building."

"You mean they'll have to go down through the bathroom?"

"Not a big job," said Nate, and though I complained and protested, a couple days later a technician in a smart brown shirt and slacks rang my bell.

I must admit I'd been planning in a strictly theoretical way, but I greeted him cordially. He was a big fellow, well over six feet, wide in the shoulders. I had some hope that he might not fit down the trap, but he shook off my concerns. "I've been in tighter places than this," he said.

I could not help hovering in the bathroom. "Straight down, right? This side of the ridge?"

He shook his head and sealed his fate. "Wish it was, but the wire comes in on the north side of the building. I'll have to get around the other side of that old roof. Your basic, screwed-up city architecture," he joked. He put down his tools and went to get his wire.

I took a heavy plumber's wrench out of the storage closet and set it handy behind the bathroom door along with a pair of latex gloves. I waited until the technician returned with his wire and had started down the ladder, then I swung at his head.

Nasty. More than nasty. Abusable drugs and alcohol had spared me the real horrors, but not this time. He groaned and fell and cried out, so that I had to scramble down the ladder after him. And raise the wrench and lower it and raise it again. A forensic nightmare. Unplanned, unwanted, inappropriate, not at all what the space required.

Legs trembling, I had to go up to the bathroom and shower before I could go down the ladder again to get his keys. I'll admit I was shaken. I had nothing against the cable guy, and the fact that he'd wound up on the flaking, hidden roof with his head smashed frankly made me nervous. I had a sense of events slipping out of control.

In my state of mind, it was fortunate that I had already made contingency plans. I lugged the big toolbox out to his truck before I could succumb to nerves. I climbed into the cab to check his work orders, then drove to within a block of his next appointment where I parked the vehicle and walked to the T. On the way home, I shopped for some large-size garbage sacks and another garment bag. I still had plenty of duct tape.

Back upstairs, I put on my caver's lamp and my heavy boots and climbed down the ladder. Mess. I would need buckets of water and disinfectant. There would be prints, blood tracked about, the obvious and to-be-expected result of the unexpected.

I got to work with bags and tape, but he was a big guy, and I could foresee trouble with the ridge, with getting him over the hump. With a major effort, I hauled him up the roof, but this time no amount of force would get the parcel between the ridge and the joists.

Around then I closed the trap, just in case someone ventured into the apartment—Nate, maybe, checking on the work, on how things had gone, on whether I had been satisfied. That would be fatal. Enemies were one thing and neutral strangers like the cable guy were another matter, but the idea of friends like Nate gave me the shivers.

Darkness, pierced by the miner's lamp. I started down the slope, letting him roll. The plastic was sure to tear, but once in place, repairs would be possible, necessary. Along the parapet was an easy walk, but what a weight! Two hundred pounds at least. Whatever made him pick a profession requiring ladders and roofs and small, confined spaces?

The gable end, heave him along, don't let him get wedged between the roof and the wall. I told myself that he'd be as well hidden in one place as the other. But no, no good. It had to be all the way to the dark side for him.

I was beginning to sweat, and my heart, always reliable in the past, began to leap and stutter with the heat and the close air and the tremendous, malicious weight of him. Deliberate, that's what it was. His weight, I mean. The space had chosen him without consulting me, without my best interests in mind. I knew it and it frightened me.

I had reached the north wall with completion, safety, and an easy return trip just yards away when, in my effort to move him around the corner, I had to lift his full weight. I staggered, thumped my shoulder against the wall, lurched toward the roof, and to keep from falling, braced one foot on the slope of tin and asphalt.

A crunching sound, the noise of something brittle resolving itself into dust. It was his weight that had done it; my left leg had gone through up to the thigh. Struggling to free myself, I put my hand down on the roof, tearing another hole in the fabric, and trapping me beneath the monstrous weight of the cable guy.

I shouted and, bracing my right leg, I was trying to extract myself when I felt a sharp pain deep in my trapped leg and then, to my horror, a warm wetness flowing into my boot. I had cut something, something large, and my blood was dripping into the attic.

I will spare you the account of my futile efforts to get free, to escape from the grasp (I can only think of it as the grasp) of the cable technician above and the clutches of the rotting metal roof below. I think you already know about that. I thought I knew what the dark space required, and I can't think how I missed it— a decorator and connoisseur of my experience—but it turns out I was wrong.

Neat and tidy and bloodless wasn't right at all, and from the first, the body required was my own.

Listen

Judith Green

"Busted the friggin' living room window right out!" Raymie Bean unzipped the blaze-orange hunting jacket he wore year round and leaned against the counter. "Figured I'd better check on the place after all that snow and wind we had on Thursday. I told Miz Littlefield she oughta let me cut that old oak tree down."

Erlon Nesbitt leaned his skinny elbows on the counter. The store was quiet at this time in the afternoon. Two men sat at one of the tables in the corner, snowmobile suits peeled to the waist, helmets on the floor beside them, eating a late lunch. Ralph Towner surveyed the rental videos in the revolving rack. Margery Easton gazed into the bakery display, deciding how badly she wanted that raspberry pie.

"Anyway," Raymie went on, "I fetched my key and went into the cabin to see could I get this big branch out without my chain saw. And that's when I saw it."

Erlon raised an eyebrow.

Margery decided against the pie, and made her way to the counter with a half-gallon of milk and a copy of the Lewiston *Sun-Journal*. "Saw what?" she asked helpfully.

"A canvas bag. Like a gym bag," Raymie said. "Stuffed full of money! Tens and twenties."

Erlon raised the other eyebrow. "Stuffed full?"

"Money?" Ralph slapped a video on the counter. "Agnes

Littlefield rents that cabin out, summers. You think one of those New Jersey people just went off and left the money there?"

"Naw. Miz Littlefield had some work done on the place last fall, wiring and stuff. Then Tammy closed up for the winter. She'd'd've seen it."

"So where is it?" Ralph asked.

"Miz Littlefield told me to take it over to the sheriff's office." Raymie dropped his voice. "She thinks it's drug money."

"Well," Erlon said, "Maine's got a helluva long coastline, 'scuze my French, Margery. Boats go in and out of those coves, and nobody sees 'em."

"Plus stuff coming down overland from Canada!" Ralph added.

Margery slid away, knowing that in a minute or two someone would inevitably ask her if there were drugs at the high school where she taught. "Can you put the milk and paper on my slip, Erlon?" she called. The bell jangled over her head as she yanked the door open.

As she slogged through the slush at the side of the road, a gust of wind chilled her face and hands, and spun a tiny cyclone of winter sand against her ankles. She climbed into her car and rested her forehead for a moment against the steering wheel. God, she hated March. It had been winter forever.

And she didn't want to think about drug money in the village. She still had a teenager at home.

She wished she'd bought that pie.

□   □   □

"Worrying about the wallpaper again, Mom?"

Margery started at the sound of Jennifer's voice. She'd been gazing out the kitchen window at the back pasture beyond the barn, where her husband sat contentedly by his fire in the gathering dusk, boiling down maple sap into syrup. As she watched, Tom roused himself for a moment to shove another log under the wide boiling pan, then returned to contemplating the flames. At a ratio of forty gallons of sap for one gallon of finished syrup, a man could pretty much count on spending every moment of his spare time in March outside by his fire, safely away from his wife and kids.

Margery jabbed at the stew beef in the skillet with a wooden spoon, turning the chunks of meat to brown on the other side. At the back of the stove, a big pot of amber almost-syrup steamed fragrantly, finishing off.

The first year Tom made syrup, when Jennifer was just a baby, he'd done all the boiling inside on the electric stove, and upstairs the wallpaper unstuck itself from the walls and flopped to the bedroom floor in great sticky sheets. The story had been told so often that Jennifer thought she remembered seeing it.

"I forgot to tell you," Jennifer said from the sink as she scrubbed at a potato destined for the stew. "I stopped on the way home from town this afternoon to see Grandma."

"That was sweet of you, dear." Margery felt a pang of guilt. She hadn't been over to the nursing home in more than a week. There was less and less point to it these days. Her mother slept most of the time. Slept right through visits. It was rare to see her mother with her eyes open, let alone to get the barest glimmer of recognition.

"It was kinda weird, Mom," Jennifer said. "She was talking."

"Talking? Your grandmother?" Margery turned from the stove to look at her daughter. "What about?"

Jennifer picked up another potato and held it under the faucet. "I'm not sure," she said, raising her voice to be heard over the running water. "She kept jumping from one thing to another. She's like, 'If only I'd been there.' Then she's like, 'He's crying!' and I'm like, 'Who's crying, Grandma?' But she's just like, 'Now it's gone! Serves him right!' Who was she talking about, Mom?"

Margery sighed. "Who knows? It could have been anyone in

the last eighty years."

Jennifer hooked her hair behind her ear with the back of her hand and turned to look at her mother. "When I got up to go, Grandma went all crazy," she said. "She grabbed my arm, and she's like, 'We need it! Get it back!' Her eyes were all wild-like, Mom. She kinda scared me!"

Margery turned back to the stove and jabbed again at the stew beef. Perhaps her mother should be on some kind of medication. She hated to think of it. Even though her mother had gone pretty much silent in the last year, Margery still liked to go to the nursing home and kind of talk things over with her. She liked to think her mother was still in there somewhere. That inside this tiny, bent old lady was the woman who had milked the cows before heading to a long day at the store. The woman who had split wood, and knit those thick, lumpy sweaters, and bandaged her children's cuts and scrapes, who pushed Margery and her brothers through their homework and absolutely insisted on proper manners at the table.

"I don't know," Margery said. "I don't know."

"Listen, Mom—" Jennifer was at the kitchen table, pushing aside a Land's End catalog and an unfinished lesson plan for Margery's senior English class. On the cleared end of the table she set down plates, paper napkins, silverware. "I don't have time for supper. Jason'll be here in fifteen minutes and I haven't even had a shower!"

The third plate clattered back up onto the shelf, and she was gone.

Margery sighed. She'd better get herself over to the nursing home tomorrow.

If it didn't snow.

God, she was tired of winter.

□ □ □

"Oh, Lord, it's leaking again!" Cyndi Pringle pointed at a damp spot in the fiberboard ceiling tile high over their heads. "We've got to get that roof fixed this spring, just as soon as it warms up." Margery took a sip of lukewarm decaf and sighed. Every Sunday, they spent the coffee hour at the back of the church after the service talking about the roof. They'd been trying to raise the money to fix it for two years.

"We've got to have a meeting!" Delbert Hiscock announced. "The oil bill hasn't been paid this month! The price on everything keeps going up, but folks don't seem to understand that anymore, when it comes time to donate to the church!"

"Maybe Agnes will give us the money!" Elsie Nesbitt said. "Have you heard? Raymie Bean found a whole suitcase full of money in that cabin Agnes has down on Back Pond!"

They all turned to look at Agnes while she shrugged into her coat and gathered up her cane and pocketbook, and then came toward them down the aisle, her big round glasses gleaming like headlights. "Well, well, Miz Littlefield!" Delbert bellowed, Adam's apple bobbing in his scrawny neck as if he'd swallowed a yo-yo. "Surprised to see you out this frigid morning. We thought you'd be halfway to Acapulco by now!"

"That money went right over to the sheriff's department, and you know it!" Agnes snapped. She brushed imperiously by him, through a silent press of people who stepped back to let her through like the Red Sea parting for Moses, and headed for the door.

"How much money was in the suitcase?" Delbert called after her.

"I don't know!" Agnes bawled from the vestibule, hands on hips. "Raymie never touched it! And the sheriff ain't talking! Besides, it wasn't a suitcase. It was a gym bag."

"A gym bag," Delbert repeated.

"Ayup. Drug money," Agnes said lugubriously. "Probably someone from New York, or one of those places. Now if you'll excuse me, I'm on my way over to Nesbitt's. I'm going to buy an Instant-Win scratch ticket," she added. "I'm feeling lucky."

Margery gazed out the church window. Across the road, the parking lot in front of Nesbitt's Store was already full of snowmobiles. She watched Agnes hobble across the road and up the front steps of the store.

"The poet had it all wrong," she murmured. "It's March that is the cruellest month." Elsewhere in the United States, birds were singing and daffodils bobbed in the breeze. Maine was still under two feet of snow.

"Do you really think we have drug dealers on Back Pond?" Mary Mills asked. "What about the school, Margery? Are the children safe?"

Margery pretended she hadn't heard. Carrying her coffee, she stepped around Delbert and made her way up the worn brown carpet to where Matt Ferguson was standing in front of the pulpit, gathering up the envelopes and loose change from the silver collection plates. "Hi, Matt," she said. "You're all alone this morning?"

Matt turned quickly at the sound of her voice, then lifted his bristly little mustache in a small smile. "Yes, Evelyn's gone back to Massachusetts for the weekend to visit her sister."

Margery watched him as he put the collection into a green bank bag and carefully zipped the bag shut. She had come to feel a bond with this quiet little man, after he and his wife had moved to the village five or six years back. Since he kept his own books for his electrician's business, he'd allowed himself to be talked into serving as the church treasurer, a job which might otherwise have fallen to Margery when Delbert gave it up. He did the best he could with it, putting the church's paltry finances on a very pretty spreadsheet. And for the past two years she'd bumped into him from time to time at the nursing home.

Esther Ferguson had never recovered from her stroke, but had never quite died, either. She just lay there in the bed, unmoving, like the Resusci-Annie model the nursing aide students practiced on at the high school. Margery could see why the nursing home staff had placed Esther in her mother's room. The two of them passed their days in absolute silence, except when an aide turned on the radio on the table in the corner. Margery would come in to find Country and Western twanging away, and no one listening.

"Matt, I was wondering—" she began.

"What?" he asked, glancing quickly toward the other end of the church, where the coffee hour was petering out.

"Well, have you visited at the nursing home lately? I was just wondering if you'd noticed any change in my mother."

"Your mother?" Matt turned back to Margery and smiled reassuringly. "She looked fine yesterday, when I was in. I mean, she was mostly sleeping, but—" He tucked the bank bag under his arm while he buttoned his suitcoat. "Our mothers. They just don't make women like them anymore."

Margery watched him as he made his way down the side aisle and slipped through the door to the vestry. Poor guy, she thought. His wife had clearly not appreciated moving to Maine to be closer to his mother. She was a city person, from the top of her well-coiffed head to the soles of her ridiculously high-heeled shoes.

His wife was gone more and more, lately. One of these days, Evelyn was going forget to come back to Maine at all.

A nurse wearing scrubs covered in pink and orange giraffes stopped Margery in the hall as she headed for her mother's room. Margery had known Sally Millett since high school. There was a lot more of Sally now than there had been back then. And the dizzy pattern on the scrubs only made her look heavier.

"Margery, I was going to call you," Sally said. "We're worried about your mother. She's become quite agitated, just since yesterday."

"My daughter told me. Did anything happen that might have touched her off?"

Sally pursed her lips. "Nothing I can think of. She ate her lunch with no problem. I fed her myself. Esther's son came in for a visit, but he's real quiet."

"Yes, I know Matt. He wouldn't bother anyone."

"What a nice man! He's in here like clockwork, Tuesdays and Thursdays after work, and Saturdays right at lunchtime. He likes to feed his mother, when she'll take anything. There just aren't many men like him. His wife, now, she hardly ever visits. And we're all just as happy when she doesn't."

Sally shrugged, and the giraffes on her blouse all jumped at once. "Don't worry. Your mother'll probably settle down in another day or two. We'll keep an eye on—Oops, gotta go!" As she hurried off after a tiny old woman who was pushing her own wheelchair down the hall, the giraffes across her buttocks leapt into a cheerful rhumba.

Margery stepped into her mother's room, which was thick with the smells of disinfectant and industrial skin lotion. Her mother was propped up in her bed. Her hands, thin and knotted with blue veins, plucked at the granny-square coverlet Jennifer had made her for Christmas, and which had already been washed so often that it resembled colored cardboard. She was staring across the stretch of linoleum at her roommate, who was dozing, or perhaps dead.

"Mom," Margery said softly.

Her mother's head snapped around. Her eyes gleamed white all the way around the faded blue irises. Her hands pleated the coverlet, folded it down, and grasped again, forming accordion pleats in the stiff fabric. "Where's the baby?" she asked. "Oh, they shouldn't let—"

"Which baby, Mom?" Margery asked. She sat down in the straight-backed chair beside the bed and slid the coverlet out of her mother's grip, smoothing it down over the knobs that were her mother's knees. "Mom, what's wrong?"

"Where's the—" her mother began. Then suddenly her eyes seemed to focus on Margery. "Ssh!" she hissed. She cut her eyes to the still form in the other bed, and then back to Margery. "Him!" she said. "Where is he?"

"Who?"

"Him! Him!" her mother whispered urgently. She cut her eyes again to the other bed. "Where is he?"

"That's a lady, Mom," Margery said. "That's your roommate. Her name is Esther Ferguson."

She glanced over at the other bed. Maybe Matt's mother *was* dead! It happened so often: old people seemed to weaken and die in March, all worn out just when the temperature began to climb above freezing.

Margery got up, crossed the bit of floor in three steps, and stared down at Mrs. Ferguson's wizened face. The old woman was gripping the end of her pink satin spread in both hands just under her chin. While Margery watched, a tiny snore puffed out from the narrow lips, which were so deeply wrinkled that they appeared to be stitched haphazardly to her face with black thread. Well, at least the woman was still alive. "It's okay, Mom," Margery said as she returned to her chair. "Mrs. Ferguson is fine. She's just sleeping."

"Ssh!" Her mother lifted a finger to her lips. Suddenly she grabbed Margery's arm, gripping it so tightly that it hurt. "You!" she blurted. "It's up to you!"

"Me?"

"You have to! It's your job! They're going away! Far away!"

"Who's going? What about my job?"

But the interview was over. "I just can't believe it," her mother said, and sank back on her pillow and closed her eyes.

"It's as if my mother is trying to tell me something," Margery told her husband that evening. "She said something about my job. But I always thought she was glad I went into teaching."

Tom sat across the kitchen table from her reading a back issue of *Harper's* he'd unearthed in his study. Now he put his broad fingertip on the page to mark his place and looked up at her. "No offense, honey," he said, "but your mother hasn't made much sense for two or three years now."

"I know." Margery sighed. "It's like she just gave up after Dad died."

"Mmm," Tom said. He went back to his magazine.

Margery finished entering the grades for her senior research class into her laptop. "You know," she said, "when my mother was church treasurer, back before Delbert Hiscock took over, she did everything by hand. She didn't even have a calculator."

"Mmm," Tom said.

□   □   □

The weather report on the drive home from school the next day called for wet snow on Wednesday, accumulation up to eight inches. At this rate, Margery thought, they'd still be in school in July!

As she came down the hill into the village, she spotted Agnes's ancient, mud-spattered car parked next to Nesbitt's Store.

And suddenly it clicked.

She pulled up right in front of the store, blocking the gas pump. Quickly, before she lost her nerve, she leapt out of her car and scurried inside. "Agnes!" she called. She rounded the humming milk cooler and headed for the canned goods. "Agnes!"

Agnes was bent over the cat food selection, reaching for a can of Kitty Platter Supreme. She looked up at the sound of her name, her eyes moving like goldfish behind her thick glasses. "Hi, Margie. How's your mom these days?"

"Agnes, you had some electrical work done this year?" Margery asked.

Agnes straightened up. She blinked, an epic movement behind the glasses. "Electrical work? Well, yes. I got Matt Ferguson to put circuit breakers into both cabins. They still had fuse boxes, and Raymie said that could start a fire. So then you know what happens? Someone breaks the living room window right in and—"

Margery was already headed for the front door.

"Did you need some gas put on your slip?" Erlon called, but the only answer was the jangle of the bell.

□ □ □

Raymie's wife, Tammy, answered the door. His mother wielded a pair of tongs, piling steaming spaghetti onto a row of plates lined up on the counter. Raymie, still wearing his blaze-orange jacket even though it was easily over eighty degrees in the tiny kitchen, sat at the table, reading the Sunday comics from yesterday's newspaper. He jumped up politely when he saw Margery.

"I'm sorry to bother you at suppertime," Margery began.

"No bother. You hungry?" Arline motioned for Tammy to get her another plate from the cupboard. "We got plenty of spaghetti."

"No, no, I can't stay. Tom'll be wondering where I am. I just wanted to ask you about finding that money."

Arline raised an eyebrow as if to say *at suppertime?* Tammy murmured something about checking on the kids and left the room. Raymie sat back down, allowing himself to drop the last inch into the chair to express his fatigue with the entire topic.

"Agnes thinks the money belongs to drug dealers," Margery said.

"Well," Raymie said.

"She says they wanted to hide the money in the cabin, so they broke the window."

"Naw," Raymie said, folding the newspaper and placing it on the floor beside his chair. "Tree branch did that. Big chunk fell off the oak tree above the cabin. I keep telling Miz Littlefield she's gotta let me cut that tree down before the whole thing comes down and breaks that cabin right in two. I've told her I'd do it just for the firewood that's in it, but—"

"So you think someone had a key?" Margery cut in.

"Ayup. Must've had a key. Wasn't any sign of someone breaking in."

"So someone—"

Raymie sighed, and went on. "There were footprints. Weren't mine. I hadn't been over since Christmas, and then I just did a walkaround."

"So—"

"So what I told the sheriff was, I think someone came in sometime last month, and they went in and out with a key. I'd've never noticed, except for the branch coming down and busting in the window. Otherwise, we'd never have gone inside until May or June, for opening up."

"And the money would have been gone, and the footprints melted, and no one would have ever known," Margery said.

"Well," Arline said, calmly ladling tomato sauce over the spaghetti, "might've been better that way."

□ □ □

The deputy sheriff, who lived down beyond the sawmill, was polite. But skeptical.

"Your mother's still at the nursing home, isn't she?" he asked. "They take good care of them over there. God, I thought she was a goner, that time she wandered off. Poor thing! When we found her, out in Delbert's pasture, she didn't have a clue where she was." The deputy shook his head.

"Now, you say she saw something. And if I went over there to the nursing home, she'd be able to explain it to me, right?"

Margery swallowed. "I guess probably not."

The deputy smiled. "We don't want to be slinging accusations unless we're sure. Right?"

Margery got into her car and jolted over three miles of frost-heaved road to home.

□　□　□

Margery lay awake far into the night, alongside the large, warm log that was her husband, and stared out the window at a handful of stars caught in the bare branches of the maple tree. It was not until Orion slid silently behind the black outline of the barn that she fell into sleep, still wondering what to do.

She called the nursing home during her lunch period at school the next day. Her mother had passed a restless night, she was told. They'd found her wandering twice in the hallway. She wouldn't eat.

Margery telephoned her husband and told him to meet her at the nursing home after work that afternoon. She needed him there, she said.

As witness?

As protection?

She didn't know.

□　□　□

Margery's mother was sitting up in bed when they came in. Her face was haggard, her faded blue eyes sunken. She seemed to have aged a half-century since Sunday. Her bony fingers worked the coverlet, folding, folding, until even the pleats had pleats.

"Hello, Mom," Margery said.

The fingers pinched the fabric, pleats within pleats.

"Hello, Celeste," Tom chimed in. "It's good to see you."

The fingers were still a moment, as if they were doing the listening. The head turned, but blindly, as if she couldn't find the source of the voice. After a moment, the fingers resumed pleating.

"Look at her, Tom!" Margery said. "What should we do?"

Tom patted his wife on the shoulder, produced a paperback copy of *Master and Commander* from his suitcoat pocket, and settled down in the armchair in the corner.

Margery took her mother's hands, which were cool and narrow and almost weightless in hers. It was hard to imagine these hands swinging a splitting maul.

Sally Millett appeared in the doorway, a stethoscope hanging out of the pocket of her scrubs. Today's theme was panda bears. "How are we doing in here?" she asked.

Margery looked up. "Has Mom eaten today?"

Sally shook her head, her blond pony tail swinging. "Nope. Not a thing." She turned, looked down the hall. "Oh, look, Esther!" she called. "You've got company! Here comes your son!" Her voice dropped. "And your lovely daughter-in-law!" she murmured.

She stepped aside, dimpling, as Matt Ferguson arrived, wearing tan coveralls with *Ferguson Electric* stitched on the pocket.

"Oh, hello, Margery," he said in a low voice. "Hello, Tom. It's been a while."

"Matt. Evelyn. Good to see you," Tom said, and went back to his book.

"How was Massachusetts, Evelyn?" Margery asked. "I'll bet the daffodils were out!"

"I didn't notice," Evelyn said. She glared at Tom, as if willing him to vacate the only chair. She tapped a fur-ruffed boot. "Matt, dear," she said, "let's get on with it. Tell your mother hello, and then we need to get going."

Matt flushed. He stepped over to his mother's bed and took her hand in his. "It's me, Matt," he said. "I've come to see you."

Mrs. Ferguson snorted slightly. Then her breathing returned to the even cadence of sleep.

"Okay," Evelyn said. "She's sleeping. Let's go."

Matt's shoulders sagged. He turned to follow his wife.

"Matt!" Margery said, so suddenly that the electrician's head snapped back. "Matt, tell me about the work you did for Agnes Littlefield."

"What?" He hunched his shoulder, hiding the little mustache. "What work?"

"Didn't you put in a circuit breaker in her cabin on Back Pond?" Margery pressed.

"Oh. Yes, I suppose—" He started to edge toward the door. But his wife blocked the doorway, her arms crossed over her fake-fur jacket. "I mean—"

"Did you have a key?" Margery asked.

"Well, I must have. Maybe. I don't know." Ferguson looked from Margery to his wife and back at Margery. "I—"

"Matt." Margery's voice quavered. In the newspapers, it was always the quiet guys who turned out to be killers. She glanced over at Tom, but his head was bent over his book. "Matt," she said, "tell us about the money."

"What money?" Evelyn's voice was harsh. "He hasn't made two cents since we moved here!"

"Matt," Margery said again, "tell us what you told my mother about the money!"

"What do you mean?" Matt asked. His face was white. The little mustache twitched and wriggled. "I just—I mean—"

Suddenly Margery's mother sat up in her bed. She looked square into his face and said, "Well, young man? What do you have to say for yourself?"

Ferguson's face crumpled. "You told them?"

"Yes," Margery said. "She told us." Sort of. If you were listening.

Slowly his knees buckled and hit the floor. He toppled slowly toward Margery's mother, until his forehead touched the edge of her bed. He buried his face in the granny-square coverlet, and wept.

Celeste reached out a hand and softly stroked his hair. Margery yearned for that touch. But Matt Ferguson needed it more.

"I didn't mean to," Matt said into the coverlet. "I could never give Evelyn what she wanted. But I thought if I gave her a vacation, a real one, to Europe, maybe. Or a safari to the Serengeti, I thought she'd—"

He moaned. "I didn't take that much. Just a little bit each week. But Delbert Hiscock started asking me about bills that weren't paid. And the withholding for the minister. He wanted to come to my house and talk about the withholding. I couldn't have the money in the house when Delbert came! That gym bag. I hated that bag. It got so I could feel it, wherever it was in the house! Delbert would have known—"

He put his face in his hands. "So I put it in that camp, just for a few days, but when I went back, it was gone." He lifted his head and turned his tear-streaked face toward the doorway. "Evelyn, I did it for you!"

The doorway was empty.

Ferguson's shoulders drooped inside the coveralls. "I had to tell someone!" he said. "My mother wouldn't listen, so I told yours. I'd never heard her speak. I didn't know she could!"

"Well, she did," Margery said. "And I'm sorry, but the church needs that money. The only way we can get it back is if you go to the sheriff and explain."

"Explain?" Ferguson sat back on his heels. "You think I can explain?"

"Well," Margery said, "you have to try." She jerked her head in Tom's direction. "Otherwise he'll have to tell them."

Slowly, Ferguson stood up. He paced to his mother's bedside, bent down, and kissed her wrinkled cheek. Then he turned and walked out of the room. Margery could hear his workboots echoing down the hall.

"That Mr. Ferguson is leaving already?" Sally asked from the doorway. Her generous bosom heaved like a soft tidal wave. "He's such a nice man. I'll just see him out." She whisked away in pursuit.

"Well, Mom, you got him," Margery said, quietly, in case Esther Ferguson could hear after all.

Her mother sank back into the pillow. Her gnarled hands relaxed onto the coverlet. "Bad boy," she whispered.

"I think he wanted to confess," Margery went on. "He just seemed to want someone to talk to."

Margery's mother closed her eyes.

"She looks happy. Don't you think so, Tom?" Margery asked. "Do you think she understands what I'm saying?"

"Mmm?" Marking his place with his forefinger, Tom looked up from his book. "The Fergusons left already?" Without waiting for an answer, he went back to his reading.

Margery gazed down at her mother's face. It was good to know her mother was still in there somewhere.

Was that a smile?

"You know, Tom," she said, "I can understand how Matt felt. It's just nice to have someone to talk to. Even when they aren't listening."

"Mmm," Tom said.

T-Boned

Clayton Emery

ATM machines in New Hampshire now make you select English or Spanish, which is stupid. There are more French in the state than Hispanics. Probably more Cambodians, Vietnamese, Chinese, Thai, and Philippinos than Hispanics.

But some Asians don't use banks. Which is why I was sitting in a McDonald's in Manchester talking to Tom Viroj.

Built like a sumo wrestler, he had a handshake gentle as a baby's. In the noon rush, people all around shoveled food and talked nonstop. I wondered about what.

"Is this illegal?" I asked.

"Uh, would you like a Coke? Or something to eat?" A slight Asian accent made him sip his words like tea.

"Illegal or not? Because if it's illegal—" Come to that, what did I care? I flipped a hand. "What's the job?"

Tom leaned forward to whisper. "My parents are very old-fashioned."

I waited.

"They don't always—follow the rules."

I stared.

Tom squirmed. "Are you mad at me?"

"What? No. My face just doesn't work right. I put it through a windshield once." That's a lie. I am mad, all the time, mad as a woman can get, but I don't need to tell a client. "Which rules don't your parents follow?"

"My parents don't believe in banks. They kept all their money at home."

"Kept."

"Yes. Someone broke into the apartment and stole it. Pushed my mom and dad around, scared them pretty bad." He was the angry one.

"You know who they are?"

"Yes."

"The Crime Prevention Division is top notch."

"My parents won't go to the police. They're afraid to get into trouble."

"Because half your relatives are illegal? And Cousin Louie's dealing drugs? And Aunt Irene runs a food stamp ring? And nobody pays taxes?"

"Not that bad." Tom slumped. His folks would freak about spilling family secrets.

"Asians ripped 'em off? Asian-on-Asian crime? And you know who."

"Kids in the neighborhood, yes."

"Gangbanger wannabees."

"They carry knives and guns."

"How much?

"$28,000."

"Hunh." I drummed my fingers on the table. My nails are blunt and rimmed black. In real life I'm a shadetree mechanic. "Why'd you call me? I live on the coast an hour away."

"I—liked your company's name. '.45 Caliber Investigations.' It sounded—tough."

"And first in the phone book." I straightened the salt and pepper shakers. "Okay, let me try it. Give me the details."

"You'll get my parents' money back?"

"I'll get your parents what they need."

□ □ □

Manchester, New Hampshire, is an old mill town. It died after the Civil War, died again after World War One, and died again in the Depression. Lately it's undergone a renaissance, which tells you something about business cycles in New England.

The West Side is three-story tenements. Autumn was windy and cold with a sky like greasy rags. I'd picked early morning because school was in and the air too cool for old folks to linger. Plus I figured my bad boys would sleep till noon. Tom Viroj had told me they drove a canary-yellow Mercedes, the only one in the neighborhood.

I'd picked up rocks at a construction site. I lobbed one at the Mercedes. It's German. Why not?

Honk, honk, honk went the car alarm. I hung back in a drafty alley and watched. An Asian big as a refrigerator came out a door. The dimwit didn't even see the pockmark on the hood. He just keyed off the alarm and went back inside.

I pitched another rock. The alarm jarred the air.

Two guys. Fridge and a little greasy guy, also Asian. The smart one saw the dings in the hood and even found the rock. But they just circled the car, scowling like stray dogs, and went back inside.

One more rock, more noise.

This time the whole gang assembled: all three. All young in matching leather jackets with some Chinese character painted on the back. The mid-sized would be Steve Buncha, the leader. He hopped up and down. "Who the fuck is throwing these mother-fucking rocks?"

"I am."

They spun. I wore soiled jeans, ratty sneakers, and an Army jacket so out of date it's olive drab. My hair is a chopped blonde mess, and as I mentioned, my face doesn't work right. Which is good, because people never know what I'm thinking.

What they noticed was my pistol. I'd slit a pocket of my jacket. With my hand inside, the gun showed just behind the zipper. It's a piece-of-shit .22 revolver, eight shot, like a kid's cap gun. But pointed at them.

Steve wasn't scared, much. "What do you want?"

"Keys."

"Fuck you. You won't shoot—"

I shot. A crack like a bubble gum bubble. The bullet hit the sidewalk between Steve and Fridge, chipping concrete. They jumped higher than the chip.

Steve held the keys on a long arm. "You want the car, take it. I can get another. But I'll get you—"

"Save it." I circled the car on the street side and used the remote to pop the trunk. Waggled the .22. "Get in."

"What?" Steve's eyes bugged. Maybe more angry than scared. "What, so you can kill me?"

"Nope. We're just going for a ride."

"Fuck—"

I shot again, not caring if I winged one. The bullet chipped a brick. Red showed on the grimy wall for the first time in a hundred years.

"I won't kill you, Steve," emphasizing his name, "because then I won't get what I want. Now climb in while you still have your kneecaps."

Growling, he climbed over the coaming into the trunk. It was big enough to hold nine suitcases. His buddies stayed put.

Standing at the far corner, I put out a hand. "Give me your gun and your cell phone."

"How do you know I've got one?"

"Tools of the trade."

Squirming in the trunk, steaming with rage, he handed over a ruby-red cell phone and a Glock 16, for Christ's sake. Before he could squawk, I slammed the trunk shut.

I popped the door and dropped behind the wheel. Without

their fearless leader, the grunts stood gawking. In a hurry, I backed the Mercedes CRASH! into a grill, cranked the wheel and WHACK! clipped a bumper, and took off like a rocket.

Greasy and Fridge came up with a plan. They piled into their blue Buick. By then I'd taken the first left, then another. Two more turns and we were alone.

I drove, sticking to the speed limit, stopping at stop signs, waving little old ladies in quilt coats and knit hats across cross-walks.

My spine crawled at the thought Steve might have a backup gun that could shoot the length of the car. But after a while no bullets came, so I took a breath.

□ □ □

I drove to the mall and parked amid cars from Massachusetts. Our lack of sales tax lures them like trout.

I went to the food court and had a McSausage with plenty of mustard and a Starbucks coffee. I looked at tools at Sears, browsed books, windowshopped. It was too early for a movie. I got bored and gave up.

I wandered the parking lot as if I'd lost my car. I circled and circled. No one watched the Mercedes, so Steve probably hadn't banged and screamed while I was gone.

On the other hand, he might have escaped. I jostled the car, felt something live thump and roll, then got in and drove.

To the industrial park at the airport. One lot was overrun by staghorn sumac. I backed the Mercedes in among them and trash bags. Standing away from the car, I pointed the .22 and thumbed the remote.

Steve Buncha just about exploded out of the trunk. He grabbed with both hands and both feet to vault when I shot off the popgun. The bullet punched a neat hole through the trunk lid.

"Stay put."

He sank into the trunk, eyes blazing.

"Here's the deal. I get $36,000, I let you go." I didn't give him Tom's exact number because he might guess my client. And for another reason.

"This is kidnapping!" Unlike Tom Viroj, a devoted son, he had no accent. If anything, he talked like Tony Soprano. "This is extortion! This is—"

"Rather than invest in cars, you should go to law school. Kidnapping, yes. Extortion, no. I'm dunning you."

He swore a while. I shot again—WHACK! off the bumper—and he stopped.

"You're a tough guy, right? Wimpy bullets like these might not even penetrate, hunh? Maybe just sting a little?

"Use your brain, Steve. I give you your phone, you call your goons, they deliver the money, we all go home happy. 36 is chump change. This car cost three times that."

"You're crazy! Crazy! There's no way—"

I slammed the trunk, but it bounced off his foot. He yelped and whipped it inside. I slammed it again.

"I have to piss!" he called, muffled.

"Be my guest!" I yelled back. "It's your car!"

□ □ □

It was a nice day for a drive. The sun sparkled among red-yellow-orange trees along Route 101. Traffic picked up, it being Friday.

I watched the picture of the car on the Space Shuttle dashboard. It would signal if my captive tried some TV survival skill such as breaking the taillights from inside to attract the police. But he behaved.

After thirty minutes I turned up the sloping roads to Pawtuckaway, a state park with a little bit of everything.

The boat ramp was busy. Weekend warriors backed trailers with a lot of fussing and seesawing. I waited for an empty slot. No one paid attention until I backed the Mercedes into the lake.

I watched out the back window as the trunk slid into the

water. The exhaust pipe bubbled, but the engine had enough guts to overcome the back pressure, I figured. Water seeped in the back doors. If the engine did stall and the car rolled into the lake—well, it wasn't my car.

About the time someone starting banging in the trunk, someone else banged on my window. A duffer with flies in his hat looked worried. I powered the window down.

"What are you *doing*?" His eyes were watery blue.

"What do you care?" I snapped. Hammering from the trunk was loud. I felt the back wheels slip on slime. The engine labored. I might lose the car yet. More guys circled. In New England we don't offer help until it's asked, luckily, but it was getting crowded. Shouting rang from the trunk.

I eased the car into Drive. It gurgled but clunked. I told the fisherman, "Oops! Forgot my boat again! Thanks!"

Spinning wheels, churning mud, I let the car drag free of the lake. Water ran out of the trunk for a mile. Clouds covered the sun. It got chilly. I turned up the heat and fiddled with the radio, stabbing Seek over and over. When did they outlaw rock 'n roll?

□   □   □

The car bumped and clunked over rocks and branches. An old logging road in South Newfields. I stopped where people had dumped couches.

This time when I popped the hood, Steve Buncha didn't even try to climb out. He was soaked and frozen and probably scrambled from carbon monoxide poisoning. But he was still mad.

I pointed the gun. "Last chance, asshole. I don't work weekends. That means I leave the car somewhere and come back Monday morning. Maybe you'll give up the $36,000 by then."

"I'm never—" he shivered, "never—"

"Okay, better idea. I tank up, park the car in a garage, close the door, and leave it running for three hours. Then I drive to Charlestown and hand it over to a chop shop for 36 grand. Those guys'll toss your body in a dumpster along with the license plates and never blink an eye."

"You think—"

I'll admit, I got too close for a pistol, even though I held it, but I saw red. I jammed the pistol barrel in his mouth. His head sank to the bottom of the soggy trunk and stopped. I leaned until my trigger finger touched his cold lower lip.

"You don't get it, do you?" I talked through my teeth, breathing hard. "You think you can do whatever you want to anybody, hunh? Steal money from old people, sell drugs to kids, rape a girl, carve somebody up with a knife if you want to? Well, I'm here to tell you otherwise, get it? Get it?"

He got it. His hands stirred. I took a deep breath and pulled the gun out of his mouth.

"I'll pay. I'll pay. Give me the cell phone. I'll pay."

He fumbled the cell phone but finally called his help. He spoke in Thai like a dogfight, but "$36,000" was clear enough.

He asked me, "Where do they bring it?

I took away the cell phone. "You'll see. Get out."

Wet, cold, and stiff, Steve crawled from the trunk and fell to the forest floor. I knelt on his back and clapped a handcuff around one wrist. The other cuff I snapped around a sapling too big to uproot.

"Stay put. I'll be back soon."

Shivering, he yanked on the handcuff and only skinned his wrist. "What if you don't come back?"

"A fox'd chew its leg off."

□ □ □

The exchange is the tricky part in a kidnapping scheme, because the parties have to meet, or at least rendezvous around the same point. Still, the kidnapper sets the rules.

Bumping out to the highway, I steered into Brentwood to a junkyard I use.

The gate was open. I stopped by the big shed. Kent Trotter tweaked a stereo from a totaled BMW.

"Kent, you still got that pile of bathtubs down in the back?"

"Hey, Sue. You working today?"

"No. Bathtubs?

Kent laid out screws in a neat line. "Last time I looked. You doing some remodeling?"

"Help me move one, will you?"

Puzzled, Kent climbed into the Mercedes. We drove down the yard to a mountain of iron bathtubs. White ones, blue ones, cracked ones, rusty ones.

"Help me load one, will you?"

"You mean, into the Benz?"

Kent shook his head as we manhandled a black porcelain-lined iron bathtub into the back seat of the Mercedes. It barely fit when I closed the doors. I walked around and looked through the rear window. The tub stuck up just past the seat. I'd thought they were taller.

"Gimme another one. That one."

This time was harder. We had to mash down the seat and wedge the bathtub under the door lintel, but we got it inside with a nerve-wracking screech.

This time when I checked from the rear, all I saw was bathtub.

"Sue," Kent couldn't control himself any longer. "What—"

"It's Susan. How much?"

He gave up. "Fifty bucks?"

I paid him, then reached in a jacket pocket and tossed him the Glock.

"Jesus!" he chirped. "Is this thing even real?"

"Hold it for me, will you?"

I drove off. Slower with five hundred pounds in the back seat.

I steered around the Mall of Manchester, found a street setup

I liked, pulled out Steve's cell phone, and hit Redial.

A goon answered in Thai. I said, "You got the $36,000?"

"We got it," growled Fridge. "You got Steve?"

"There's a stupid question. Now listen. Put the money in a backpack, gym bag, something like that. Drive out toward the mall. There's a Dunkin' Donuts on Mammoth Road near Shaw's. Go through the drive-through. A dumpster sits just at the corner of the building. Set the bag on top and drive away. I'll turn Steve loose once I count it."

"What if you don't?"

"You'll have to alert the authorities. Move." I hung up.

I parked in the supermarket parking lot between two SUVs. I hoped that was enough cover. The yellow Benz was damned conspicuous. I left it running.

By and by the crappy blue Buick skulked along. The goons didn't see me. They entered the drive-through and popped out the other side—onto a one-way street.

I spun into the parking lot, ignored the talking purple box, and skimmed through the drive-through. A black backpack sat on the dumpster. I powered down the window and snatched it. I goosed through the lot to hang a right—

—when a godawful racket exploded behind my head. Lead pinged and pranged off the bathtubs. Iron chips spattered my head and the front windshield.

I scooched my neck and mashed the gas. Narrowly cutting off a pickup truck, I hooked right, ran a red light, hooked right onto the highway. Gunning it, I raised the bar to 80 and checked my mirrors. No blue Buick.

I hoped those assholes hadn't punctured the gas tank. I was in no mood to shoot it out with two dickheads while commuters cruised by in their minivans.

One-handed, I fished in the backpack. Porno mags and *Sports Illustrated.*

"Big surprise."

Checking my mirrors again, I took the next exit and stopped on a parallel street open at both ends.

The car had been hit about sixty times. Bullet holes stitched the trunk from lower left to upper right. The taillights were red and white chips. Two bullets had crazed the back window.

I squatted and sniffed, but didn't detect any gas leak. Mount a cannon on a Benz and you can go to war.

Fingering the holes, I imitated Manny, my slow-bear boss at the garage. "Gonna take some wicked work t'pass inspection this yeah."

□ □ □

"Sorry to keep you waiting, dear. Macy's had a sale on shoes."

Steve Buncha glared like a raccoon in a trap. He was dirty from lying in leaves. The sapling was scarred round and round by the handcuff. "Did you get the money?"

"Nope. Got a spiffy backpack out of the deal, though." I tossed it in his lap. Magazines spilled out.

"Those shitballs couldn't even get that little bit together?"

"It's worse than that, Steve, but I'll tell you later. For now, we got a change in plans. You're gonna come up with the money."

"How do I know you didn't take it already and stick in these books?"

"That's the trouble with being dishonest. You can never trust anybody." Aiming the .22 at his middle, I uncuffed him. "Cheer up. You get to ride in front like a big boy."

He balked as I led him around the passenger's side. "My car!"

"Hammered, hunh?"

"What's with the bathtubs? Ha! They tried to kill you good!"

"Good thing they didn't, or you'd be bear shit. Get in."

It took some doing, but I squoze Steve into the passenger's kneehole with one hand cuffed to the lower seat frame.

Hunchbacked, he had to crane his neck to see me. He didn't. I'm nothing to look at.

"Why should I give you the money?" he asked the floor.

"C'mon, Steve. After all we've been through? You know I'll just keep bugging you till I get it."

Back on the West Side, I circled three times looking for the blue Buick. Finally I parked. I was amazed I hadn't been pulled over for the bullet holes and cracked window and fried taillights, but maybe the cops watched the highway, it being Friday.

I shifted Steve's handcuffs behind his back with the chain through his belt, and prodded him with the .22 up the stairs. The tenement smelt of red pepper oil and ginger and oranges. A woman looked at us and looked away. Probably figured I was a hooker.

The gang's apartment was a rathole. Steve showed me where to kick aside dirty laundry and pull up a floorboard. Underneath was a cereal box stuffed with cash. I counted out $36,000, counted it again, and put the rest back.

Steve goggled. "You're not gonna rob the rest?"

I buttoned the money into the many pockets of my Army jacket. "It's worth the rest just to see the look on your face."

Back in the car, I handcuffed Steve a little more comfortably. Tracked back and forth through side streets. Checked the dash clock. 2:30. I handed over his cell phone.

"Call your heroes and tell them to meet me at Bridge Street and Elm."

He sniffed as if I were the stupid one. "They'll kill you in a second."

"Thanks for the warning, but call 'em anyway. They must be worried about you."

Steve dialed, spoke in Thai, then added, "Steve, asshole." He relayed instructions.

I felt sorry for the guy. His whole life had changed, and he didn't have a clue.

He hung up. I let him keep the phone. I pulled my tech knife, flicked it open, and jammed the blade into the dash. I propped the .22 in my lap. He watched, wary.

2:50. Show time.

We skimmed over the bridge and approached Elm. The blue Buick jumped out of a parking space after us.

I flipped Steve a small key from my shirt pocket. "Take off the cuffs and pitch 'em out the window. But sit tight. I'll pop you if I have to."

The Buick came fast behind. Once they thumped the bumper. I hoped the airbags didn't blow out.

"Hang onto your hat."

Banging a left and a right, careful not to run the lights and lose my hound dogs, I zoomed up a side street—

—stomped the brakes—

—cracked the wheel hard—

—and skidded to a screeching halt, rocking sideways, blocking the street.

The Buick T-boned us square.

Front and side airbags deployed like the Macy's Thanksgiving Day Parade. Alarms buzzed like hornets. I ripped the tech knife from the dashboard and slashed all three airbags. Then I hit the Unlock button and shoved Steve Buncha into the street. I climbed after.

The Buick was locked against the Mercedes. Greasy, not wearing a seat belt, sat behind a bent steering wheel clutching a bloody nose. Fridge climbed out limping.

And five hundred cops stood around, blue as the ocean. It was dead-on 3:00. Shift Change at the Manchester Police Department Headquarters.

I pointed at the Buick. "Watch 'em! They've got guns!"

The magic word. Pistols spun out of holsters. Four of us

faced a circle of black holes. I dropped to my knees. I knew the routine. I'd done it to others.

Proned out, covered, secured, handcuffed, searched and disarmed, then hauled to my feet, I felt suddenly tired. It had been a long day.

"Mind telling us what this is all about?" The cop in charge was Bigda. Steely eyes behind steel frames. Body like a gorilla.

"These morons tried to kill us," I told him. "They shot the shit out of our car."

"This bitch kidnapped me!" Steve shrilled. "She stuck me in the trunk and wouldn't let me out—"

"Idiot! I saved your life!"

That shut everyone up. With my hands cuffed behind my back, I pointed with my nose.

"Check out the back of your car, dummy. It looks like a Swiss cheese. Your goons never shot at me. They drilled the living hell out of the trunk because they thought you were inside! Your guys double-crossed you, Steve. They wanted to keep the money and the business!"

A cop shook bullets out of my crappy .22. "You got a permit to carry concealed?"

"Yes."

Another counted the contents of my pockets. "What's with all the money?"

"It's money. It's not illegal to carry money."

"Not unless it's evidence." Officer Bigda hoisted me to tiptoes. "Come on. Everybody inside."

I talked fast as we were frog-marched across the parking lot and around back to the Booking Room. They'd separate us for interrogation. "Steve, I saved your life! You got any complaints?"

"Uh, no. I mean, I dunno."

"You were driving recklessly," said Bigda. "You caused an accident."

"The wheel spun in my hand. And nobody got hurt."

"We got bullet holes. And what's this about kidnapping?"

"He's delirious. I raced to get here—at the speed limit—in time for shift change because I thought our lives were in danger."

"You're gonna need an attorney," said the cop. "I suggest you let him or her do the talking."

Concrete walls surrounded us. I remembered the smell: must and polish and disinfectant and cordite. The booking officer was Sergeant Doughty. Gray-bald, looks like he's had his ass kicked. He blinked. "I know you. You used to be a cop."

"Used to be."

Other cops nodded, remembering the stories. The female cop who got sliced to ribbons and was quietly mustered off the force. All forces.

"Take these damn handcuffs off, will you?" I sniped. "We're innocent. Steve Buncha here didn't trust his bodyguards. He hired me to investigate. I did. They tried to kill him. I kept him alive. You've got the bad guys, convicted felons packing guns. Book them. Steve and I should be free to leave. Right, Steve?"

"Uh, right, right. I don't want any trouble." The poor guy looked stunned, having lost his two best friends.

"This is some kind of bullshit, but I don't know what kind." Officer Bigda waved the other cops off to their homes: their wives and husbands and kids and BBQs and TV sets and beer. Or to a shift: radar tuning forks and an AR tucked against the roof and pepper spray that needed to be shaken before you tucked it in your belt and jokes over the radio.

I had trouble talking, choked by a heartache I couldn't believe. I wished I could go with them. Any of them.

Sergeant Doughty tilted the computer screen. "Name?"

"Blake. Susan Marie. I'm in the files. I'm a licensed PI."

"I wouldn't bet on that," muttered Bigda.

Steve slumped on a bench, trembling like a man

reprieved from the electric chair. Then he shook his head. "Hey. What about my car?"

"I'll give you a good deal." I sniffed. "I'm a mechanic now."

□ □ □

Tom Viroj sat at the same table in McDonald's. Beside him sat his parents, slim and elegant as royalty amid yellow and orange plastic.

"You got my parents' money back?" He couldn't believe it.

"I got them what they need."

I set a passbook, cranberry red, on the table. I kept my finger on it. Tom's parents looked bewildered. They queried Tom in Thai: growl, gutter, growl.

"This is a bank book," I said. "The account has $28,000 in my name. If your parents want the money, we go to the bank and add their names to the account. Take it or leave it."

Tom talked to his parents in Thai a long time, pleading, I thought, while they frowned. But they came back quick. Growl, growl.

"They'll take it."

Cat's Cradle

Skye Alexander

The summer of my twenty-seventh year I got involved with a woman twice my age who was dying of cancer, which would have been troublesome enough if I hadn't already been involved with her daughter, and if the daughter hadn't been married to a man who wanted to kill me. Only one thing can get a guy into such a complicated mess—thinking with the little head instead of the big one.

Let me back up and explain. I wasn't looking for a job when I wandered into All Booked Up that sunny July morning in '71. But the bookstore's owner, a fifty-ish blonde with the tiniest teeth I've ever seen, heard the beach calling. When I handed her two bits for a used copy of *Tropic of Cancer* she asked, "Do you know what ISBN stands for?"

"International Standard Book Number."

"You're hired." She held out her hand. "Welcome. I'm Helen Dietz."

"Max McCoy," I replied, thoroughly confused.

"If you sell anything, put the money in the Valentine candy box in the desk drawer." She rummaged through a battered leather purse the size of a duffel bag and pulled out a set of keys. "Lock up at five. I live at the end of the street, the yellow house with the purple door—just drop the keys through the mail slot."

Before I could protest, she was gone.

I spent the next two hours unpacking boxes of books with postmarks dating back to last year. Around lunch time, my first customer sauntered in, a chick about my age dressed in full hippie regalia: bellbottoms, tie-dyed t-shirt, peace sign belt buckle, and love beads. Her caramel-colored hair was parted in the middle and hung straight down almost to her waist.

"Is Helen around?" she asked.

"She took off," I answered.

"You working here?"

"Looks that way. I don't know exactly. Helen just handed me the keys and split."

She nodded. "Sounds about right. Well, then, can you recommend a good mystery?"

"Sorry, I don't know much about mysteries. Sir Arthur Conan Doyle? Agatha Christie?" I suggested, throwing out the only two names I could think of.

"That's okay, I'll just look around."

I'm usually pretty good at chatting up chicks, but so far I'd only managed to display my ignorance to this one. I decided to try a different tack, let her show me what she knew. "Are you a mystery buff?"

She plucked a book from a shelf, fanned the pages, then put it back. "Not really. I only started reading them a couple years ago, after my father was murdered."

"Wow, I mean, I'm sorry. What happened?"

"My father was Philip Austen—you must have heard about it."

I shook my head. "I just moved here from L.A. a week ago."

"Oh. Well, it was a pretty big deal. The first murder in Rockport since last century." She sounded proud of the notoriety. "He was shot at close range with a .38. My mother heard the shot and found the body in the backyard. They still don't know who killed him."

"Do they know why?"

She pulled another paperback off the shelf and flipped through it. "The police figured robbery—his wallet was missing. Maybe he discovered someone trying to break into the house. But my father was a political figure. I've always wondered if he was assassinated."

I thought she was being a bit paranoid. Conspiracy theories abounded in 1971—the murders of JFK, Bobby Kennedy, and Martin Luther King still loomed large in the public's mind. Russia was still the Evil Empire and Sean Connery was still James Bond.

"I hope they catch his killer," I said.

She laid a copy of *The Big Sleep* on the counter. "I'll take this one."

□ □ □

Helen stood on the fourth rung of a ladder, shelving the books I'd unpacked yesterday. When I asked about Philip Austen and his hippie daughter, she dropped a field guide to birds of the Northeast, practically hitting me on the head.

"Hey, watch it!"

"Sorry," she apologized.

I waited for an answer that was a long time coming. Finally she said, "Philip Austen was the Prince of Rockport."

"A real prince?"

She sighed, slid a couple books into place, then backed down the ladder. "Philip was a big fish in this little pond—a retired ambassador who'd traveled to foreign countries, met with world leaders. He was brilliant, handsome, and charming, and awfully pleased with himself. A terrible gossip and a name-dropper, and he liked to make himself look good by putting other people down. To Philip, us small-town folk were a bunch of peasants." She shook her head slowly. "Nonetheless, he was my friend and I miss the son of a bitch."

"His daughter—what's her name?—said he was murdered."

Helen nodded. "Catherine, everyone calls her Cat. Her husband, Torry Blake, handled the case. He was in the District Attorney's office then. They never arrested anyone for the murder. Doesn't look like they ever will."

Husband has never been one of my favorite words and I felt a slight letdown hearing it linked with that cute little chick, even though I'd only known her for about 5.5 minutes. "Cat thinks maybe he was assassinated," I suggested to see if the idea had wings.

"Cat likes intrigue. She has a vivid imagination." Helen sat down behind the old oak schoolmaster's desk where she kept the bookstore's paperwork and the Valentine cash box. "Most victims are murdered by someone they know, not hit men."

"But Austen wasn't an ordinary person; he was famous. And it sounds like he was kind of a prick."

Helen raised an eyebrow. "If every guy who's a prick got killed for it, the human race would soon die out." She smiled, showing her little girl's teeth. "Doesn't look like we're going to be flooded with customers today. Why don't you take the afternoon off."

□ □ □

I spotted Cat as I passed Front Beach, a sliver of sand and rocks on the edge of town that's usually crawling with tourists. Absorbed in the mystery novel I'd sold her, she seemed oblivious to the sunburn spreading across her shoulders. As I approached, she jabbed her cigarette in the sand, completing a spiral she'd made of butts.

"Hi," I said. "How's the book?"

She looked up, recognized me, and scooted over, making room for me to join her on her Grateful Dead beach towel. "Not bad, except I already know who the killer is. I always figure out whodunit after about twenty pages. I must have a criminal's mind."

"Or a mystery writer's. Maybe you should try your hand at it."

She shook her head and laid the book aside. "I don't have the patience or concentration to plot a murder. Writing children's books is about as much as I can handle."

"You write children's books?"

She shrugged. "Now and again."

She was wearing a multicolored bikini that looked like macramé potholders tied together with string. Cute little body, nice legs, nice ass. Not cute enough to attract a second glance on Venice Beach, but enough to hold my attention. Her long brown hair was twisted into a knot on top of her head and pinned in place with a chopstick.

"Your shoulders are getting burned. Want me to put suntan lotion on them?"

Cat handed me a bottle of Coppertone and I squeezed some into my palm. Taking my time, I massaged her shoulders, arms, and back, stroking her smooth skin and kneading her muscles until I half expected her to start purring.

After a few minutes she asked, "What did Helen say about me?"

"What makes you think we talked about you?"

"She was one of my father's favorite friends, even though they didn't have a thing in common. My mother can't stand Helen, but I've always liked her."

"She said you have a vivid imagination."

"Was that supposed to be a compliment?"

"I'd say a vivid imagination is essential for someone who writes children's books." I ran my thumbs up and down her neck.

"Mmmmm," she murmured, leaning into my caresses. "That feels nice."

The shadow that fell over us would have been the perfect cinematographical metaphor in a Hitchcock film. I looked up at a man who personified a Howitzer shell: gunmetal gray hair, stainless steel eyes, and the sleek, hard, no-nonsense body of someone who knows his way around the gym.

Cat pulled away too quickly, leaving my hands hanging empty in mid-air. She squinted at the ominous presence and said, "My husband, the great criminal lawyer Torrance Blake. Torry, this is Max McCoy. He works for Helen."

She must have asked around about me, because I hadn't told her my name. I stood up and held out my hand. Torry gripped it harder than necessary, his hackles bristling as we squared off like two cougars scuffling over a fresh-killed jackrabbit. I had a few inches on him and about fifteen years, but he seemed like a guy who'd fight dirty and the pressure on my hand said I didn't want to test his right hook.

"Nice to meet you," I lied.

Cat handed him a towel and he dried his face without taking those metallic eyes off me. Time to bow out, I decided.

"Well, I guess I'd better get going. See you around, Cat."

As I turned away, Torry muttered, "Dead man walking."

□ □ □

I ran into Cat again the next evening. She was smoking on the front steps of the Community Center and waved me over.

"Sorry about Torry's manners," she said.

"Does he threaten every guy you talk to?"

"Just the good-looking ones."

"Am I taking my life in my hands here?" I asked, only half-kidding.

Cat laughed. "His bark's worse than his bite. Anyway, he left this morning for Chicago—some very important meeting with some very important people."

"What are you doing with a guy like him? You seem like an odd couple."

"You know what they say, opposites attract." She shrugged. "Torry provides me with security and he lives out his bohemian fantasies vicariously through me."

"So what are you up to now?"

"Being a supportive daughter." She nodded at the Community Center, where half the residents of Rockport seemed to be gathered. Snippets of conversation and polite laughter drifted out the front door. "My mother's hosting a fundraiser for animal rights. Come inside, I'll introduce you."

Cat took my arm and led me through a crowd of men in navy blazers, gaudy plaid pants, and topsiders, and women wearing summer dresses and too much perfume. Old money. As we passed a linen-draped table laden with hors d'oeuvres, I snagged two glasses of wine.

"Mother likes animals better than people," Cat explained.

"So do I," I said, handing her a glass. "Most of them are more intelligent and better behaved."

She pulled me toward a group of octogenarians arranged around a tall, thin, very pale woman with short silvery hair, dressed in a black silk sheath. Her skin seemed almost transparent. When the woman saw us, her tired smile shifted to one of relief.

"Ah, Catherine, dear," she said, holding out a bejeweled hand.

Cat grasped her hand, frowning as she studied the woman's pallid face. The woman nodded almost imperceptibly and Cat's frown disappeared.

"Mom, I'd like you to meet Max McCoy. He's new in town. Max, this is my mother, Elizabeth Austen."

I noticed she didn't mention my job at the bookstore. Cat placed her mother's cool, delicate hand in mine and I said, "Pleased to meet you, ma'am."

Occasionally, I encounter someone I feel instantly drawn to, for no apparent reason. The Buddhists would say we'd known each other in a past lifetime, but I'm not a religious man. All I knew was that Elizabeth Austen's fragile elegance made me want to cherish and protect her, as if she were a rare Ming vase.

"Let's skip the 'ma'am' business, shall we? Mrs. Davenport, here, you can call ma'am," she smiled at the elderly dowager standing beside her, "but please call me Elizabeth."

Her directness and her voice—deep, sultry, and raspy as a blues singer's—surprised me. Cat might purr when content, but I imagined Elizabeth uttering the low, gravelly growl of a lioness.

"You're doing an admirable thing here," I said. I didn't know what kind of animals she was trying to save—whales, baby seals, gorillas, or homeless puppies—whether she was a representative for one of those acronym organizations like PETA or a lone loony with eighty cats at home, but I wanted her to like me.

"Are you an animal lover?" she asked.

"I like animals."

"Do you have any?"

"I had a dog, until a couple months ago. Actually, he was half-wolf."

"What happened to him?"

"Some redneck out in the Ozarks shot him. Didn't like my long hair and wanted to make sure I got out of town fast."

"Wow," said Cat. "You're lucky he didn't shoot you."

"Come for dinner, day after tomorrow," Elizabeth said, touching my arm. "We'll talk."

She turned back to Mrs. Davenport and company, politely dismissing me. Cat took my hand and steered me through several rooms packed with old Yankees consuming copious quantities of wine. We ended up in the kitchen.

"You made an impression," she said. "Mom doesn't see many people these days, outside of functions like this."

"Why not?"

"She isn't well. Three years ago she was diagnosed with breast cancer. She had a mastectomy. After chemo, she went into remission for a while." Cat paused, twisting a strand of hair around her finger. Her blue eyes clouded. "Lately her white blood cell count has been climbing."

That explained Elizabeth Austen's wan appearance. I felt a twinge of sadness and fear that seemed excessive considering the woman was a virtual stranger. "I'm sorry. Can she do chemo again?"

Cat shrugged and dropped what was apparently a painful subject. "I hope you like Indian food."

"I do. Why?"

"That's all Mom cooks. She and Dad lived in Delhi for several years, before I was born. It was the happiest time of her life."

I couldn't shift gears as fast as Cat. I was still processing the transition from cancer to curry when she made her next move—a move that caught me totally off guard: she grabbed my crotch.

"What are you doing?" I gasped, glancing around nervously to see if anyone had witnessed it.

"Gosh, I thought it was pretty obvious." She smiled sweetly at me. "Let's get out of here."

"What about your husband?" I'm not in the habit of rejecting the advances of pretty women, but I value my life. Torry Blake wasn't the first jealous guy to threaten me. I'd looked down the wrong end of a gun barrel before and I didn't ever want to do it again.

"I told you, he's in Chicago."

"Let me make one thing clear, Cat. If your husband ever comes after me, I'll consider him armed and dangerous. I'll strike first, ask questions later. I hope your conscience can handle the consequences."

"You're being a bit melodramatic, don't you think?" She looked up at me with those big blue eyes. "Come home with me, my pretty stray, and I'll give you something good to eat."

In moments like this, lust speaks louder than logic. It only took me about 2.2 seconds to overcome my reservations. At twenty-seven, we still think we're invulnerable. Later in life, I would exert a great deal more energy to avoid what I feared than to obtain what I desired, but not today. The risk, I think, even heightened the thrill.

I shook my head. "My place." At least I had the good sense not to follow her into the enemy camp. "My place."

□ □ □

Elizabeth Austen lived in one of those old estates you can't see from the road, a massive stone affair right out of *The Great Gatsby* with about forty rooms, Corinthian columns, a carriage house, formal gardens, and sweeping views of the ocean. Cat parked her MGB near the kitchen door and told me not to be too impressed by the house.

"It's a hand-me-down," she explained. "My maternal grandfather made his money the same way old Joe Kennedy did—bootlegging."

I followed her into a kitchen the size of a gymnasium, with stainless steel commercial appliances and at least an acre of blue-and-white Delft tile. Pretty excessive for someone who rarely entertained and cooked only Indian food, I thought. Elizabeth stood at the stove, stirring something in a copper pot. When we entered, she turned and held out her hands, taking Cat's in her right one and mine in her left. Her face, flushed from the heat, seemed less spectral than I remembered. Tonight she reminded me of an angel, pure and ethereal in a white blouse and long white skirt.

"How nice to see you both. Thank you for coming."

"Thank you for inviting me," I answered. "It smells wonderful. Let me guess . . . lamb *saag*?"

"Very good. Catherine told me you like Indian food."

"I visited India a few times. I didn't think I'd enjoy it, but the country surprised me."

Elizabeth nodded. "I expected filth and poverty and oppressive heat. I wasn't prepared to also find a land of incredible beauty and delightful people. And wonderful food. The only thing I never got used to were the bandicoots. Philip and I had to shoot several that got into the house." She shivered, remembering.

"That was before she became an animal rights activist, of course," explained Cat.

"Perhaps I'm trying to undo my bad karma," Elizabeth said. "And now, if you'll excuse me, I have to get back to my cooking. Please help yourselves to some wine."

While her mother fixed dinner, Cat showed me around the mansion, which looked more like a museum than a home. Each room displayed treasures from foreign lands—Persian rugs, African masks, carved Japanese chests, jade Buddhas, Aztec pottery. As we toured the place, it occurred to me that if Elizabeth died, all this would pass to Cat—and because Massachusetts is a joint-property state, Torry Blake stood to inherit a bundle, too.

"I used to slide down this banister," Cat said as we climbed the curved staircase to the second floor. "And this used to be my bedroom. How about a quickie?" She flopped down on the four-poster bed.

"Your mother's downstairs." I grabbed her arm and pulled her up. "C'mon. We'd better get back."

"Spoil sport." She stuck out her bottom lip in a mock pout and I could easily imagine the little princess who'd slept in this room.

We ate dinner by candlelight, at a Chippendale-style mahogany table that could have seated the entire President's Cabinet and their wives, laid with English bone china, Austrian crystal goblets, and gleaming silverware. In addition to the lamb *saag*, Elizabeth served me *kabuli channa* laced with ginger and garlic, creamy *matter paneer*, and *poori* bread that looked like a fried pillow. In between the spicy dishes, I cooled my tongue with cucumber and yogurt. It wasn't the best Indian food I've eaten, but better than I'd expected from a Yankee Brahmin like Elizabeth Austen.

Each time she spooned something onto my plate, she made a subtle point of touching my hand. In the candles' golden glow, she seemed younger and healthier, and I tried to envision her hosting gala parties here for visiting dignitaries. During dinner, we talked about the places we'd seen—Tibet, Senegal, Yugoslavia, Madagascar, Chile, Iceland, Cape Breton—trying to outdo each other. I was the only one who'd been to Vietnam. Cat played footsie with me under the table, nestling her bare arch against my crotch. With the two of them directing 99.9 percent of the conversation my way and vying for my attention, *I* felt like a visiting dignitary.

Somewhere between Tahiti and New Zealand, Elizabeth grew quiet and rested her chin on her hands. I noticed, even before Cat, that she was fading.

"Do you want to lie down, Mom?"

Elizabeth shook her head. She pushed herself up from the table and Cat reached for her hand, but Elizabeth grabbed my arm instead. "Why don't we sit in the den? There's an old movie on TV that I'd like to watch."

I grabbed the wine and guided Elizabeth into the adjoining room, settled her on an enormous leather couch, and sat beside her. Cat flipped through the channels until she found *The Postman Always Rings Twice*, then sat on the other side of her mother. As John Garfield ambled into the café to meet his destiny, I refilled our glasses.

"I love this scene," said Cat as Lana Turner's lipstick rolled provocatively across the floor. Evidently she'd watched this flick quite a few times, because she chimed in on about half of Lana's lines and pointed out all sorts of details she didn't want me to miss. If I hadn't already seen the film her backseat directing might have annoyed me, but I knew she was using the script as foreplay and the steamy chemistry on the screen intensified the erotic tension in our own dicey triangle.

As John and Lana took their first moonlight swim together, Elizabeth laid her head in Cat's lap. I angled my body and leaned against the arm of the sofa, making room for Elizabeth to stretch out her legs behind me. She patted the couch and said, "You can put your feet up here if you want, Max."

I slipped off my sandals, swung my legs up onto the sofa alongside Elizabeth's reclining body, and tucked them under Cat's knees. Cat stroked her mother's head with her right hand and my ankles with her left. Elizabeth rested her arm on my knees. Long before Lana tried to whack her clueless husband in the bathtub, the three of us were curled up together like a litter of kittens, nuzzling and rubbing each other while fantasies dirty danced in my head.

My hopes for a *ménage à trois* fizzled, however, when Elizabeth started snoring softly.

"Can you carry her upstairs?" Cat asked.

I scooped up the sleeping woman, surprised at how little she weighed. Cancer had consumed so much of her flesh that her bones were as sharp and delicate as dried sticks beneath skin like wilted rose petals. Cat turned back the covers of Elizabeth's bed and I laid her down carefully. While Cat undressed her mother, I went back downstairs to watch the rest of the movie.

Just before the final scene, Cat came in and shut off the TV. "I hate the ending," she said, unzipping my pants. "If I'd been the author, they would've lived happily ever after."

"But they killed a guy," I pointed out.

"They did it for love."

"I think you're confusing lust with love."

She lay back on the couch and pulled me down on top of her. "Confuse me," she purred.

□ □ □

Still wet from the shower, I pulled on a pair of gym shorts and answered the door. Elizabeth Austen stood on my doorstep with a manila folder in her hand. I couldn't have been more surprised if the Pope had come calling.

"Sorry I nodded off last night. You must think me quite rude," she said.

"Not at all. But you missed the end of the movie."

"I've seen it before." She smiled, her neon-blue eyes lighting up her ashen face. "May I come in?"

I stepped back to let her enter, self-consciously aware of my rumpled hair, morning breath, and the Zen-like barrenness of my crummy little apartment. I'd given away most of my furniture when I left L.A. and hadn't gotten around to replacing it yet. "I was just about to make coffee. Want some?"

"That would be nice." She handed me the folder, her excuse for being here. "I thought you might enjoy these recipes. They're some of my favorites, collected while we were in India."

"Thanks."

"I hope you don't mind my coming here uninvited. I didn't want to bring them to *that store*."

The way she spat out the words "that store" roused my curiosity, but I sensed this was territory I shouldn't venture into right now. Instead, I said, "I'm glad you're here," and set about fixing the coffee.

Elizabeth seated herself at the kitchen table, watching me. Studying me was more like it. As I placed a steaming cup in front of her she said, "I like you, Max. May I speak candidly with you?"

"Of course," I answered.

"I suppose Catherine told you I have cancer."

I nodded.

"Three years ago, I had a breast removed. I underwent chemotherapy and lost all my hair. Afterward, my husband withdrew from me completely—he found me repulsive. My self-esteem plummeted. I no longer felt like a woman."

She paused, searching my face for a reaction: empathy or disgust. I'm not a very compassionate person, but my heart went out to her. I thought Philip Austen had gotten what he deserved.

"Now it seems the cancer has moved into my lungs," she continued. "I'm going to try chemo again, but the prognosis isn't good, I'm afraid." She reached for my hand. "I know I'm being terribly forward, but the proximity of death has caused me to dispense with many of the formalities of etiquette. I have a favor to ask of you, Max. Will you make love to me?"

I led her into my bedroom, regretting its total lack of ambiance—the mattress on the floor and the orange crate nightstand were hardly befitting a woman like Elizabeth Austen. My hands shook as I undressed her. The kinky fantasies I'd entertained last night dissolved, replaced by a mixture of tenderness and apprehension. For the first time since high school I had performance anxiety.

Like most things we fear, the reality wasn't half as bad as the anticipation. Instead of being repelled, I found her asymmetry exotic and exciting. I thought of the Amazon women who, according to mythology, removed one breast so they could draw their bows without interference. As I ran my tongue along the crescent moon scar, she uttered a low, guttural sigh. Not a growl, exactly, but close enough.

□   □   □

For the next few weeks I was busier than any man has a right to be, trying to keep mother and daughter from finding out about each other and Torry Blake from finding out anything at all. Mostly I worried about Cat giving us away. A loose canon, she enjoyed taking risks. Helen was right—Cat liked intrigue. The thought of two men fighting over her and maybe killing each other turned her on. And while I was all for turning Cat on, I had no intention of dying for her. Before she left my apartment, after one of our afternoon romps, I made sure she showered and douched and brushed her teeth to remove all hair, fibers, and body fluids from her person. Torry Blake was a criminal lawyer, after all, and I figured those razor-sharp eyes didn't miss much.

I had a few anxious moments one night when I ran into Cat and her husband at the movie theater and she lit up like a Las Vegas casino. Torry grabbed Cat's arm and maneuvered her away from me, positioning his body between us. I half expected him to pee on her leg.

"You're still in town?" he sneered.

"I'm settling in nicely," I replied. "Rockport already feels like home."

"Most accidents happen near home, you know. Don't get too comfortable."

My ego goaded me to take the arrogant prick down with a couple of well-placed punches, but I had enough common sense to restrain myself. If I so much as sneezed on Torry Blake, he'd stick me behind bars on an assault charge and slap a lawsuit the size of the National Debt on me. I refused to let him trick me into playing his game.

Avoiding situations that might bring me together with Cat and Elizabeth at the same time was a bit harder. When Cat suggested another dinner at her mother's house a few days later, I declined, saying I had tickets to a Red Sox game. When I spotted them at the supermarket, I hurried into the next aisle and out the door before they noticed me. It's hard to hide in a town of six thousand. Restaurants, the drugstore, the post office all became venues for awkward encounters.

With Elizabeth's health waning, Cat dropped in to check on

her mother every day—sometimes in the evenings, too—usually unannounced. More than once I listened from the bedroom as Elizabeth tried to get rid of her daughter without rousing Cat's curiosity. My place wasn't any safer—Cat popped by whenever the urge struck her, and it struck her several times a week. About the only place I knew Elizabeth wouldn't set foot was All Booked Up, which worked out fine for a while since Cat liked the idea of getting it on in the storeroom while customers milled around out front.

Then one sultry afternoon I was reciting passages from *Tropic of Cancer* to Cat in bed, punctuating Miller's words with physical demonstrations, when she suddenly shouted "Ow!" and rolled away.

"What's the matter?" I asked.

She plucked something from between the sheets and held it in her palm, scrutinizing it the way an entomologist might study a rare beetle. I gazed down at the sapphire and diamond earring in her hand and knew I was in deep shit.

Cat glared at me. "Motherfucker."

□ □ □

I phoned Cat several times over the next few days, but she didn't pick up. Once Torry answered and I hung up. When I tried to reach Elizabeth, her housekeeper told me she was resting and promised to give her my message. Elizabeth never returned the call. Finally, I drove over to the Austen mansion and was met at the door by the housekeeper. "Mrs. Austen is out," was all she'd tell me.

I hoped Cat and her mother were just pissed off—they'd get over that eventually. More disturbing was the possibility that Elizabeth's illness had worsened; perhaps she'd been hospitalized. I considered asking Helen if she'd heard anything, but there seemed to be some sort of animosity brewing between the two women and I didn't want to stir the pot. Like in the children's game "Cat's Cradle," I found myself caught in a web of strings. Then one afternoon at the bookstore I was making change for a twenty and knocked the Valentine candy cash box on the floor. Coins and bills scattered, and the paper lace doily at the bottom of the box slipped out. When I picked up the box, I noticed the inscription inside: "To my dearest Helen, with all my love, Philip."

Bells and lights went off in my brain, like a pinball machine registering hits. After I closed up that evening, instead of slipping the keys through the slot in Helen's front door I let myself in and snooped around. Framed photographs of Helen with Philip Austen, hanging on the walls in her bedroom, confirmed my suspicions. I wondered how much Cat and Elizabeth knew and how long they'd known it.

☐ ☐ ☐

I was so glad to see her that I didn't notice the gun at first. When I invited her in, she raised the .38 and aimed it at my crotch.

"Say good-bye to your balls, baby boy," she hissed.

As I lunged for the revolver it went off.

☐ ☐ ☐

Cat was sitting beside the hospital bed when I woke up. My whole lower body throbbed with an amorphous, morphine-dulled pain. I jerked the sheet off and stared in horror at the bandages swathing my hips and left thigh.

"You're a lucky man," she said. "A few inches the other way and you'd have been singing soprano."

"Your mother . . ."

"If it hadn't been for Mom, you might have bled to death. She told me how she went over to your place to break things off and found you and called the ambulance." Cat stood, picked up her purse, and kissed me on the forehead. "It was fun while it lasted, Max, but it couldn't go on forever."

I tried again, my mind and tongue slowed by the drugs. "Your mother . . . "

"She's downstairs now, getting a chemo treatment. She told me to tell you that if she feels well enough afterward, she'll come up and visit you."

With acknowledgments to Dan Brown for the sentiments expressed on page 57, lines 4-6.

Death of a Good Wife

Susan Oleksiw

Anita Ray leaned over the breakfast buffet table of Hotel Delite, an empty plate in her left hand and a serving spoon in her right, surveying the various offerings. Breakfast at her aunt's South Indian resort hotel was always a treat. She decided to have two *iddalies*, coconut chutney, and a large dollop of plain curd, and then have a small bowl of papaya. She was about to begin serving herself when the sound of rustling cloth caught her attention. Her Aunt Meena leaned toward a camera sitting by a steaming cup of tea, then pulled back, as though the strap were a cobra ready to strike. When she saw Anita, she straightened up and smiled broadly.

"Anita, I have an idea."

"Goodness, Auntie, I thought you swore off having ideas." Anita joined her aunt at the table.

"Eh? What? Never mind. This is a good idea. You could get yourself one of those little cameras the size of a cigarette case and use that one and put it back in your pocket like the tourists do and they would think you're one of them."

"Now, why would I want to do that?" Anita asked as she sat down and pushed the camera away from her plate.

"Well, it would be like a disguise. You would pretend to be a tourist."

"And you would pretend what? That I'm normal?"

"Don't be hurt, Anita."

"I'm not hurt, Auntie."

"It's just that people ask questions, and I, oh dear, I have nothing I can say."

"Poor Auntie." Anita grinned sympathetically.

"I only meant— Anita, why do you have that look on your face?"

"You know, Auntie, you may be right. I could use a disguise now and then. And I could get some of those beach clothes the tailors make." Anita pulled the newspaper toward her and propped it up against her camera. Her aunt gasped.

"You don't have to go that far. Those clothes— Why are you agreeing with me? What do you see in the newspaper?" She leaned over her niece's shoulder and scanned the headlines.

"Oh, no, no, no. Please, Anita, you mustn't ask questions about all the deaths of people I know. Couldn't you just ask questions about strangers?"

"Goodness, Auntie, if I could only talk to people you don't know, I'd have to go back to the States."

Aunt Meena grabbed the newspaper and fled the room.

□ □ □

"Okay, Ravi, what happened?" Anita snagged the waiter as soon as he approached her table. It was still early, before 7:00 A.M., and although the buffet was laid, few hotel guests appeared at breakfast before 8:00 A.M., a source of disgust for the Brahman cook, who rose at 3:30 to perform *puja* before turning to the commercial activity of his day. "Why did my aunt run off with the newspaper, and what happened to Mr. Pillai's daughter-in-law?"

"I am forbidden to speak of it." Ravi glanced around to see if anyone might be watching.

"Ah, I see. My aunt must know the family well. Who is it? Tell me, Ravi. If you don't I'll find out some other way and Auntie will blame you."

Ravi gasped. "All right. It was that girl who married Jayan, the young cousin of your mother's teacher's wife's sister." Anita sighed, wishing people would just be known by their names in India instead of their lineage. It would make things so much clearer—and explanations shorter. "Your aunt was very fond of him, very fond. He is such a good boy, and now look what has happened to him. She cannot believe it. Good is rewarded with evil—that's all she'll say."

"Nonsense," Anita said. "My aunt dramatizes everything. Still, it wouldn't hurt to ask a few questions."

The hotel guests were filling up the dining room by the time Anita had finished her breakfast, found a map of Garuda Nagar, where Jayan and his family lived, and decided on a course of action. She stuffed her papers into her purse and headed for the front door, her camera dangling against her chest.

"Where are you going?" her aunt asked imperiously, her chin thrust out to hide any weakness.

"Now, Auntie. You know what such questions can lead to," Anita said.

"No! I forbid it. Every time you go out with such a look on your face you come back with such tales—I cannot believe I know my own neighbors anymore."

"Well, you don't, do you?"

"Anita, how you talk. Of course I do, don't I?"

Anita left her pondering this conundrum.

Garuda Nagar was a new development on the outskirts of Trivandrum made up of modest bungalows enclosed by a series of small temples to various deities—the most common were dedicated to Shiva and Devi, but a few honored Krishna with small shrines cut into compound walls or set up along the road. Anita followed the lanes until she came to Priya House, and rattled the gate to announce her arrival.

"What is it? What do you want?" A bearer appeared from around the side of the house and changed his tone as soon as he saw who it was. Anita asked to see Jayan's parents.

"His mother is crying in her bedroom and his father is sitting in his visiting room glaring at anyone who comes near him."

"Where is Jayan?" Anita asked.

"In his room. Where else would he be?"

Anita considered the reply. Well, if my spouse had just died, where would I be at this time? She asked to see Jayan's father. Mr. Pillai made no secret of not being interested in seeing her, but since she was the niece of the owner of Hotel Delite he had no choice; one family cannot insult another family of long association.

"Your aunt has mentioned you many times," Mr. Pillai said, and not warmly in Anita's view.

"How nice of her," Anita said with a smile. "I came to express our condolences. You have had a terrible loss, a young daughter-in-law too." Mr. Pillai shrugged and picked up his paper, making a great show of folding it so that all the creases lined up.

"Yes, a great loss. You want tea?"

How could she turn down such a gracious invitation? "Yes, that would be lovely." A few minutes later Anita sipped her tea and knew she had better get to the point because they were both getting tired of small talk. She put her cup down and said, "It is tragic that she was so young and her death was so strange."

"Strange? Strange? You think it is strange that a woman who turns to prostitution is beaten to death by her customer? You think it is tragic? Ha! It is simple justice!"

"Prostitution?" Anita said. She had wondered what was so odd and distressing about this death, but prostitution had never entered her mind. "How do you know this?"

"How she was found," he said, "how she was found. That's how I know."

"And how was she found?"

"Someone saw her go into a house of those ladies and passed the word. I sent a policeman to get her back—why I do not know—and he found her all bloody and dead on the floor of the bedroom, only a rope cot and some rags for sheets there with her. A filthy, low place—and a fitting tomb for her sort."

Anita had seen many angry men before, and had listened with the patience of a childless woman, but Mr. Pillai's anger was different. It scared her, and she pulled away from the canyon of his despair.

"They had not been married long, is that true?"

"Only a few weeks," he said, rubbing his hands together.

"And so young. I wonder how it happened," she said more to herself than to him.

"She was a slut. That's how it happened." He looked at her as though she had insulted him.

"Does she have family in this area? I want to offer my condolences to them too."

"No family here. My son met her in college in Cochin. They married there, just there last month."

"Ah, just last month."

"A slut has seduced him. A stupid boy." Mr. Pillai shook his head in dismay over the behavior of his only son.

At the door, Anita turned to the bearer and asked if she could express her condolences to Jayan. The bearer shrugged and disappeared. A few minutes later a young man no more than twenty came shuffling down the stairs and onto the veranda. He looked absently around him until his eyes came to Anita, and he gazed at her with no curiosity. Anita thought he might be drugged or sleepy or dull—it was hard to tell which. His face was soft and unformed by decision-making or any other challenges, and his dark wavy hair made him seem too pretty to have character waiting to be called forth. Anita introduced herself.

"Thank you for your kind words," he said quietly. "It is so sad for me. I hardly know what has happened." He looked around him, with his hands hanging at his sides while the crows grew brave and skittered onto the veranda.

"You haven't been married long," Anita said.

"Barely a month." Jayan blushed.

"You met at the College?"

"She was living in the Women's Hostel and became friends with Meenakshee Thoma, a childhood friend of mine. She introduced us."

"Tell me what happened the last time you saw your wife," Anita said.

"The last time?" A warm smile came over his face, and he looked even younger. "It was nearing midnight. You know it was the night before Pongaala Puja, on March 6?"

"Isn't that the *puja* when young women get a new pot and some rice and take everything to the Attukal Bhagavathy Temple in Trivandrum for a blessing?"

"It's more complicated than that," Jayan said with shy enthusiasm. "Lots of temples have Pongaala Puja this time of year, but the one at Attukal Bhagavathy is the biggest. The morning puja is elaborate and at noon a whole troop of priests sets off with water to bless all the pots and then they pass along fire from the temple to start the cooking fires. The streets are lined with women kneeling behind their pots set on the three bricks and a small fire. The women come from all over Kerala."

"It must look like the city is on fire," Anita said.

"They make their rice." Jayan paused and smiled. "It's quite good—with jaggery and banana and cashew nuts. Anyway, when the rice is done, the priests come again and bless all the women and their cooking. It's supposed to ensure a good kitchen for the rest of the year, so a happy home."

"Is that why she wanted to go? To get your marriage off on a good foot, so to speak?"

"Bija said it was so important that she wanted to be sure to get a good spot. Thousands of women go to this every year. She was so happy. She had a new pot and three new bricks to sit it on, and I collected just the right firewood for her and she bought expensive rice and other ingredients. And a new saree, just for this."

"When did she leave here?"

"Near midnight, so she would get a good spot. There was a special bus running from the villages around here. She was going to be near Overbridge Junction, she thought."

"Overbridge," Anita repeated, "and with thousands of other women. Sounds like the proverbial needle in a haystack."

"No hay in this cooking."

"What? No, of course not. You were happy with your wife?"

Jayan blushed and hung his head. Lord, he's just a boy, and an unformed one at that, Anita thought.

□ □ □

Anita had to walk through several lanes before she encountered an unengaged autorickshaw. She waved it down and gave the driver Meenakshee's address. Anita found her sitting on the veranda sifting rice for the evening meal.

"You are going about telling everyone you are sorry to hear about Bija's death, aren't you?"

"You seem very skeptical," Anita said.

"She had no friends here. Why would you care?"

"Do you?"

Meenakshee shrugged. "I am sorry she is dead, but I didn't know her very well. We were not bosom buddies, growing up together. She had no family here except her husband's, but she was a nice enough girl."

"Were you surprised when you heard she had died and the way she died?"

"Oh yes. That did surprise me. She was very naive." Meenakshee glanced up at Anita, sizing her up.

"And?"

"And, more than naive."

"How so?"

"When she told me that she and Jayan had just married, she giggled and blushed so much that I had to ask her how she had fared on her wedding night, and she insisted that it was the rule to wait a few days and they were waiting. I think she was too frightened of sex to plunge right in, and Jayan certainly isn't worldly enough or strong-minded enough to insist on anything of the sort. Not him, that's for sure."

"You have known him a long time?"

"Since we were children." She gave the rice a vigorous toss.

"I see." Anita looked around at the modest house; Meenakshee's parents had invested a great deal in their daughter's education compared to what they seemed to have. "Were you surprised when you'd heard she was married?"

Meenakshee glanced at Anita, and she felt a chill across her shoulders.

"It was impetuous of them," she said.

"Not a good match?"

Meenakshee shook her head, but kept her eyes lowered as she picked through the rice.

"I suppose you might have been more suitable."

Meenakshee's hand paused in midair, then dropped into the rice once again and deftly removed a small pebble. "I have known him all my life."

"And she stole him from you?"

The pain in Meenakshee's eyes was all Anita needed to see.

□ □ □

The traffic between Overbridge and East Fort was enough to drive the sanest person mad if he or she spent any time there; it was best to consider it a circle from Dante and charge through it as best one can. Anita ordered the autorickshaw driver to stop in front of an alley and wait while she stepped out into the foot traffic. She strolled back down to the main intersection, studied the sidewalks and other buildings, then strolled back to the auto.

"Find a tea stall that was open on the night before Pongaala," she told him.

He gave her an impatient look but set off. Within a few minutes he was back, pointing to a stall a few storefronts away. They drove down to it. When the custom cleared, Anita approached the tea *wallah* and looked over his offerings.

"Tea?"

"Hmm. Tea." He set about serving her.

"You are well placed for the pilgrims for Pongaala and other *pujas*, aren't you?"

He nodded, not ready to commit himself.

"Have the police already asked you for information about that night? You know that a woman died just over there?"

"Yes, I am knowing this."

"Have they questioned you?"

"Not me. I am only a tea *wallah*."

Aha, thought Anita, his pride is hurt and he knows something. "Their mistake, isn't it?"

He smiled and winked at her.

"So, let me guess," Anita said.

"You would guess wrong."

"What would I guess that is wrong?"

"She is not dragged kicking and screaming along the road."

"No?"

"No. She is walking along pleasantly chatting with two men. Happy to see them."

"Who are they?"

"Common thugs."

"Then . . ."

"Does she know this?" he asked, anticipating her question.

"Ah, she doesn't know who they are. Okay. But why, then?"

"Ah, that is the question," he said with a sly smile.

"Did you see them again?"

"No, but I am hearing her. She is screaming her head off and making such a racket."

"What sort of racket?"

"It sounds like she is tossing the furniture at the walls."

"Does no one come to the aid of a woman calling for help?"

"Sometimes."

"But not with those men. Is that it?"

He smiled and winked.

"So why did she at first go willingly with them?"

"You might ask the other women."

"What other women?"

"The ones also cooking on the sidewalk, saving their place by sleeping rough so they are well placed in the morning."

"Did she leave her cooking materials there with them?"

"Ah, yes, now that you mention it, she did."

"And do you know them?"

"I heard one of them say she is coming all the way from Vizingham for the *puja*."

"Then I shall find her," Anita said. "I know the village very well indeed."

□ □ □

By the time Anita returned to Hotel Delite, darkness was falling and guests were filling up the dining room. Most chose to settle on the sand patio, where they could look out over the waves crashing onto the rocky coast and watch the village men hunting for crabs with their torches lighting up the night.

The Brahman cook stood by his stove checking the various dishes in different stages of preparation. He muttered a greeting to her without looking up, barked a few orders to an assistant chopping vegetables on a nearby table, and took a deep sigh before picking up another spoon and turning over pieces of eggplant sautéing in an iron pan.

"If I had not heard your venerable aunt just now, I would think you have come to sneak a free meal."

"How can you say that of me? Don't I work too?"

"Doing what?"

"Getting publicity for this place," Anita said with a sly wink. The Brahman shook his head and stifled a laugh. "Tell me what you want."

"The girl Bija, the one who was found murdered in a slum in Trivandrum during Pongaala. She is from here, isn't she?"

The Brahman gave another order and the assistant scurried from the room. "He is a terrible gossip, which is not so bad but he never gets it right. He is useless. How can I start important rumors or even send ordinary messages if he is such a bad listener and worse reporter? It is worse than no help at all."

"Okay, I'll see what I can do to get you a better assistant."

"And one that can cook a little too. Eh?"

"Okay, a good gossip and a good cook."

He waggled his head and smiled contentedly.

"So, about Bija."

"Ah, the village girl who was murdered. Yes, very strange."

"Why?"

"She was raised in an orphanage by the nuns. Her father died in a fishing accident and her mother threw herself off a bridge when she heard, so the nuns are taking her. She is very bright, so they are helping her get scholarship to college. It is in Cochin she is studying, yes?"

"So if she grew up around here she must have friends here."

"The nuns have recently arranged marriages for three of their girls, and they must have gone to Pongaala too."

"Pongaala is for Hindus."

"Girls are girls. They all want a good marriage. And if they were Hindus when the nuns took them in, they would not forget everything. And some nuns are here a long time." This seemed to please him and he gave the eggplant a gentle tap before laying down the spoon and turning to a meat curry.

Anita gave the autorickshaw driver a ten-rupee note without even looking at the meter charge, and missed the surprised and pleased expression on the driver's face. He turned the auto and gave her one last smile before merging into the traffic. The small hut had been hard to find, since she had not known the last names of the three girls recently married by the nuns and had to go casually from store to store in the tiny junction until someone recalled hearing about the weddings and asked a neighbor who knew very well each of the three brides and sent Anita off to the nearest one. Sarah pulled aside the curtain hanging in the front door and peered out. Anita introduced herself as a slight acquaintance of Bija's from Cochin. "I heard the news and was very distressed, so I have come down to see for myself."

Sarah peered at her. "You are from the Hotel Delite, isn't it?" Anita frowned.

"Hmm, well, yes. You're sharp. I didn't think anyone out here would recognize me."

"Oh, but you are so well known. You have come about Bija's death, so there is a story here, isn't it?"

This girl was proving to be more than a little interesting, thought Anita as she waited for a cup of tea. When Sarah had done all that she felt necessary to welcome her notorious guest, Anita rested her cup on its saucer and said, "Did you know that Bija had gone to Pongaala Puja that night?"

"Of course I knew. We went up together on the bus, she and I. The nuns don't want to let us go to such things, but we are married now, we can do what we want. So she and I are going together, for safety."

"Did you sit together when you arrived?"

"Yes, we are having our bricks with us and our firewood, and everything, and we are sitting on the Main Road, M.G. Road, at Overbridge. We couldn't get any closer, but at least we are not at Statue Road. It is so far out, people there are afraid the priests will not go so far. They cannot traipse all over Trivandrum in the one noontime giving blessings to housewives, can they? But we are close enough. There are so many women cooking after us, we are not worried."

"Bija must have been very excited."

"She is thinking this will make her marriage perfect."

"Was she worried about it?"

Sarah twisted her face into a grimace and frowned. "She is worrying. Her father-in-law is not liking her—she has married his son secretly in Cochin without family blessing and he is angry that his son has gone off and done this on his own."

"So the *puja* was important for making the family happy too."

"Yes, that is why she was so excited when she is arriving there. She is setting up her pot and getting ready to sleep on the ground with all of us when two men are coming from her father and telling her that she is not needing to sleep on the ground. They are having a room for her and one will hold her place there. She is not to worry about it."

"They had a room for her?"

Sarah nodded vigorously. "A room!"

"Did some people do that?"

"Yes, there are lodges there and some people are staying in them so they don't have to sleep on the street, but we are poor so we are sleeping on the street with our pots. But Bija is so excited. She is happy, not for the room, but because it means that her father-in-law is happy for her and wants to please her. This is momentous!" Sarah threw back her head, her eyes wide in amazement.

"Yes, it is momentous." Anita could only agree. "Which house did she go to? Do you remember?"

Sarah thought hard, and described watching Bija disappear into a narrow alleyway near a certain shop.

□ □ □

The alleyway stretched before Anita, growing darker not for lack of sunlight but for the dirt and grime thickening its walls. Anita took a deep breath and headed in. She knocked on the first door but no one answered. She waited; a window opened and a woman missing two front teeth peered at her.

"The house where the girl was found?" Anita asked. The woman nodded for her to go on and shut the window with a slam. Not a friendly neighborhood, Anita thought. Anita came to another door and knew this was the one—a string of police tape still clung to one of the door hinges. She pushed the door open and headed up the stairs. At the top she faced two doors, one locked with a shiny metal padlock and the other closed with a new wooden bar. She pulled out the wooden bar, and pushed the double door open. To the right of the door she found a light switch and turned it on. She gasped.

"That poor girl," Anita said to herself as she surveyed the room. "That poor girl."

The room contained a wooden bed and a small table and a stool; the stone floor was a dull black, but the dirty walls were the shock. Splattered all over them was dried blood, drops flying out in strings, splotches the size of a shoulder, smears as long as an arm. Everywhere there was blood, from floor level rising nearly to the ceiling. All four walls were covered with blood. Anita couldn't move. She could only stand and wonder at the cruelty of it all. "That poor girl," she muttered again and again.

□   □   □

"What are you doing here?" A voice screeched at her from the bottom of the stairs. Anita turned and instead of wanting to find some lighthearted excuse to defend her behavior and mislead the other, she stamped down the stairs and confronted the other woman.

"Who are you? Do you live around here? Hmm? Answer me!" The woman backed away. "Do you know about that room?' Do you know what happened there?"

The woman waggled her head but slowly, as though not sure she wanted to admit that she did.

"What do you know?"

"Only what is happening here."

"What happened here?"

The woman looked around her for a way of escape but Anita had backed her into the corner at the end of the alleyway.

"Tell me."

"A girl is angering her customer and he is beating her to death."

"How do you know that?"

"I am hearing it, aren't I?"

"What did you hear that night?"

"I am hearing her yelling and screaming and she is going on and on. Yelling and screaming. Why wouldn't he beat her? Nicely beating, she is deserving."

"The men. Do you know them?"

She began to say no, but Anita took a step toward her.

"They are ordinary men, just workers like anyone else."

"What did they look like?"

"Ordinary men. I don't know. One is short and slight and the other is the same but he has big ears."

"What did they do when they came out? Where did they go?"

"They are running down the stairs and out the alleyway and driving away."

"Driving away?"

"In their car."

"What kind of car?"

"A car. I am a poor woman. What do I know about cars?"

"What kind of car?"

"The new Maruti. White. It must have a mark on it because one of them drove too close to the wall."

"Did you tell the police this?"

She spit on the ground. "Why? I am not stupid. I'm not making trouble for myself. She was a whore; whores get beaten to death. What is it to me?"

Anita clenched her fists but held her tongue. Barely able to contain her anger, she turned on her heel and hurried out of the alleyway.

□ □ □

All the way back to Hotel Delite Anita was so wrought up she could barely think. She knew her anger against the woman in the alley was misplaced, but still she was angry. How many others had heard Bija's cries and done nothing to help her? How did we get to such a place that we can her a woman cry and do nothing? How have we lost ourselves? By the time the auto was pulling into the Hotel Delite compound, Anita had turned her thoughts to more practical matters. A new white Maruti was pretty common in these parts, she thought despairingly, but fired up by the woman's dismissal of Bija's calls for help, Anita pigheadedly determined to find every single one in the district.

"Anita, what has happened to you? You look ghastly." Anita's aunt grabbed both her arms and looked her over squarely. "And you are filthy. Where have you been?"

"Where I should not have been, Auntie."

"Ah, Anita, that is always true. Come, eat supper with me. I can't decide if it is better not to know where you have been or to know and face a heart attack. But at least if you have supper with me, I will know where you are for a little while."

☐ ☐ ☐

Anita settled down to a *masala dosa* with sambar and chutney, letting her mind drift far away from her recent encounters. Her aunt lost herself in trying one dish after another, critiquing them all and passing small judgments on each one, till the waiter rolled his eyes and sighed and shifted from foot to foot, bored with the predictability of it all.

"You know, Auntie, Brahman's cooking might improve if he had a little help, someone with some energy and interest."

"Energy and interest? What on earth does that mean?"

"It means he's getting cranky and he wants a change. Get him a new assistant, someone young he can boss around and complain to and can ill treat and disregard as he feels the need, someone who will talk mindlessly about the village and the other hotel cooks and know everyone's flaws and mistakes and talk endlessly about them, with great delight in other people's foibles."

Anita's aunt stared at her aghast. "And where will I find such a person, assuming I would even want one like that anywhere near me?"

"Try the local orphanage. The nuns always have girls looking for work."

"You are serious!"

"Auntie, you must keep the cook happy!"

"And the rest of the town will be miserable. It is your doing, isn't it?"

"He is a man full of information for me."

"I shall forbid him to talk to you!"

"Then I shall ask you questions!"

"No!" She clapped her hands over her ears. "You will pollute my mind and then I will be tortured. And not tonight, Anita. I am going to Mr. Pillai's house to offer to help Jayan's mother; she hardly knows how to cope since Bija's death." Anita's aunt bustled out of the dining room; Anita followed her.

"You will make me late, Anita."

"Not to worry. I'll tell the driver to wait."

"I am going in Mr. Pillai's car. Our car is taking guests to the airport for departure."

"Then I'll tell Mr. Pillai's driver to wait for you while you get ready."

Anita sauntered out to the compound where the light blue hotel car was waiting to take guests to the airport. Another car pulled in—a white Maruti covered in dust. Anita stepped back and watched it. A small man in a khaki uniform stepped out. Anita studied his ears, his very large, well-shaped ears. He nodded and smiled to her and she told him her aunt would be slightly delayed.

"Is this Mr. Pillai's car?"

The man nodded yes.

"And you are the driver?"

Again he nodded yes while Anita circled the car, taking note of what appeared to be a recent repair to the paint job on the rear right fender.

"It must be nice work, driving a car for Mr. Pillai. He doesn't go out much, does he?"

"Not so much. But he has me driving others around for him."

"Ah, so you get to see much of the district too."

"I have been all over the state, madam. All over the state."

Anita nodded, carefully phrasing her next question. "He must trust you exclusively."

"Yes, only me," he said with evident pride.

"No one else can drive this car."

"No, no one else." Just as he was about to puff up even more, he paused and looked at Anita, just now aware that there may be more to this than flattery. He began to back away.

"Others see this car and know that only you may be driving. Yes?"

"I must tend to the car, to be ready for your aunt."

"And that means they remember you. They remember the car and they remember you."

He blanched. Bingo, thought Anita.

"Tell me about the other night."

"What other night?"

"Tell me or tell the police." Anita spoke softly and the man turned pale as beads of sweat spread across his forehead and upper lip.

□ □ □

The driver's hand trembled as he picked up the cup of tea; a few drops sloshed over the edge and dribbled down the side. He leaned down to the cup and sucked up the creamy liquid, but he was too tense to drink. He put the cup down with a clatter into its saucer.

"You are going to tell me what happened," Anita said.

"I don't want to think about it. It is too ugly."

"It will torment you forever unless you do. What happened? Why did you beat her to death? What did she ever do to you?"

"I did not beat her to death."

"All right, then, your friend did. Don't try to trick me," Anita said, leaning forward. "I saw the room. I saw the blood. I saw the furniture too covered in blood. What you did was beastly."

"But I didn't. She did that."

"What are you talking about?" Anita studied him. He didn't seem to be lying, but he wasn't making any sense. "You beat her. The evidence is there."

"No, she did that herself. We took her there, and when we got her upstairs—she followed us without argument—we told her to take her clothes off. But she wouldn't. She went wild. We were just to make her look compromised, like a slut. But she went wild. She threw herself away from us, against the wall and said no, she would never. We tried to take her clothes, but she started to scream and yell. She was like a mad woman, throwing herself against the walls and the floor and running from corner to corner to get away from us. She tried to throw herself out the window, but we pulled her back and threw her down onto the floor." He took a ragged breath, and drew his shoulders in.

"And then?" Anita asked.

"Nothing," he whispered. "Nothing. It was all silent. She didn't move, she didn't scream, she didn't do anything. She must have hit her head one last time. We didn't know what to do. We ran."

□ □ □

"I have listened to your story, and you have told me the truth, I think," Anita said after he had calmed down. "But one thing is not clear."

The driver looked up at her, drained of all the fear he had held inside himself for the days since Bija's death. "There is nothing more."

"I think there is," Anita said. "Why did you go there? Why did you want her?"

The man's face blanched and he looked about him as though there might indeed be a path of escape. "It is my job, isn't it?"

Anita nodded; it was the answer she expected. "And the other man?" The driver grew increasingly agitated. "One of us is going to give this information to the police," Anita said. "Which one of us do you think it will be?"

□ □ □

Aunt Meena wiggled deeper into the seat and grabbed the door handle as the driver careered around a corner. She shut her eyes and began to mutter.

"Thomas, slow down!" Anita called out to the driver.

"I don't see why the driver couldn't wait for us. Mr. Pillai specifically sent him to collect me. Now I'll have to pay for a taxi to take the guests to the airport. It makes no sense. He should have waited."

"It's just as well, Auntie. He was rather agitated when he left here; we probably wouldn't have survived the trip anyway."

"But he is a good driver."

"People have their off days, Auntie."

"And since when have you become so concerned about Mr. and Mrs. Pillai's sorrow? You're not up to something, Anita. Anita?"

"Ah, I think we are arriving." Anita peered out the window at the metal gate, its wrought-iron image of a lotus in white and red swinging aside to invite them in.

□ □ □

Mr. Pillai accepted their condolences with the stoicism expected of the head of a sprawling household, and offered them tea. Before Anita's aunt could launch into her prepared speech, Anita said, "You know, Mr. Pillai, we came in our own car."

"How is that? I sent my driver to you."

"Anita!" her aunt said. "Hush. He has other things to think about."

"I just thought he should know. He will be inconvenienced for some time to come."

"What?"

"Auntie, I think I hear Mrs. Pillai weeping."

"Oh? Eh? Oh, I must go to her." Aunt Meena hurried off.

"What is this nonsense about my driver?"

"He is not here, is he?" Anita said. Mr. Pillai gave a shout, and another servant came hurrying in. After a rapid-fire conversation in Malayalam, Mr. Pillai dismissed the servant and turned to Anita.

"So, he is not come back. Where is he?"

"At the police station if he is smart." Anita was gratified to see Mr. Pillai's eyes widen. "I guess I don't have to tell you why."

"What do you mean? What do I know about this fellow's doings? He is only a casual employee."

"Oh, I think he is more than that."

Mr. Pillai walked to the door leading into the back rooms and shut it, then turned around to study her. He was not a large man, but he had presence. Shorter than Anita, with thinning black hair, smoothly shaved, and wearing a pressed white shirt over a lungi, his well-filled stomach testament to his wealth, he was indignant at the mere idea of being challenged.

"The driver has told me all I need to know, and he will tell the police the same. Perhaps even a little more, depending on how frightened he is." Mr. Pillai glared at her. She continued, "And when he is done, the police will find his partner and then they will come here. They will come here, Mr. Pillai, to talk to you. Just as I have."

"You did all this?" He let go a low growl. "It is messy, but you are no one and I will manage this."

"Don't be so sure. I have more than my imagination behind me." Anita leaned back. "She was not good enough for your son, is that it?"

"She was not good enough for anyone! She was from the orphanage!"

"But your son fell in love and married her."

"What does he know about the feelings of adults. He is but a boy."

"Yes, I agree with that. He is but a boy."

"He has no more spine than the stalk of young grain in a warm breeze. How could he get himself into such a thing?"

"But you got him out of it."

He almost spat at her. "She showed her true colors."

"Mr. Pillai, she showed her true colors by fighting to the death two men who meant to harm her."

"Ah, nonsense. She went off with two men to a brothel, and there the police found her. What sort of woman goes off to a brothel with men she doesn't know?" he said.

"A girl who is told the two men are sent from her father-in-law to see she has a place to sleep through the night while waiting for Pongaala Puja next day," Anita said.

"A foolish girl who goes off with strangers can't be respected."

"I don't know what the crime is for bringing a girl to her death, but you withheld information from the police, and set those two men on her. You will have to face charges. That is some satisfaction to those who cared about Bija."

"No one cared about Bija," Mr. Pillai said.

"I fear, Mr. Pillai, that in this household that is true."

□ □ □

Anita found Jayan sitting morosely on the veranda staring at the dusty compound. She thought about leaving him there and letting him find out about his father's treachery from the police, but that seemed unnecessarily cruel. But more, she wanted to know how he would react to the news. If he took it hard, she could at least feel that Bija's love was not misplaced. Anita pulled a chair up close to his, and began in a low voice.

"I'm sure your father was thinking of your welfare and didn't stop to think about what sort of girl Bija really was," she concluded at the end of her tale.

"Father says she is a slut. That she just tricked me into marriage and that she could never be a good wife. She had no family, no background. She was just a slut."

"She grew up in an orphanage, but she was a sweet girl."

"Yes, well, my father knows more about these things than I can at my age."

Anita bridled. She could not imagine herself ever having been as stupid and as spineless as this young man. "The police will be coming to talk to both of you, but especially your father."

Jayan leaned forward in his chair and clasped his hands in front of him. "He knows more than I do. He has told me about her, how she was found and what it means. And now you are saying something different. Well, I can't just jump onto your bandwagon, can I?"

A sweeper came into view around the corner, one arm resting behind her back and the other swinging the reed broom with all the grace of a dancer, back and forth, back and forth, then up in the air to tighten the string, tapping the end on her hip to bring all the reeds into alignment, then down onto the dusty ground, back and forth, back and forth. She moved forward without looking up or ahead, just swinging her broom in the manner she had learned as a child.

"Well, I can't, can I?"

"No, not you," Anita said.

□ □ □

A police car pulled up to the compound gate just as Anita and her aunt were pulling out. As they passed into the lane, Anita's aunt turned around to look through the rear window.

"Anita, they're going into the Pillai compound."

"Yes, Auntie, I expect they are."

"Anita, did you have anything to do with this?"

"Possibly."

"Anita, you must stop this. You must stop. If you don't stop this sort of thing, it will be impossible for your family to find you a suitable husband! Even advertising in *The Hindu* will not succeed."

"Really, Auntie, do you think so?"

"I am telling you, aren't I?"

"Dear Aunt Meena, you do say the nicest things."

Her aunt stared at Anita with her mouth open. "You want to get married, don't you?"

"Actually, Auntie, no. I consider myself far too old to be interested in such matters."

Anita gave her aunt a good slap on the back as the older woman began to choke and sputter.

Security Blanket

Toni L.P. Kelner

Living through a science fiction convention is incredibly intense. In less than forty-eight hours, from Friday evening to Sunday afternoon, you can experience everything in fast-forward: friendship, romance, rivalry, hatred.

In my case, I went from admiring Pinky, to being embarrassed by him, to disliking him, to mourning him, to solving his murder.

□ □ □

Naturally Pinky saw the situation before anybody else. He moved to intercept even as he used his walkie-talkie to alert me. "Regina, we have a toucher—repeat, a toucher—moving in on Masters. Older female, blue sweatshirt, white hair."

I buzzed the rest of the available redshirts, but though we immediately headed in that direction, the room was filled with fans hoping to catch a glimpse of someone famous. By the time Andi, Donna, Elliot, and I made our way through, Pinky had blocked the toucher's access to her goal: the guest of honor, William Masters, who'd played the recurring role of Bane, good-guy werewolf on the TV show *Werewolf Hunter*.

In a polite-but-firm voice, Pinky said, "I'm sorry, but other fans are talking with Mr. Masters right now. If you'll show me your ticket, I'll let you know when you'll have an opportunity to speak with him."

"I just want to give him a quick hug and kiss." The silver–haired woman looked more like Bane's grandmother than one of his fans, but you really can't judge fans by their appearances. "I know he won't mind."

"Mr. Masters himself requested that there be no unauthorized touching," Pinky replied. "The rules were included in your registration packet." He reached into his belt pouch. "I've got a copy here, as well, if you've lost yours."

"I don't need your damned rules," the woman spat, destroying the illusion of grandmotherhood. "I paid my money, and I came a long way to meet Bane, and that's what I'm going to do."

Pinky said, "You'll get your chance to meet Mr. Masters when it's your turn, but there will be *no* touching. May I see your ticket?"

"I've lost it," the woman said unconvincingly.

I'd have bet my favorite *Werewolf Hunter* t-shirt that the woman had never even seen a ticket, let alone paid the extra fee for a personal meeting with Bane. Still, as head of security, I had to play nice, so I asked, "Is there a problem?"

Pinky actually kept a straight face as he said, "This lady lost her ticket for her meeting with Mr. Masters."

"I'm sure we can take care of that." The woman's face brightened, but only until I turned to Andi and said, "Can you take this lady out to registration and see about getting her a replacement ticket?"

"Sure thing, Regina." The woman was trying to come up with another lie as Andi escorted her out, but I knew she'd be kept out of the way until the meet-and-greet ended. Fortunately, Bane hadn't even noticed the uproar and continued speaking to one of the legitimate ticket–holders in that Australian accent fans found so irresistible.

I let Elliot and Donna go back to working the room and said, "Good catch, Pinky."

"I shouldn't have had to catch anyone," he retorted. "There should never be a ticketed event in the middle of a meet-and–greet. You can't do decent crowd control this way."

"I know," I said, annoyed. "Ted said there wasn't enough in the budget for a separate room." Ted, the chairman of the convention, had refused most of my requests.

"If you can't afford decent security, you shouldn't put on a convention."

Again he was stating the obvious, and I ran my fingers through my bangs in exasperation. "We've only got half an hour to go. Maybe we'll make it through without any more problems."

"If Shannon pays attention, that is. I saw that toucher a mile away—she should have, too."

I turned to look at Shannon, who was serving as Bane's personal attendant. Rather than keeping an eye on the people nearby, she was staring at him in rapt attention. "Star–struck?"

"Big time."

Security crew members, known as redshirts, were supposed to maintain objectivity, not stare in adoration at the guest of honor. But it was hard sometimes—we were fans, too. I'd purposely kept my own distance from Bane because I was such an admirer. "It happens," I said.

Pinky grunted, and I knew what he was thinking. It had never happened to him, and never would. Even as we talked, his eyes were constantly moving, watching for trouble. He didn't look that formidable—he was plump with glasses and thinning hair—but his devotion made him a much sought-after security team member at conventions up and down the east coast. I'd been delighted when I found out he was willing to work at FullMoon, a small convention for fans of *Werewolf Hunter*, especially since I was taking my first stab at running security. By rights, he should have been in charge, not me, but he'd said he'd rather not. At the time, I'd thought that meant he had confidence in my abilities. Now I wasn't so sure.

"Did you realize Shannon was so inexperienced?" Pinky asked.

"She's not inexperienced," I objected. "Ted says she's worked plenty of conventions in the midwest."

"Ted says? When you've worked as many conventions as I have, you learn to check out your team members yourself."

"You're probably right," I admitted. It was something else I'd have to remember for the next convention, assuming that I didn't screw up so badly this weekend that I never got another chance. "I'll keep an eye on her."

"Does she have an exit strategy?"

"A what?"

He assumed a pained expression. "A strategy for getting the subject—that's Masters—out of the room expeditiously."

Everybody else called the actor by his character's name, which Masters himself encouraged, but Pinky insisted on using his real name. "I'm sure Shannon has a plan," I said. "She's worked as a personal attendant before."

Just then, an exuberant fan grabbed Bane by the neck and loudly kissed him, while Shannon watched in a blend of horror and envy.

"Maybe you should go see—" Pinky was gone before I could finish. "And I didn't even get a chance to thank him," I mumbled to myself.

"Did he say when he's going to destroy the Death Star?" asked Elliot, who'd appeared at my elbow.

"You mean Pinky?"

"Who else but fandom's answer to the Pinkertons?"

"He's helping Shannon with her exit strategy. I can't believe I forgot to check on her exit strategy."

"I can't believe you just said 'exit strategy.' Look, Regina, that guy may think he's the Terminator crossed with a Klingon warrior, but the rest of us are just volunteers with walkie-talkies, doing the best we can. And you're doing fine."

"Then how come I nearly let that toucher get through?"

"Nearly only counts in horseshoes and hand grenades. By the time Granny Goodness gets away from registration, Bane will be back in his suite drinking Fosters."

"Granny Goodness?"

"The toucher."

Security people tend to attach nicknames to troublemakers. This one came from the DC comic book universe. Granny Goodness, like our toucher, was not nearly so nice as she appeared.

I noticed a flurry of activity in one corner of the ballroom. It was probably nothing, but it was best not to take chances. "Can you check that out?"

"You're the boss," he said with a mock salute, and sauntered off. Unlike Shannon, I knew Elliot could handle anything that came up. We'd worked together before, and though I didn't know him as well as I wanted to, I had hopes. Of course, even if he were interested, it would have to wait until after the convention.

True to his word, Pinky had Bane out the door at the stroke of ten, confounding the fans lingering in hopes of personal interaction. Shannon was left behind, too, though I wasn't sure if it was on purpose or because she couldn't keep up. Either way, Pinky was right. It was only Friday night, and Bane had a slew of events scheduled for the weekend. Shannon just wasn't up to being his personal attendant.

The rest of the redshirts and I waited until the room cleared out, with most people heading either for a marathon showing of the first season of *Werewolf Hunter* or to their rooms to get some sleep. I checked in with the other redshirts distributed around the hotel, and was relieved to hear that everything was calm. I sent most of them off-duty, which left me and Elliot as the only ones active. Elliot had volunteered to stay on call for the night, and I figured I'd be on call until the last fan dragged himself out of the hotel Sunday evening. Pinky, of course, said he'd keep his walkie-talkie on, too, even though he was doing his overnight on Saturday.

After that, I was almost done for the day, but I still had to stop by Bane's room to make sure he had everything he needed. This was annoying for two reasons. First, to ensure Bane's security, he'd been given a suite that was only accessible by going outside and up a steep flight of stairs, so it was completely out of the way. And second, it was a waste of time anyway because Bane wasn't alone. He and a happy crowd were noisily partying. As I'm sure Pinky would have told me, the location of Bane's room should have been kept a secret, but I suspected Ted the con-chair, who was in the thick of it, had been less than discreet. I noted resentfully that he didn't even have his walkie-talkie with him.

Shannon was at the party, too, sitting as close as possible to Bane, and laughing too hard at everything the actor said. Not that she was the only one. Bane was known for being the kind of wolf that didn't need a full moon to bring out his animal side, and there were several other women there hoping to be chosen for the night. Bane waved me over when I saw him, but I just smiled and shook my head. I'd spoken to the man earlier, and tripped over my tongue so badly that I wasn't inclined to repeat the experience. Drinking an extra-large Australian beer wasn't likely to help.

On the way to my much less plush room, I walked down the corridor designated for room parties, and made sure the hosts knew to keep noise down, avoid serving beer to minors, and refrain from recreating famous chase scenes from *Werewolf Hunter* in the hallways. Lastly, I checked in with the hotel's night security man to let him know things seemed under control.

Then I went to bed.

□   □   □

The first thing I did the next day was meet with my team over donuts and coffee in the control room, the function room reserved for convention business. We were all wearing our uniforms—jeans and blood red shirts with white bulls' eyes on the front and the word "SECURITY" on the back. The shirts were easy to spot, and I'd been told it was a good color to set off my dark hair and eyes. I wondered if Elliot agreed.

We reviewed the day's schedule, which included morning panel discussions with writers and artists connected with *Werewolf Hunter*, autograph sessions for those writers and artists, an afternoon talk by Bane that we expected the whole convention to attend, more panels, and a werewolf-themed costume contest that was likely to be our biggest headache. Ongoing were the art show, video room, dealers' room, and hospitality suite where Bane would meet with the rest of the people who'd bought private tickets.

I was dreading the next part, so I kept my eyes on my clipboard as I said, "I've got some assignment changes. Shannon, I'm switching you to morning panels and autographs. Float between the panel rooms, and keep the lines moving in autographs. Pinky, you'll be with Bane."

I paused, waiting for an outburst, then looked at Shannon. She was nodding, maybe a bit annoyed, but there wasn't a tantrum in sight. Pinky just looked smug. I breathed a sigh of relief. "Okay, people, get out there and keep things secure." They headed for their first assignments, leaving only me and Elliot, who had the morning off in return for his being on duty overnight.

"Good call," he said.

"I'm surprised Shannon didn't make a fuss."

"Didn't you hear what happened last night?"

"What now?" I asked, sure that I'd let something slip.

"You know there was a party in Bane's room, right? Well, Shannon practically threw herself at the guy, but when the party ended, Bane invited a different girl to spend the night with him."

"Ouch. So that's why she was willing to switch. At least we won't have that problem with Pinky. Unless . . . Elliot, Pinky's not gay, is he?"

"Who can tell? The only one who shares his bed is his walkie-talkie. I hear he even puts it into a plastic bag so he can take it into the shower with him."

□ □ □

Though the morning had started out well, the lull didn't last long. A wannabe writer showed up at the first autograph session with a stack of copies of her manuscript, intending to shanghai as many authors as possible into reading her *Werewolf Hunter* novel and then forward it to their agents and editors. It wasn't an unusual situation, and Shannon should have been able to handle it. Unfortunately, she wasn't where she was supposed to be. It was Andi, who was stationed in the dealers' room, who heard the commotion and buzzed me.

By the time I got there, the aspiring writer and Marilynn Byerly, well–known author of *Werewolf Hunter* novelizations, were having a shouting match in the middle of the room, lobbing phrases like "incompetent amateur" and "sleazy hack" at one another. Plus the signing lines were in disarray, with people pushing and shoving their way to the front. I yelled, "Linus in the signing room!" into my walkie-talkie—that was the code word that meant that all available redshirts should blanket the room with security.

Needless to say, Shannon showed up late, after the rest of us had things back in order. Wanda Wannabe had been sent off with a warning that she'd be ejected from the convention if she approached any more authors with her manuscript, and Ms. Byerly had been soothed with a Coke and the promise of a good seat at Bane's talk. As for the lines, Pinky had people queued up like Catholic schoolchildren, and I'd been both too busy and too embarrassed to see how he'd managed it.

Shannon didn't even have the good grace to look winded. "What's up?" she said.

"Where the hell were you?"

"I had to go to the bathroom. I was only gone a minute."

"Then how come I've been here for ten minutes, and the people here said there was nobody here when the session started twenty minutes ago? Why didn't you tell somebody you were going to the bathroom? That's what your walkie-talkie is for. And why didn't you come when I called the Linus?"

"I left my walkie-talkie in here."

I was furious. Not only had she been away from her post and out of contact, but she'd left an expensive, rented walkie-talkie unattended. If I'd had anybody to replace her with, I'd have fired her, but the convention was too far along to scrape up another volunteer. "Then since you've had your break, I don't want you to leave this room again until one."

"What about the panels?"

"I'll take care of them."

"What about Bane's talk? I want to work that."

I just glared at her, then turned to see Pinky shaking his head in disgust. I wasn't sure if it was at Shannon, me, or both of us.

The next disaster was right before Bane's talk. It was scheduled for one-thirty, which meant that most of the fans were skipping lunch so they could line up for good seats. While they waited, under the watchful eyes of most of the redshirts, Bane was enjoying a private buffet with a few privileged members of the convention staff. Naturally, the invitation list for that meal had caused more dissension than almost anything else during convention planning. I'd stayed out of it. Just being in the same room as Bane got me flustered—I could only imagine what would have happened if I'd tried to eat in front of him.

Through my careful planning, Elliot and I both had the noon hour free, and were headed for the hotel restaurant when we saw Pinky being confronted outside the door where the VIP lunch was being held.

"Should we give him a hand?" Elliot asked.

"He hasn't called for backup," I said.

"I know, but that's the woman Bane took to bed last night."

The woman in question was blonde, buxom, and swearing like a sailor. Since she'd been Bane's Friday night conquest, I mentally tagged her Girl Friday.

Elliot and I joined them, and I asked, "Anything wrong?"

"Nothing I can't handle," Pinky replied, keeping his security guard face firmly in place.

The woman appealed to me. "I'm supposed to go in there to meet Bane for lunch, but this fascist won't let me in."

"It's by invitation only," Pinky said, "and she's not on the list."

"Bane didn't know me when the list was made," the woman argued, "but when I asked him to meet me for lunch today, he said I could come if I wanted to." Presumably realizing that wasn't the most enthusiastic invitation, she bolstered her authority with, "It was early this morning—when we got up—so he probably forgot to add my name."

More likely he didn't remember her name, I thought to myself. "Pinky, have you checked with Bane?"

He gave me a look. "There's no need to disturb Mr. Masters."

Since I knew there were twenty people already in there, I didn't think one more would hurt, especially since it was a buffet. "I'll go ask him." But Pinky continued to block the door.

"Don't bother. Mr. Masters informed me that he doesn't want to spend any further time with this woman."

"You're lying!" Girl Friday shrieked. "Bane would never say that."
Pinky just stared at her.

"You're lying," she said again, her voice cracking. Then her
face crumpled, and she ran off down the hallway, sobbing like a
woman betrayed by her idol.

"Geez, Pinky," Elliot said. "Do you think you could have said
something to make her feel worse?"

"I wouldn't have said it if Regina hadn't interfered."

"Regina is head of security," Elliot snapped. "Doing her job
is hardly interfering."

"Regina assigned me to Mr. Masters, and I'm meeting my
obligations the best way I know how. If she wants me to step
aside . . ."

They both looked at me, finally acknowledging that I was
right there, even though I wished I weren't. "No, Pinky, you keep
doing what you're doing."

He nodded, mollified, and I started toward the restaurant,
with Elliot close behind.

"Who does he think he is?" Elliot wanted to know. "Why are
you putting up with him?"

"Because he knows what he's doing," I said, leaving unsaid
the thought that maybe I didn't.

□   □   □

The rest of the afternoon went reasonably smoothly. We had to
defuse a couple of arguments over seats at Bane's talk, but the
talk itself was a big success. The afternoon's panels went fine,
too, and a gap in programming at dinner time meant we redshirts
could meet for pizza. Except for Pinky, of course, who was maintaining watch over his subject, and Shannon, who'd announced
that she was in the costume contest and wouldn't be helping with
security for the night. By the time we'd eaten and planned the
evening's coverage, it was time for the masquerade.

□   □   □

The first part of the costume contest went fine. Of course, getting the contestants into the right order was the masquerade staff's headache, not ours, and the tech crew was in charge of setup, lights, and sound. All we had to do was make sure nobody snuck into the ballroom early and resolve the inevitable arguments over seats. After that, we got to relax and enjoy the show.

Though I wasn't all that happy with her, I loyally cheered for Shannon, who was dressed as a woods-dwelling sprite who'd lured Bane to her tree in Season Two. Or rather, undressed, because sprites wear fur bikinis with boots. At least Shannon could carry off the skimpy outfit, unlike some of the other contestants.

Once the procession of werewolves, werewolf hunters, miscellaneous lycanthropes, and other *Werewolf Hunter* characters had paraded across the stage, the judges retired to deliberate while a band came on stage to perform "Werewolves of London," "Bad Moon Rising," and other appropriate songs.

All the judges were supposed to go to the control room, which had been emptied for that purpose, but after they left, Pinky buzzed me on the walkie-talkie.

"Regina? Pinky, in the main corridor with Mr. Masters, en route to his suite. He prefers to deliberate on his own, and will join the other judges later."

"He's going to get a beer, isn't he?" I said.

I could hear laughter when Pinky keyed his walkie-talkie, and realized Bane had heard me. "Affirmative," Pinky said dryly. In the background, I heard Bane say, "After looking at that lot, I deserve it!"

Feeling like a complete idiot, I asked, "Do you need backup?"

"Negative. The halls are clear."

"Good enough. Call me if you change locations."

"Roger."

Then I checked with Elliot, who'd accompanied the other judges. Since they hadn't expected much input from Bane, they were perfectly willing to carry on without him.

The band was followed by a demonstration of sword fighting, but despite the display, the crowd was fidgety. There was a constant flow of people going to the bathroom, or to grab a Coke from a machine, or just deciding they'd rather party now and find out who the winners were the next day.

I knew the contestants had to be sweating bullets. Competition is always fierce, but the stakes this time were higher than usual. At the con's closing event, Bane was going to act out a scene from the opening episode of *Werewolf Hunter's* next season, and he'd promised to pick one of the contest winners to perform with him.

About twenty-five minutes into the wait, my walkie-talkie buzzed again. "Regina, this is Pinky, outside Bane's room."

"Go ahead, Pinky."

There was no response.

"Pinky?"

There was a burst of noise, which I later decided was from the button of the walkie-talkie hitting something, and a horrific yell.

"Pinky!"

Now there was nothing.

"Linus! Outside Bane's room!" I barked into my walkie-talkie. Then I ran as fast as I could, not knowing or caring who I ran into. Elliot, who was closer to Bane's room, beat me there, and was at the bottom of the stairs leading toward the suite. When he heard me coming, he turned to stop me.

"There's nothing you can do, Regina."

Elliot was six-foot-something to my five-foot-four, but I pushed him out of the way just the same, and saw Pinky's body at the foot of the stairs. I'd thought our shirts were blood red until

I saw real blood staining his. His walkie-talkie lay on the sidewalk next to him.

"There's no pulse," said Elliot, who was an EMT in real life. "He must have fallen just the right way to break his neck."

More like the wrong way, I thought.

Shannon padded up behind me, still wearing her fur bikini and boots. The other redshirts came on her heels. "Andi," I said, "get hotel security. Donna, call the cops."

Bane stood at the top of the stairs, looking down at Pinky, swearing fluently. I wondered what the fans would have thought if they'd heard him, because for the first time all weekend, he'd dropped his Aussie accent.

□ □ □

The hotel's security man got to the scene first, and, ignoring Elliot's protests that Pinky was dead, insisted on checking himself, getting bloody in the process. Ted showed up, too, but just dithered uselessly.

Eventually the cops arrived, followed by a doctor to examine Pinky's body and take it away. The police were visibly tense at first, but then got more relaxed, and I realized that they'd decided Pinky's death was an accident. But it didn't seem right to me.

Pinky had buzzed me to tell me he was on his way to Bane's room, and presumably he'd gotten there without incident. So why had he buzzed me later? Why would he have been heading down the stairs? I mentioned my questions to the cops, but they figured he was going to get a drink or take a break, and was going to let me know. They didn't understand that Pinky would never have left Bane's door unattended, and they didn't think there was anything odd about him buzzing me just before he fell—one officer even suggested that he might not have fallen if he hadn't been using the walkie-talkie.

Bane was no help. "I should have let the bloke come into the room," he said apologetically, the accent back in place, "but I was fagged out and wanted a minute alone. He didn't seem to mind."

"Did you hear anything?" I asked.

He shook his head. "Not a sound. I was in the WC at first, and I had music playing. Poor bastard. Has he got any family or anything? I'd like to pay my respects."

"I don't know," I said. "I only met him yesterday. There wasn't really time to get acquainted." But that wasn't true. One of the best things about a convention was the way you could go from stranger to close friend in just a weekend. Only Pinky had been all business. Not to mention the fact that he'd intimidated the heck out of me, and annoyed me even more.

"Bruce," one of the cops said, Pinky's wallet in his hand. "His first name was Bruce."

I hadn't even known that.

□   □   □

The cops didn't stay long, and looking at my horrified team, I realized I had to get them moving again. "Elliot, will you take Bane for the rest of the weekend?"

He nodded.

"Good. Ted, what's the status on the masquerade?"

"The judges are ready, but maybe we should cancel."

"No, Pinky would want us to go ahead."

"You've got to be joking," Bane said.

I glared at him. "Haven't you ever heard 'The show must go on'?"

"Yeah, but—" He stopped. "Right. Let's do it. But I want to say something about Pinky afterward."

"Good idea," I said. I turned to the rest of my team. "Okay, the crowd is going to be restless. Our job is to keep things running as smoothly as possible. Andi, you and Donna roam the halls, make sure nobody's been taking advantage of our absence. Everybody else will work the masquerade with me."

"Shouldn't I go back backstage?" Shannon asked hesitantly.

"I mean, I'm still in the contest. That's where I was when you called the Linus."

I stifled a sigh. Clearly her job in security was secondary to a chance to act out a scene with Bane. At least she'd responded to the Linus. "Fine, we'll handle it."

As I'd expected, most of the fans were milling around, spreading stories that had nothing to do with what had really happened. I heard half a dozen people who claimed to know the real story: everything from a drug bust to an orgy to a government crackdown to alien infiltration. We tried to reassure them and got people back into their seats as fast as possible. Once we had them situated, we brought in the judges, including Bane, and got the show on the road.

The judges dutifully announced the winners, including Shannon, who got an award for "Most Daring" for her scraps of fur. The way she rubbed against Bane when she accepted her ribbon made it plain she hoped to supplant Girl Friday.

Once the awards were over with, Bane solemnly announced what had happened to Pinky, and said some kind words about him. I saw plenty of tears, but I also heard speculation about whether or not the death had really been an accident. I tried to tell myself that the idea was ridiculous, but it sounded all too believable.

It wasn't just the oddness of Pinky's death, it was the faces around me. Granny Goodness actually looked glad when she realized that Pinky was the one who'd kept her away from Bane during the meet–and–greet. Wanda Wannabe was there with a satchel, and I'd have bet dollars to donuts that she had a copy of her manuscript with her, hoping to corner a writer in the bathroom. Then I saw Girl Friday, bawling loudly where Bane could see. As he left the stage, he took pity on her and let her sob on his shoulder. That wouldn't have happened if Pinky had still been alive.

I'd heard that when somebody's been a cop for long enough, everybody starts to look guilty. Now I understood what they meant, because suddenly it seemed as if anybody in that room could have pushed Pinky down those stairs. If it hadn't been for the walkie-talkie in my hand, offering me instant aid from the rest of the redshirts, I think I'd have run screaming from the room. No wonder Pinky had been so attached to his. For one morbid moment, I considered suggesting that the walkie-talkie be buried with him, which led to the even more morbid idea of him sending me a message from the grave.

Then something occurred to me, almost as if Pinky *had* sent me one last message.

□   □   □

Though the plan had been for Bane to choose the person who'd be acting out the scene with him at the end of the costume contest, under the circumstances, it had been forgotten, and I heard people muttering about it. That gave me the idea about what to do next.

I buzzed Elliot, and told him to take Bane someplace where I could talk to him privately. Then I buzzed Ted, and told him to announce that Bane would be picking somebody momentarily. Both of them sounded taken aback, but they didn't argue.

Leaving the rest of my team to keep watch, I went backstage, which was mostly empty now that the masquerade was over. I was happy to see that Elliot had managed to detach Girl Friday, so he was the only one who heard me tell Bane what I had in mind. For once, I forgot that Bane was a celebrity and the most handsome man I'd ever met. From that point on, he was just another member of my team. I told him what I wanted, and why, and made it plain that I expected him to agree. He did.

I buzzed Ted again, told him Bane was ready, and listened as he told the same to the waiting throng. There was a hush when Bane stepped on stage, and I could practically hear fingers crossing.

"I know the timing is awkward," Bane said in that delectable accent, "but a lot of people have come a long way to hear tomorrow's program, and it's fair dinkum that Pinky wouldn't have wanted them to be disappointed."

There were enthusiastic sounds of approval.

"Now I'm hoping one particular sheila will be willing to share the stage with me." Now there were shrieks, giggles, and more than one shout along the lines of "Pick me!" Bane, who was an actor after all, paused dramatically. Then he named his choice. "Come on up here, luv."

There was a delighted shout, and scattered applause as Bane's leading lady accepted his invitation. From the catcalls that followed, I think there was physical contact between them, too.

Still playing to the audience, Bane said, "Of course, we're going to need to rehearse, and tomorrow morning is pretty well booked. Do you think you can spare me some time now to go over the scene? We could work in my room."

There were even louder catcalls, and I didn't need to hear the woman's answer to know she'd agreed. That was my cue to get in position and make the last arrangements.

I'd told Elliot not to rush, so I had plenty of time to get to Bane's room. Too much, in fact, because I had time to reconsider what I was doing. Twice I reached for my walkie-talkie, ready to call the whole thing off, but then the door opened, and Elliot escorted Bane in. Along with Shannon.

She was nestled under the actor's arm, looking at him so lustfully that it took a while for her to notice I was there, long enough for Elliot to close and lock the door. When I'd told Elliot he didn't have to stay, he'd insisted strongly enough to make me think it was more than professional loyalty, but it was the wrong time to think of that.

Finally Shannon saw me. "Hey, Regina. Did you hear? Bane picked me. I guess I'm not going to be able to help out with security tomorrow." She actually giggled.

"That's okay," I said. "I don't want you on the team anymore anyway."

"Hey, I know I haven't been at my best, but—"

I forced a laugh. "No, I think this was your best."

"Now, now," Bane said soothingly, "I'm sure Shannon's been trying."

"Then how did that woman nearly get past her at the meet–and-greet? And you never saw the mess she made in the signing room."

"That wasn't my fault!" she protested.

"Maybe not, but you didn't show up to help, either."

"I told you I didn't hear the call."

"That's right, you forgot your walkie-talkie, didn't you?" I said with a sneer. "Where'd you leave it this time—there sure as hell isn't anyplace to put it in *that* getup."

"You know I'm not on call tonight," she said defiantly. "It's locked up in my room!"

"Then how did you hear the Linus when Pinky fell down the stairs?" I asked.

She went white. "What?"

"For once, you were where you were supposed to be—you got there faster than Andi. So how did you know there was a Linus?"

"Someone told me."

"Who? I'll buzz whoever it was right now to confirm."

"I . . . I don't have to tell you anything."

She was right, of course. I wasn't a cop, and I wasn't going to beat it out of her. Fortunately I didn't have to, because Bane took her in his arms, looked at her with those indescribably blue eyes, and said, "You didn't mean to kill him, did you, luv?"

"No," she whispered. "I mean, it wasn't me."

He gave her the smile that had melted the heart of the werewolf hunter herself, not to mention countless fans. "Of course it was, but you didn't mean for him to get hurt. Just tell me what happened."

I was almost afraid to breathe. If she hung tough, I didn't think there was anything else we could do. But she was a fan, through and through. She'd killed to get close to Bane—she couldn't lie to him. As long as she basked in his attention, Elliot and I might as well not have existed.

"I didn't mean to," she said in a tiny voice. "I only came up here to talk to you about using me in your scene, but Pinky wouldn't let me come in. He said he knew I was lying about working security. He found out which conventions I'd said I'd worked at, and he actually called to check up on me. Can you believe that?"

Bane shook his head in shared dismay.

"I've worked at other conventions, honest I have, but I was just a gopher, and I knew a gopher wouldn't get to see you up close. I just had to meet you."

He nodded understandingly.

"Then Regina got mad at me, and you and that other girl—"

"She meant nothing to me," Bane said convincingly, both because he was an actor and because it was true.

"I know, but Regina had already given you to Pinky, and I knew tonight might be my last chance to talk to you. That's all I wanted. But Pinky said I was a phony, and that you wouldn't want to waste time with me. He was going to buzz Regina to tell her about me. So I knocked that damned walkie-talkie out of his hand. It fell down the stairs, and when he reached for it, he lost his balance and fell. I tried to grab him, really I did. I didn't push him."

Bane nodded again, but I'm not sure if she saw it, because she'd looked away from him at last, either from shame or guilt. "Then what happened?" he prompted.

"I meant to get back to the masquerade, but I saw all the red-shirts coming, and knew Regina must have called a Linus. Since I couldn't get back without them seeing me, I acted as if I'd come with them." She looked at him imploringly. "You believe me, don't you?"

I didn't give him a chance to answer. "What he believes doesn't matter nearly as much as what the cops believe."

"Bane would never turn me in," she snarled. "It's your word against ours."

"Don't be so sure of that," Bane said, stepping back from her.

"Besides," I said, "we're not the only ones who heard you." I held up my walkie-talkie so she could see that I was holding the button down. Every redshirt had heard her confession, and they all heard me say, "Linus outside Bane's room." Then I put down the walkie-talkie to say, "Elliot, call the cops."

"You're the boss," he replied.

"Damn straight I am."

Flotsam

Michael Milliken

The weatherman explained it as the whirl of a draining tub. After the hurricane shot off Cape Cod to the open Atlantic, where the winds took on moisture and slowed, the storm settled over the coast of Maine. For two days the gray drain churned overhead, some hundred miles centered at the coastline, transferring ocean to land. Below the clouds, every crack and depression bloomed rivers and ponds, flooded the coast of the state.

But on the third morning, the thinning clouds broke in the west. As the rain slowed, James Johnson pushed open his front screen door to see what damage had been done. On the porch, he placed his hands between his belt and the snug rubber of his camouflage waders, arched his back and drew in the dampness of the air. Broken limbs and leaves lay thrown about the lawn, a bronze-bladed beech across the dirt drive. It seemed that the land had saddened, drooped a bit. He didn't know why—just something about the trees, dark and storm-battered, something about the heft of the air.

He stepped down and turned to take in the house, both sides of the rented duplex. "That shutter needs to be straightened," he said, smiled because the house had fared well. On a squat hill, good, hard earth, the rain had washed over the sides, spread out south toward its source. He knew that Miller's Creek, a two-minute trudge through the backyard tamaracks and barbed undergrowth, had taken much of the water, filled its ravine. Thanks to the creek, Johnson's Buick and snowmobile were safe and there were only a few puddles in the basement. Still, the creek worried him.

Murphy, a retired man who Johnson had known for years, lived down where the creek backed up into Mill Pond, then passed under the road through an elevated culvert. Johnson wanted to walk down the road and check on Murphy, who had recently taken on a stiff leg, but Sheila wasn't ready yet, still strapping on a pair of Johnson's boots in the living room. Already the girl borrowed most all of his things since moving in two weeks ago. Johnson didn't mind. It was nice to have her in the house, someone with whom he could talk, share a meal, laugh out loud at the TV.

When Sheila opened the front door to the porch, Johnson chuckled.

"Pencil thin and lead-footed." She sprouted from his big black boots, thin legs and knob knees, all beneath the hemline of a pilled pink dress. Johnson didn't mean to stare at her body, and when he caught himself he shook his head, blinked hard and turned away.

"You told me to wear the shit-kickers." Sheila lifted a boot, laughed, and stomped it on the porch. "I just need to get out after all that rain. And what about you?" She pointed at his rubber waders.

"I'm prepared," he said. "And you took my boots."

□ □ □

When they came upon Murphy's house, the shock wasn't that the land was dry, no silt film swirling from a flooded pond, nor the two cop cars parked in his driveway. The shock was the blue van between them, white letters spelling out Forensics.

"Goddamn," Johnson said, then spotted Murphy standing at the end of the street where the bridge had washed out.

"Seems your friend's fine," Sheila said. "I'm heading back. Can't stand another second in these boots."

Johnson walked toward Murphy, who soon turned and hobbled over while waving one arm.

"I seen it," he hollered. "I seen the whole thing happen."

"Now what happened?" Johnson hollered.

Murphy slowed, stopped, and pulled his left leg straight with the other.

"I'll tell you. I was in the living room this morning and all of a sudden I heard this rumbling in the ground." Murphy's arms rose, fists clenched, and shook. He had a tendency to embellish his stories, with physical gestures too. "Now I thought there was a quake coming, like the earth was going to tear open and swallow me, but I realized that the rumbling was coming from the bridge, so much water backed up and trying to get through that little hole, water up to the road itself.

"Well, I'm just standing out there minding my business and all of a sudden that culvert shoots out like a silver missile." Murphy opened one hand and fanned it across the sky. "And the road on top just caved all in—out comes the culvert, out comes the water." With each outpouring, Murphy's arms swooshed before him. "And then out comes this huge plastic bag riding that water.

"You'd never guess what's in it." Murphy shook his head. "The bag landed in the crook of one of them swamp maples in the gully. And I looked real close," Murphy leaned in and squinted, "and I saw hanging out of that bag a human arm."

"You're kidding." Johnson held his words to a flat tone.

"And I'll tell you one thing," Murphy said. He shook a finger. "I bet you it's that neighbor of yours—that Palmer boy who took off. That's why the van's over here."

They walked to the edge of the road where the bridge had collapsed and Johnson saw that Murphy's story was true. Joey

Palmer's soon-to-be identified body hung in a tree, one blanched arm out of the bag. Johnson just stood and looked down into the gully at a man in a gray coat writing on a clipboard and two policemen stringing yellow tape in a wide circle.

□ □ □

Johnson thought of his duplex as a mirror image, one side a reflection of the other, like crouching down over the edge of Mill Pond and staring into your own eyes. He loved its seclusion from the road, the farmer's porch and extra toilet off the kitchen. Of course, the place had always been home. After his mother died, he took over the lease at reduced rent because he agreed to shovel and rake, do any repairs he could handle, and those of the neighbor too. But he didn't love the mirror-reflection design two weeks ago, when lying in bed, he couldn't sleep. Yesterday, his neighbor, Joey Palmer, had brought in some tramp, lean and angular with black, straw hair, and soon Johnson could hear the sounds of their union through the wall—slaps and yelps, the occasional dull thump of their headboard behind his pillow. He decided, though, not to complain. After all, it was Joey Palmer who saved his sister's life a year ago.

□ □ □

That morning, a year ago, Johnson arrived at Enchanted Acres, a public home for the retarded where his sister lived and Johnson worked. An ambulance blocked the front door. He parked, hurried out of the car and ran. An ambulance was a common sight, all the residents so ill, but Johnson always felt a rush of fear when he saw one—the chance that it came for Gayle. Inside, he saw the EMTs, two guys in their twenties, talking to weary-eyed Joey Palmer who was closing in on the end of his shift. The charge nurse, Denise, stood behind them, writing on a clipboard.

"I was in the middle of changing her," Joey said. "I really didn't think about the training. I should have, but I've never seen death coming on like that. It's not the same in the training videos."

"What happened?" Johnson asked.

"She's okay," Denise said, put her hand on Johnson's shoulder.

"So I jumped on the bed, hoisted her up and started the Heimlich. You know, one hand over the other. Maureen was at the door not long after the rag came out of her throat."

"Why was the door shut?"

Denise spoke up. "We require doors to be shut for privacy."

"Had you yelled for Maureen's help?"

"Yeah, but she was on her smoking break and there's no one else at night."

"My God," Johnson said and left for Gayle's room.

There, his sister lay in bed, flushed and sweaty, black hair matted at the back. Johnson leaned over the bed, the metal railing pinching his stomach, and stared, silent, into the stillness of her eyes. At that moment, he wished, more than any time before, that Gayle could speak, tell him exactly what had happened, what she thought, just what her life was. But Gayle had never been able to speak, born into the world backward and ill, never weaned from mashed foods, bedrails, and diapers. But she was alive, looking up at him. Joey Palmer saved the last bit of Johnson's family.

So that night, a year later, Johnson lay in bed, trying not to hear the sounds through the walls. He didn't blame Joey. Men had certain natural desires and he understood them. It had been some time since Johnson had touched a woman, even a short slap or pull from the girls in Portland who swung around poles and bent over for tips. And Johnson could never get a woman to stick around, though he had tried. Thinking about it all brought a strange comfort to the noises on the other side of his bedroom, lulled him to sleep with the thought that the possibility still remained out there for him, as it did for Joey Palmer.

But Johnson soon woke up. A scream pulled him up and out

of some phase of slumber, after which he couldn't decide if he had been asleep or just on its edge. He rose and rubbed his eyes and a scream came again, long and shrill, nothing like he expected from a couple, any couple, making love. And then he heard a crash, something thick but fragile thrown against the wall and Joey Palmer hollering. Johnson threw off his blanket, put his feet into slippers and walked outside to Joey's front door with the master key.

Inside, he turned on the living room light and walked to the bedroom. There, Johnson stopped, held his shaking hand over the doorknob. He had never entered the other side without knocking and, after all, he respected, even admired, Joey Palmer. But there had been screams. From behind the closed door, Johnson listened, heard nothing but silence, worse, he thought, than hearing the screams again. And when the screams came, Johnson pushed open the door and stepped inside. There, he saw Joey Palmer and the girl on the bed. Joey was naked and the girl wore a short velvet dress, thick makeup, a handkerchief around her throat. Joey held her bent over, one arm around her waist, the other holding a gun behind her head.

"Damn it all," Joey said, looked at Johnson.

As Joey turned his head, the girl screamed again, loud, filled the room with a sting of pain. She twisted her body, reached up and wrung the gun from Joey's hand, fell to the floor. Joey reached down to take it back, but Johnson lunged and placed his leg between them.

"Johnson, get the hell out of here," Joey yelled.

Johnson couldn't respond. He saw the girl pointing the gun at Joey Palmer. He saw Joey Palmer naked on the bed. But all Johnson could think, a thought so strong he couldn't lift his foot to kick the gun as the girl fired it, was that the position in which he had first seen them was the same one Joey used to save Gayle's life.

The girl dropped the gun when Joey's body fell backward, his throat open and red. Johnson picked up the gun, though he knew, somehow, that she wasn't going to touch it again. He stuffed it in the pocket of his pajamas and reached down, lifted and cradled the girl in his arms. Sheila cried, a black trail over one cheek, another thin and red down one leg.

"It really hurt," she whispered.

Johnson carried Sheila next door, inside his living room and up the stairs to Gayle's old room. When he set her onto her feet, she fell, sat on the bed's edge. Johnson sat down too.

"I couldn't help it," she said, bent over and cried into her hands. "I'm not foolish. I knew he would want something, but I didn't think that."

Johnson looked at her, that mass of black, straw hair draped over her hands.

"Where are your parents?" he asked, placed his hand on her shoulder.

"I don't live with them. I can't," she said. "He offered me a place to stay. He said he worked with disabled people, that he helps people out. I figured he'd want something. I just didn't think . . ."

"It's okay," Johnson said. He said those words just as much for Sheila as for himself. Johnson knew there had been time to kick that gun. He could have saved the man's life. But the thought of his sister had held him back, or he had held himself back, which, though, he couldn't figure out.

"I'm going to jail," she said, rubbed her hands over her eyes.

"No, you won't," Johnson said. "You did that in self-defense."

"Or back home. How do you know?" she asked, lifted her face. Their eyes locked—two sets of brown eyes in silence—and Johnson thought, for a moment, that he was looking into Gayle's eyes, looking at his reflection in Mill Pond. And through her tears, Johnson could see, wanted to care for, this girl's young but hard heart.

"We'll take care of it together. Clean up like nothing happened." Sheila fell into him, slid her long arms up his back, cried on his shoulder. "It'll be all right."

"You'll do that for me?"

He nodded.

Then Sheila lowered her face and Johnson felt the warm press of her lips move up his arm, inch after inch her soft kisses on his skin. He knew it wasn't right, just wasn't right to find any pleasure in a young girl, this young girl who had learned only one way to thank a man. Johnson stood up, shook off her body.

"Let me show you where the bathroom is," he said. "You need to clean up. Then we'll both deal with next door."

Downstairs, Johnson washed his hands, gathered cleaning supplies and a black leaf bag. When Sheila appeared in the living room, the two walked next door, silent, and placed Joey's body in the bag. They scrubbed and vacuumed the bedroom, tossed around a few worn clothes, then dirtied up the carpet, just a bit.

And that night, beneath a sliver of moon, they hauled Joey in a canoe under the tamaracks and down to the edge of Mill Pond, tied up the bag with a chain and two cinder blocks and rowed toward the bridge where the pond ran deep. There, on the sludge bottom, Johnson knew that the poor guy's body would bloat, then slowly rot, piece away downstream toward the ocean. That thought didn't bother him too much, because, if nothing else, the guy had really hurt this girl. Still, when the storm came later, Johnson couldn't help but think that Joey Palmer somehow rained all around him.

"What the hell are we going to do?" Sheila asked, leaning against the living room wall, staring at Johnson as he returned from checking on Murphy.

"I don't know," he said. "There's a new renter next door, so I can't believe they'll find much, not after us, then the cleaners who came."

"But there will be questions."

Johnson thought hard. It was Sheila, really, who had killed. Yes, he had that moment to kick the gun, but he didn't send the bullet to Joey's throat. Still, Johnson had cleaned and covered up, told Joey's boss at Enchanted Acres tall tales.

"I'll just stick to the story. It still works," he said. "Some woman, long blonde hair, sunglasses, drove up and Joey jumped into the car, a Caprice, and left. Haven't seen or heard from him since. And how much I liked the guy because he saved my sister and paid his rent in cash, which was overdue last month. Makes sense he might skip out."

"I need to think," Sheila said. "I'm going to my room to sit down, alone, and think."

□ □ □

When Sheila returned downstairs, Johnson stood up from the couch.

"You can't go anywhere," he said. Sheila's backpack hung from her shoulder.

"I'm leaving." She headed toward the kitchen where she opened a drawer and took out the keys to Joey Palmer's car.

"You can't take his car."

"You took the keys." She stared at him. "Didn't you?"

"I didn't know what else to do with them."

Sheila walked over to Johnson, stood in front of him. He regretted letting her stay upstairs, giving her time to think of such a foolish thing as leaving.

"We'll just tell them the story," Johnson said.

"You'll just tell them."

Sheila walked around him and Johnson wanted to reach out and grab her, shake her hard, but he couldn't. He knew she had been through a lot, and he had only known her for two weeks.

"Wait a minute," he said. Sheila turned around, the door half-open, while Johnson reached into his back pocket. "Here, a little gas money to get you someplace far."

Sheila nodded, took the money and pocketed it.

Johnson walked out to see her off, but the girl didn't look back, just got into Joey Palmer's car, turned on the engine and left for the road. He sat down on the porch, leaned against the railing and drew in the air. He didn't know where she would go, someplace, he suspected, where people didn't care to ask questions or know the truth, someplace where people weren't tied down. For a moment, he thought he'd like to go there too, but someone needed to look after Gayle and Murphy and the house.

And then Johnson exhaled, pursed his lips and thought that he would just tell the truth if she were ever found. He couldn't stop that girl from shooting Joey Palmer and he couldn't stop her from leaving.

Being Karen Cooper

Catherine Cairns

She pulled into the underground garage and killed the engine. It was a good day to go shopping. She could feel it in her bones. Flipping open her wallet, she surveyed the crop of shiny new credit cards tucked into the sleek leather openings. Karen Cooper was printed neatly on each and every one just waiting to be swiped through a number of machines to make a variety of purchases: a new ankle-length winter coat, woolen, or maybe even cashmere; expensive jewelry, gold and diamonds; a couple of handbags—Fendi or kate spade, and of course, a few cash advances.

The fact that Karen Cooper wasn't her real name was of little consequence to the slender brunette. Andrea Skinner had been stealing identities for the past year and living off unsuspecting victims. For a sizeable kickback, an old school chum who worked at the Registry of Motor Vehicles just outside of Boston gave Andrea the personal info that enabled her to become someone else.

Andrea knew she had to be careful. This was her first time being Karen Cooper, and she didn't want to mess up. She glanced in the rearview mirror, checked her lipstick, and then tried the name on for size.

"Hello, I'm Karen Cooper." With an international flair, "Bonjour, je suis Karen Cooper." Then with a drawl, "Hello, they-a, I'm Karen Coopa."

Andrea grinned, enjoying the rush that always came when playing outside the law. The sensation swam through her veins like a good martini, exhilaration mixed with satisfaction and topped with a splash of paranoia just to keep her on her toes. She got high from shopping on someone else's dime, but it was damn risky. An acquaintance of hers got picked up for cashing stolen checks three weeks before. Andrea had no intention of letting that happen. To avoid suspicion, she had donned the attire of a wealthy young shopper in black leather pants, white cashmere sweater, and gray woolen cape.

Dressed as she was, no one would ever guess a year ago she had been working for minimum wage serving pizza and burgers to blue-collar grunts. Never again, she thought, as she stepped out of her car in the most exclusive shopping mall in the area. She'd had more than enough canned soup and stale crackers to last her a lifetime. And it was that working-class poverty that had ignited a fire in her gut and enabled her to learn the business quickly. Since many credit card companies had built-in protection for their customers, Andrea didn't think of it as stealing. More like sharing the wealth.

Shutting the driver's side door, she checked her surroundings, then pressed the remote, locking her car. One could never be too careful.

Her first stop was Tiffany's.

Andrea did wonder about the real Karen, at least for the few moments it took the cashier to run the credit card. She wondered what the real Karen was doing right now. Was she at some meeting making executive decisions that would siphon corporate profits into her bank account? Or was she at home changing diapers and wondering how she was going to afford the rent?

Andrea brushed strands of her dark brown hair from her face and, just as quickly, the thoughts of her victim from her mind.

"Ms Cooper?" The round-faced clerk wore that impatient, raised-eyebrow stare that said she'd been trying to get Andrea's attention.

"What?" Andrea asked, slightly rattled to be caught daydreaming.

"I asked if you would like the necklace gift wrapped," the clerk said, over-enunciating her words.

Andrea reigned in her nerves and tossed out a careless chuckle. "Oh, no, dear, just put it in a bag."

The clerk's face remained impassive, having been trained to respond deferentially to wealthy women like Ms Karen Cooper. Andrea knew all about catering to the rich. She'd worked Macy's cosmetics counter one summer and dealt with wealthy dowagers who constantly demanded makeovers from the cosmetics staff. Ancient women who were gullible to the insincere flattery of a sales clerk offering a line of makeup that could take years off their faces. The kind of women that store management loved and sales clerks had to kowtow to.

The thought of that summer of humiliation prompted Andrea to smile at the clerk. "Have a nice day," she said with sincerity.

Andrea reached for the little blue bag when she was bumped from behind. She whirled around to see a heavyset man in an ill-fitting trench coat lumber past. He turned slightly, showing only his profile, and muttered something she imagined was an apology. Then he veered left at the door. Immediately, she took inventory of her personal belongings: handbag, wallet, and Tiffany's bag, everything still where it should be.

Pay attention, she scolded herself. Knowing where everyone was within fifty feet of her was essential. Any one of them could be an undercover cop. She'd also have to be more careful about responding immediately, yet calmly to her new name. With those thoughts, she continued on her shopping spree.

Two hours later, she stood at Macy's cosmetics counter, testing perfumes. She had already spent several thousand dollars on a few carefully chosen items she planned to fence. Now, she wanted something for herself.

After a careful perusal of the store's most exclusive cosmetics line, Andrea handed the saleswoman an armful of makeup items imported from France. "I'll take these," she said, and then noticed a distinguished looking man a few feet away sniffing various bottles.

"That will be three-hundred and sixty-seven, fifty, please," the saleswoman said.

Andrea opened her wallet, this time selecting Karen Cooper's unchristened MasterCard, and handed it to the saleswoman. Her gaze traveled back to the handsome gentleman.

She watched him spray the air with another perfume, sniff and then grimace, and hurriedly replace the bottle on the counter. He glanced up, catching Andrea's eye, and broke into an embarrassed grin.

"I really don't have a clue what I'm doing," he called across the expanse of the spotless glass counter, his British accent smooth and cultivated like old prep schools and family money. "Do you have any recommendations?"

"I'm partial to that perfume by Givenchy," Andrea said, pointing to a bottle on the counter to his right.

"Would you sign here, please, Ms Cooper?" the saleswoman said presenting the credit receipt.

For a moment the name puzzled Andrea, and then recognition dawned like the proverbial light bulb. She slipped a pen from her purse, preferring to leave as few prints behind as possible, and pressed the tip to the receipt in front of her. When she felt her fingers swooping upward, as she would when writing the first letter of her real name, Andrea froze, feeling the clerk's eyes upon her. But she recovered quickly and changed the almost A into an angled K, averting a possible disaster.

"Thank you," Andrea said moments later, and collected her bags just as the British gentleman gave her a wave.

"You were right," he said smiling, "the Givenchy is quite lovely."

"Glad I could help," Andrea said, and felt a sudden letdown as she stepped away from the counter. In her line of work, she couldn't afford to act on chance encounters with strangers, even if they were good-looking guys with British accents. She couldn't be too careful. He could be a private detective or an undercover cop.

Most of the guys she had dated were somehow connected to the business. Her last boyfriend ran a chop shop, specializing in high-ticket foreign cars. He'd snagged her a good deal on a nice car. But two months into their relationship, one night after a few beers, he started pushing her around. The evening ended at the emergency room with her arm in a cast. She didn't need anything else broken to get the message, so she split. Since then she'd resigned herself to running solo until she could put aside enough money to live independently. After that she'd get out of the business and start over. She'd build a normal life for herself; a calm, safe life, maybe like the one belonging to the real Karen Cooper.

"Ms Cooper. Oh, Ms Cooper," a voice called from behind.

Andrea froze, her self-pitying musings muscled out by a stab of panic. The possibility of being caught was a constant companion and she'd had a few close calls over the past year. Was this her unlucky day? Plastering on a confident smile, she turned back to the counter, all the while scanning her surroundings for the best escape route.

"Ms Cooper, you forgot your charge card," the saleswoman chirped in a singsong fashion as she waved the card over her head.

Andrea let out the breath she was holding and strode back to the counter.

"Thank you," she said, inserting the card into her wallet.

Christ, I need a drink, she thought, exiting the store.

But she settled for coffee and five minutes later was sipping a mocha latte at a corner table in Java Paradise. She liked the soft lighting and the opulent atmosphere reflected in the metal of the thousand-dollar espresso machines and executive travel mugs.

In her head, she ran through the list of items she had purchased, marketable items she knew could be easily and profitably unloaded. And although she'd bought herself the makeup, she hadn't yet bought any trinkets to keep. Maybe she'd buy one of those pricey espresso machines, she thought sipping her coffee. Why not? It was well within her budget now that she was using someone else's money.

She had just placed her oversized cup on the table when she noticed the bulky man who had bumped her earlier enter the shop. He stood out from the other customers with his two-dollar haircut and his ten-year-old trench coat. He had a head like a bowling ball and no neck to speak of, and reminded Andrea of a cartoon character she'd seen once. She raised the latte to her lips again, comfortable that the large cup covered a good portion of her slender face, but still allowed her to observe him.

This overweight Columbo wannabe could be tailing me, she thought. Then again, maybe I'm just being paranoid. The guy is probably just trying to find his wife so he can go home and watch the ball game.

Tubby Trench Coat scanned the shop, his eyes resting for a brief moment on a woman sitting at the table next to Andrea's. He let out an exasperated sigh, then turned around and stormed out the door.

Andrea lowered her cup and watched him walk away. But just as he was about to disappear from view, his round head swiveled in her direction, and he stared at her through the display window. She quickly turned, feigning interest in the contents of her handbag, averting her face from his scrutiny. When she looked up again, he was gone.

The quivering hairs on the back of her neck told her it was time to get out. After waiting ten minutes, she collected her things and exited the coffee shop from the side entrance. She stepped into the main aisle of the mall, keeping close to the storefronts, and surveying the area. She slipped into a tiny shoe store, hovering around the displays, all the while keeping an eye on the door for the worn and wrinkled trench coat.

"Can I help you, miss?"

"What?" Andrea jumped at the sales clerk's question.

"I'm sorry, I didn't mean to startle you," the young man said.

Andrea sucked in air, her throat tight with panic. Get it under control, she told herself.

"I'm just looking," she said finally, and went through the motions of handling some shoes.

"We just got some new Italian boots in, and I'm sure we have your size." The clerk leaned back and eyed Andrea's feet. "I'd guess you were about a seven, right?" He didn't wait for her reply before he scurried off toward the back room.

Andrea opened her mouth to decline his offer, when she sensed something to her left, moving at the edge of her peripheral vision. She turned quickly, but no one was there. Spooked, she hurried out the door.

Merging into the crowd of shoppers, Andrea criss-crossed the mall as she headed toward the garage. Halfway to the exit, she caught sight of the man in the trench coat again standing by a kiosk that sold watches. Beside him was a woman wearing a long coat in an odd shade of green that reminded her of something her late aunt Doris might have worn twenty years ago.

Mrs. Columbo wannabe, Andrea thought, as she passed the kiosk, keeping her face averted.

A safe distance away, she slipped into a clothing store doorway and glanced back. The lady in green was still standing there, but Trench Coat was gone. Apparently, they weren't together. He'd probably positioned himself next to the lady to give the illusion he wasn't alone. And that he wasn't stalking Andrea.

She picked up the pace as she headed toward the parking garage. All along the way, she swore she caught glimpses of the ugly beige trench coat whipping around corners and ducking into storefronts.

I'm being ridiculous, she thought, pushing open the heavy metal door that led to the garage. But she didn't slow down as she fumbled in her coat pocket for her parking ticket. P-17, it read, and she scurried down the two flights of steps to that section.

It was nearing dinnertime and fewer vehicles filled the parking spaces, and she easily spotted her car beside a mammoth SUV. She fished her keys out of her handbag, isolating the car key between two fingers.

The garage seemed darker now, and she noticed the light over the sign P-17 had blown, making it difficult to make out the letters. Elevator doors whooshed open a few feet away, as she aimed the key for the car lock. Misjudging the distance, she dropped them on the ground.

"Shit." She bent to retrieve them, her fingers grazing the keys, when she heard footsteps. The fear of getting caught propelled her forward, and she snatched up the keys and jammed the largest one into the lock. The lock clicked open as a vaguely familiar voice spoke behind her.

"Hello, we meet again." Andrea spun around. A flush of relief poured over her. It wasn't Trench Coat, but the handsome Brit from the perfume counter. She couldn't help but smile.

But the gentleman didn't smile back, and she suddenly felt a wrenching pain in her gut that said something was wrong. Like she had been running from the wrong man.

"Are you Karen Cooper?" he asked.

"Oh, crap," she muttered. This was it. She was going down. This guy was the cop, not the loser in the trench coat. How else would he know her name? What a dope I am, she thought, dropping her packages at her feet and letting out a long frustrated sigh. "Yes," she said finally.

Andrea watched him reach into his tweed overcoat, most likely for a set of cuffs, she thought. But when she saw his hand again, it held a gun.

Andrea stared at the weapon, and then looked back at his face. "All right, I give up. You don't have to shoot me," she said, sarcasm weighting her words, as she extended her wrists in surrender.

"Oh, but I do," he said, and pulled the trigger.

□ □ □

The British gentleman took the emergency staircase to the street where he vanished into the Saturday afternoon crowd. He waited until he reached his vehicle, a black sedan, nondescript, except for its tinted windows, then flipped open a cell phone.

"It's me," he said, all traces of the accent gone. "The Cooper case is settled." He switched the phone to the other ear. "And one more thing, tell your sources they're slipping. She wasn't a flaming redhead, she was a brunette."

Life-Long Game

Elizabeth Armstrong

When they started the Newton Indoor Tennis Club, Stella and I were first in line to join. We were veterans of the Parks and Recreation Department tennis program run on the outdoor courts of Newton. In good weather, a group of us played in drop-in games on Monday and Friday mornings, which if you took a Wednesday lesson, pretty much gave you your tennis for the week. Stella and I were ecstatic when they built a bubble over the courts in Newton Center and began accepting winter memberships.

Kenny, the head pro, began organizing a league for women as soon as the bubble went up. Kenny was the moving force behind the indoor club—he knew he was losing major bucks during the winter, when all his loyal outdoor players drained off to indoor clubs in downtown Boston, Wellesley, or Dedham. Kenny was short, stocky, and even-tempered, which made him a good buffer for all the emotion that can surround tennis. Tennis is a life-long game, he always said. Take care of yourself and build on your skills and you can enjoy playing for the rest of your life.

I was disappointed the day Kenny rated me for the league. My elbow was stiff and my serve was soft. My forehand returns kept going over the baseline, and even my backhand went into the net several times. "Diane," Kenny said, "I know you can do better, and I'll re-rate you later. For now I'm going to have to put you as a 3.5."

I gulped. That was the very bottom qualifying rating to play in the league. "I don't know what's wrong with me today."

Kenny glanced down at his clipboard. "You volleyed well. Don't forget to ice that elbow."

I didn't answer and Kenny shot me a sharp glance. "Remember, Diane, you have to take care of yourself. Because tennis is what?"

"A life-long game," I said.

"That's right."

Stella got a 5.0 rating. She played on the tennis team in college. Stella isn't flashy, but man, she's steady. "You'll move up," she said coolly. Stella doesn't waste sympathy on trivial matters. "You just had a bad day."

"Yeah," I said. "Well, it's not like it's a big deal. It's just a game."

My bad day got worse when Steven, my youngest, came home from school with his report card. He got a C in math and a D in health. The math grade was expected, unfortunately, but I couldn't get past the D. "What did you do?" I asked him. "Light up a cigarette in class? Refuse to shower or brush your teeth? How do you get a D in health?"

He blushed. "I don't know, I guess I'm just bad at health."

It didn't really matter, I told myself. He's still in eighth grade, it's not the end of the world. Then Sarah came home from high school with her PSAT scores and they were much lower than we'd expected. *Much lower.* She was upset, and I reassured her that we'd get her into a prep course and there are plenty of good non-Ivy schools to go to. Then I swallowed two Aleve dry and took my ice bag to bed.

When the league got going, Stella started playing with different people, while I was mired down in the lower ranks, looking for a doubles partner. It took me a while to get used to playing inside the bubble, which is like a big-top tent, with strange diffuse light that made me squint. I loved playing outside. The air on my arms, the sun on my face. The sense of total well-being as I drove home from the courts was something I experienced rarely these days.

After my husband, Paul, got promoted and began to travel all the time, we agreed that I should stop working, at least for a few years. To fill up the days, I volunteered in the public schools, sorted used clothing at Rosie's Place, and took up guitar. I spent a year balancing do-gooding with self-fulfillment, until I realized that people were competing to be on the curriculum committee and what Rosie's Place really needed was fat checks. I let my new neighbor Susan take my place on the school committee—she'd told me how hard she found it to break in, moving to Newton from Wisconsin, and since she was a former school principal who was now staying home with her kids, she was the ideal candidate. When it came time to sign up for the next quarter of volunteering at Rosie's, I doubled my contribution instead. Then Jamal, my guitar teacher, told me he was moving to L.A. and I realized that what I really liked was sitting in a small windowless room with Jamal for thirty minutes a week, not playing guitar per se. I missed having fingernails. I grew my nails out and booked my first manicure in a year. French.

Steven was taking tennis lessons and I signed up for an adult beginner session so that I could hit with him. Soon I was bribing Steven to practice with me with sodas from the vending machine at the Exxon station next to the courts. I kept a basket of balls in my car and dropped by the courts to practice my serve whenever I could. When I advanced to the intermediate class I met Stella. She and I were on opposite sides of the net when I dove for a low volley and shredded the skin on my right knee. I rolled, jumped up, and raced back to try to hit the lob she'd sent over my head. I missed it, but she applauded my attempt. "Good hustle."

"Thanks." I dabbed the oozing flesh over my knee with my wristband. "Deuce, right?"

"Don't you want to take a break?"

"Nah."

Her eyes narrowed. "You should get some real tennis shoes instead of those running shoes. It makes a difference."

The next lesson I showed up in K-Swiss Glaciators with a patch of Tegaderm over my healing knee. At the end of class Stella told me about the drop-in games on Mondays and Fridays. I gave her my e-mail address. Soon she was picking me for her partner. At first I thought she was just being welcoming, but then I realized that we had an unstoppable chemistry on court. No one wanted to win more than Stella and me. I missed playing with her when the league got going, but I understood. She really should play with people who were rated near her.

□ □ □

Vivica was always late, which was why I never set up a game with her. We all have our little emergencies, but Vivica was *always* late. She was subbing for Dawn that day and Petra, Susan, and I had warmed up and played two games of Canadian doubles by the time she pulled back the thick green rubber curtain and scurried onto the court, calling, "Sorry! Sorry!" Her bulky body was bloused in nylon pants and a flowered sweatshirt. She took her time stowing her carryall and unzipping her racquet case, checking her cell phone messages, putting on lip gloss. She bundled back her waist-length coarse hair with a hot pink scrunchie, then bounded onto the court, her homely face creasing with pleasure and anticipation.

My heart sank when she joined me on my side of the net. I wished I didn't feel so uncharitable toward Vivica. Something about her mare's face reminds me of Ronadene Youngquist from the toddlers' class at Grace Presbyterian. One of my earliest memories is pushing Ronadene off the stage at a Sunday School production, after realizing I couldn't share the platform with someone whose stubby legs ended in lacy socks and saddle shoes.

Since she hadn't warmed up, Vivica played poorly during the first set, calling "Whoops!" again and again as Petra and Susan took each game. "No worries," I said. Then, "It's okay, V, you don't have to apologize." Finally, "Vivica, it's only a game!"

The second set I played with Petra. Vivica was warmed up by then and hit some decent shots, but I was on fire. This is what we play for, those brazen moments in the zone where timing and technique are effortless, and we are fearless and fierce. I fired a forehand down the line and Vivica tumbled toward it, barely getting her racquet on it as she staggered. I could see it all as the wild return arced in the air and I lined up sideways to it, racquet overhead, left hand pointing at the ball. I saw Vivica recover and return to position, I saw my infant self in a blue dress with smocking and puffed sleeves, I saw Ronadene squalling in front of the stage, her mother glaring at me as she knelt to comfort her. I slammed the ball as it descended toward me, accelerating through it with the force of a first serve. I watched as if in slow motion while it traveled its trajectory, hitting its mark in the flowered puddle of Vivica's soft gut.

She crumpled like newsprint in a flame. "My God," cried Petra, rushing toward her.

Susan got to her first. "Are you all right?" she crooned, cupping Vivica's elbow and pulling her to her feet.

All eyes shifted to me, frozen in sullen silence. "Sorry," I muttered. "So sorry, Viv."

And I was sorry. I should have aimed at her feet. Stupid, I said to myself. Save the body shots for the tournament.

□ □ □

Jelly was a dumpling of a woman, four-eleven and thick-legged, with a year round tan and simmering eyes. She said her name was a childhood corruption of Julie, but you looked at the cellulite on the back of her thighs and you just wondered.

She lived around the corner from me and asked me to invite her as a guest, since she's a single mom and didn't want to come up with the membership fee. Technically you weren't supposed to come as a guest if you lived in Newton—they were trying to pressure people to join—but how were they going to know? Of course, I told her. Jelly moved well and her ground strokes came at you low and fast. Stella had complained that Jelly tried to coach her, which was not cool, and she had a habit of calling close balls out instead of giving the benefit of the doubt. When a shot smoked up the middle, she always said the same thing: "That was yours, babe."

Jelly and I were paired up against Cate and Margaret. We were down one game to five, though each game had gone to deuce. "This one has to be ours," she said to me. "Keep your backswing short on the return of serve and be sure to follow through."

I nodded, though I didn't need her to tell me that. Cate's serve had pace and angle, and my first return sailed beyond the baseline. I didn't look at Jelly. She got the next serve into play but when the ball came back deep, she hit it into the net. She let out a low barking laugh. "Down love-thirty. Come on now." Like it was all me.

Short backswing, follow through, I mouthed soundlessly. Short backswing, follow through. Cate's first serve was wide; her second serve brushed the corner of the box and I blocked it back and watched it sail beyond the baseline. Jelly bellowed, "Out!"

I tried to hide my surprise. Cate cried, "What?"

"Out," Jelly called firmly. "The serve was out. Right, Diane?"

I shrugged. "I didn't see. If you say so."

Cate looked away for a minute, chewing on her lip, then returned to the base line and served up two aces to finish the set. We trooped to the bench to swig water and readjust the aircasts on our forearms. When we rotated for the next set, I was with Margaret. "How's Willie?" I asked as we took the court.

"Great," she said. "Do you mind if I take the deuce court?"

"No, that's fine," I said. "Does he like Miss Freelander? Steven had her in fifth grade and loved her."

Margaret opened her mouth to answer, but Jelly cut in.

"Chit chat, chit chat," she said, smiling coldly. "One thing you can count on when you play with Diane is lots of talk."

"Who, me?" I looked at Margaret, who rolled her eyes. Jelly bounced a ball on her racquet, once, twice, three times. Cate kept quiet.

I decided to leave it. I got in position on the base line and put my racquet up. I moved to net as often as I could that set, keeping quiet and smashing volleys at Jelly's feet. Margaret and I took the set 6-3. Jelly was steaming, though she kept making pseudo self-deprecating remarks like, "I don't remember the last time I double-faulted on an add-in point, what's wrong with me today?" and "I played so well last week, guess it's my turn to have an off day."

Shut up, I thought. Shut up and play.

Cate and I took the next set 6-4, which meant that everyone had lost when they played with Jelly. No one had booked the court for the next hour, and Margaret and Cate decided to stay and play singles. As Jelly and I zipped our racquets into our bags, I couldn't help feeling vindicated. Follow through, indeed. Jelly looked at her watch and said, "Gotta pick my kids up, catch you later," and fled.

I strolled to the admin desk and took a square of paper and a pencil stub. "It has come to my attention that a Newton resident is coming regularly to the club as a guest," I wrote. "It seems unfair that some of us adhere to the policy and others don't. Jelly Grant is a Newton resident who lives on Farber Avenue." I signed it, "A Concerned Member" and folded it in half, dropping it in the suggestion box.

□ □ □

The first tournament was coming up and I still hadn't found a doubles partner. Kenny suggested I play with Freda, who used to go out to Weston but was giving the Newton club a try. She had bushy black hair without a thread of gray and the kind of complexion that burns and peels. Even in the dead of winter she looked a little scaly. Freda was friendly enough at first, but after my return had gone out several times, she stepped toward me with a stern look. "Don't forget to follow through," she said. Then, after I'd muffed an overhead into the net, "You should take some private lessons."

All the mistakes weren't mine. Freda had a way of folding in long rallies, returning some tough shots but not closing. I wondered if she was losing concentration or if it was an endurance problem. "You should spend some time on the treadmill," I thought of saying. But didn't.

Freda bent over to retie her shoes, facing the back of the court so the other team couldn't miss that she wasn't ready to receive serve. I jogged to the sideline to get a drink of water. Freda's keys lay next to her tennis bag, seven shining shapes in brass and nickel with a sterling scripted "F" attached. I glanced at the other team, Lydia and Paula. They were huddled together, discussing strategy *sotto voce*. As I raised my water bottle, I pushed the keys toward my bag with one toe. Bending over to put my water bottle in its mesh pocket, I folded the keys into the deep side flap of my tennis bag. I would have to find a doubles partner myself— Kenny obviously didn't know Freda very well.

□ □ □

I called Stella that night. She had partnered up with Mona, one of the regulars from our outdoor games. I wilted with envy as Stella talked about Mona's serve—incredible topspin—and her fiery net play. "Girl, we've been smokin'!"

"You're playing together in the tournament?"

"Oh, yeah. D'you find a partner yet?"

"Still working on it," I reported glumly. I took out the league list and considered my options. Vivica needed a partner, of course. I had put off asking her, but now it was desperation time. I willed myself to dial her number. She answered on the first ring.

"Oh," she said, when I asked her if she was entering the doubles tournament. "I didn't think you . . . well, Jelly just joined up, and I promised to play with her."

"Jelly joined the league?"

Vivica's voice was high and girlish, but it had an edge to it as she said, "They told her she couldn't come as a guest anymore. Someone reported her to the club for being a Newton resident."

As I hung up, I considered calling Freda, but discarded the notion. She'd glared at me across the courts ever since the day we played together, though I told her I had no idea what happened to her keys. Cate and Susan had entered the tournament together, as had Margaret and Petra. Everyone had a partner but me.

I lay on the bed, staring into space. Mona was a good player, but she wore one of those fussy little skirt dresses, and she tended to brag about her children. It was too bad Stella had gotten cornered into playing with her, all because of my lousy and unfair rating. Kenny had re-rated me a 5.0, but by then it was too late to undo what had been done. It was such a shame, because when Stella and I played together, we were something else.

□   □   □

The week before the tournament was the coldest in Newton since 1882. The year before, all snow. This year, all ice. It took some talking to persuade Mona to go skiing with me at Wachusett. I knew she loved to ski, and had overheard her in the locker room complaining about how little slope time she'd had this year, since her daughter was captain of the volleyball team and senior class president and applying to college—all Ivies, no safeties—and her son had the lead in the Newton South production of *Macbeth*.

"I have these day passes," I wheedled. "My sister was supposed to come in town and we were going to go, but she had to cancel."

"It's so cold, Diane," she said. "I've got a busy week."

"Oh, I know, but I hate to waste these passes. And it is fun to go on a weekday when the kids are in school. So much less chance of a snowboarder coming out of the trees and clocking you."

"Well," she said. Long pause.

I played my trump card. Mona is cheap. "Of course I already bought these passes and you'd be my guest. I'll pack a lunch for us and drive. We'll leave after the kids are in school and be back by three."

□ □ □

Mona and I had warmed up on the green trails, then advanced to blue. "Let's take one more run before lunch," she said. "I'll do some black diamonds this afternoon—you're probably not ready for those."

Does a life of crime always have its defining moment, when venal misdemeanors flower into felonies? My small sins and cruelties up to then had been catalyzed by resentment and fueled by my competitive spirit. Was this where I crossed over to malice with motive? As Mona and I rode the ski lift together I looked out over the crystal landscape, made icy and bright by the continual freeze. I told myself I still hadn't decided when Mona heaved off the chair lift too early, hitting the packed ice with a wobble. I launched after her, submitting to the instincts and actions that had brought me to this bright, dark place. Ducking my head and bending my knees, I swooped after her like an eagle toward a sparrow.

□ □ □

After Stella and I won the doubles tournament, we toasted one another with mocha lattes at Peet's. "It's so crazy," she said, "the way it all ended up. Mona's leg. You not having a partner." She wrinkled her nose. "I guess I forgot for a while how much I love playing with you, Di."

"Yeah," I said. "We really bring out the best in each other."

"It's tennis. Tennis brings out the best in us both."

I took a long sip of my coffee. "The great thing about tennis," I said, "is that it's a life-long game." Sitting with Stella, I knew I had many more adventures ahead.

Salamanna Grapes

Kevin Carey

James Tierney lay on his back at the edge of the Rossi and Keller
land, his head resting against the blood-blackened roots of tall
grass, his eyes slits against his pale skin, and his mouth stuffed
with plum-colored grapes from the arbor nearby, so many grapes,
in fact, that his lips pursed around them like a stuffed dinner-
beast.

Later that night, when Tierney lay naked in the cellar of
Bell's funeral parlor, next to a half-empty bottle of Four Roses
whiskey, his eyes a little more sunken, his dark curly hair matted
on one side with dried blood and dirt, his cheeks settled into his
face, Ralph Bell covered him with a clean white sheet, folded the
corners around his toes and head, then slid him from the table
onto a gurney covered by an open heavy-canvas bag. He had
planned to get to work on him right away for a Monday wake but
the inspector had come before he got going.

"Inspector," Ralph asked, "to what do I owe the pleasure?"

"Sorry to bother you so late. It's about the Tierney boy."

They stood in the foyer surrounded by pink wallpaper. A
small, crystal chandelier hung well above their heads. "We need
to take him in town," the inspector said.

"The medical examiner?"

"They just want to be sure. Procedure."

Ralph lowered his head. "The radio says the Nazis are on the move again."

"So it seems," the inspector said.

Ralph put a finger to his lips, turned and walked toward the parlor. "It's good I haven't started yet. I'll put him away."

After he zippered the brown bag shut over the center of the boy's body, he pulled the cork from the bottle of whiskey and poured a good belt into a water glass. "My, my," he whispered, throwing one back and swallowing hard with a grit of his teeth.

□ □ □

Because he was declared 4-F by the Army after graduating from high school, James Tierney had taken a job down the road at the Forbes Plant as a press feeder. "They ever print any good news?" he'd joke with the boss. "Maybe if I slide myself under the rollers I can make the front page, huh."

"You just keep feeding, hot shot," the boss would say, slapping him on the back like an old pal.

On the weekends James liked to hang around with some of the younger guys and make a little hay. Stealing grapes was a cheap way to pass the time. It was also one of the challenges he invented for himself, now that the challenge of war wouldn't have him.

Last Friday night he and a few other boys had gathered at the bottom of Curtis Hill. The boys sat on the curb and watched while James paced back and forth in front of them. He had stuck a small square piece of black paper under his nose and yelled with a fake German accent. "The key to victory is walking quietly," he said, "like this." He stepped lightly on his toes. "The enemy has donkey ears."

The boys all laughed and one of them jumped up, clicked his heels together and threw up his arm, "Jawohl, Mein Herr." Soon the boys were marching around in a tight circle stomping their feet on the pavement.

James liked the grape raids, even if it was a game. It reminded him of playing football, a sport where he'd enjoyed some success. "He was steady," his coach had once told the local newspaper, "not easy to knock down."

The boys walked quietly up Curtis Hill until they disappeared into the lot next to the grape arbor.

□　□　□

Carmen Rossi never returned to Italy after he left his Piedmont village home over thirty years ago, but he remembered as if it were yesterday, mixing piles of compost and ash and rich black soil, which he packed in mounds around the base of the *nebbiolo* vines, then carefully pruning the tough two-year bark off the wire fences like his father had shown him. He could still smell the plump red grapes that made the *barolo*, his father sitting in a straw chair beneath the thin criss-crossed shadows of the arbor, popping a few off the vine into his mouth while he told the stories, stories of long-ago vendettas, The Blood Feuds of Corsica, The Revolution. But mostly Carmen remembered the village folktales and the way his father's hands moved like fans in grand theatrical sweeps when he told them, as if he were seeding the vineyards with his history.

Once there was a king who owned all the vineyards in the valley. He had a very beautiful daughter who wished to get married. Three young sons of the neighboring king were all interested. To be fair, the girl's father proposed a contest: "Travel the world for six months and he who returns with the finest present shall have my daughter's hand."

When Carmen had been fifteen, the phylloxera hit and chewed through most of the roots in the vineyard. The vines eventually withered and dried to dust and before long there were hardly enough grapes to make wine for the table. Soon after, his father sent him to the states with his cousins, promising to follow.

But he never did. Carmen often pictured him finishing the last bottles, his favorite white hat pushed back on his head, watching the sunset with a fistful of grapes, the dry red juices running between his fingers.

After pouring cement for enough years, Carmen bought his own home and a yard that he split with his neighbor, Ben Keller. The two of them agreed to use the land for gardens, the centerpiece of which was a grape arbor. He looked at it now out the kitchen window, and resented the short northern growing season and having to commit to beta or Concord grapes that could stand up to the early spring chills.

Though so much had changed since his childhood, it was still the pests that took down the crop. Only now instead of the phylloxera, it was the high-school pests who vandalized the vines and took what they could carry for their own selfish games.

□   □   □

The inspector lifted the receiver and listened to the dry voice of the medical examiner. Though he'd known him for many years they never spoke to each other with anything but the official repartee their jobs required. In a strange way, it was as if they resented each other, the examiner resenting the fact that he was brought bodies he was forced to probe, and the inspector resenting the violations of the human body needed to answer the questions he asked.

"A head trauma," the examiner said. "The idea that he suffocated just isn't true."

"You're sure?"

"He bled to death, believe me."

"The grapes?"

"It's possible he was running with a mouthful when he struck his head." He paused.

"Or."

"Or they were put into his mouth post mortem."

The oldest brother came upon a man selling carpets. "Magic car-pets," the man told him. "They will take you great distances." The brother purchased one and flew it home over the mountains where he waited for the contest.

The middle brother came upon a man selling telescopes. "With these you can see hundreds of miles and through walls as well," the man told him. This brother also returned home with his gift.

The youngest boy was on the last day of his journey and had not yet found a worthy gift when he heard a fruit vendor calling, "Salamanna grapes for sale."

"What are these grapes?" the boy asked.

"There are no finer grapes in the world, my son," the vendor told him. "They work a special wonder."

The inspector tipped his soft hat back on his head, scribbled something onto a notepad. Ben Keller sat in a straw-backed rocking chair in front of him. There was a bad wound between his eyes and scratches on his forehead. He'd lived here for thirty years without any trouble, but today he felt the neighborhood was probably thinking him some kind of monster.

"It's the right thing to do," the inspector said, "the fair thing, I mean."

Ben took a deep breath. "Friday night I heard Mr. Rossi shout to me."

"Your neighbor?"

"Yes. He yelled that the boys were at the vines. I rushed out the front door and caught sight of some of them. We started after them, he in one direction and I in another."

"Did you catch them?"

"The lamp in the front of the house was out. It was dark and I stumbled and fell." He pointed to his wound. "I only chased them a little way." He looked away and shook his head. "I'm sorry the boy is dead."

"You saw something later on. What time, Mr. Keller?"

"Early," he said. "Around five in the morning."

"And he was leaning?" The inspector bent over. "Like this?"

"Yes. Yes." He sobbed.

"What exactly did you see him do?"

"He looked like he was putting something in the ground, like seeds or something, one at a time. I don't know really. Had I known then what he was looking at . . ."

The next morning, the sidewalk in front of Rossi and Keller's land looked more like the beachfront boulevard a few miles away, with people promenading with unusual regularity, slowing to whisper to one another.

Carmen Rossi answered his door in a sleeveless t-shirt and a pair of gray trousers. He was unshaven, his eyes bloodshot. He turned away and left the door open. The inspector followed him down a hallway and into a small kitchen.

They sat at a table by a wall of glass-front cabinets filled with different size jars. Some of the jars were packed with fruit, others were empty. The walls were white stucco and bare, except for a small, framed watercolor of a man praying over a loaf of bread.

"Tea, Inspector?"

"No, thank you."

"My father always started his day with a cup of tea." He poured the steaming kettle-water into a teapot. "He'd call me over when he poured the cream, make me watch the clouds in the cup. He told me I could see the future in them."

"I'm here about the past this morning, Mr. Rossi. I need to know."

"I saw him fall, but I didn't kill him."

"You didn't help him either, did you?"

"Not then," he said, looking out the kitchen window.

Last Friday night when James heard Rossi and Keller chasing the other boys, who had scattered in different directions, he couldn't resist turning back by the arbor for one more swipe. He grabbed another handful then headed toward Curtis Street. After several steps his feet got tangled and he spun backward and landed hard, his head striking a rock jutting from the roots of tall grass. He lay there still and warm, smelling the grass, listening to someone yelling, then the noise became muffled and distant, and he became aware of a shadow standing over him. It seemed to hover there, then pass away like a warm breeze, leaving only the moonlight, dimmer and dimmer.

The inspector walked the handcuffed Rossi down the stairs and across the crowded sidewalk. The crowd parted as the two men made their way to the police car. A commotion came from the back of the crowd. "Murderer, stinking murderer." A gray-haired man ran forward and banged the trunk with his fist. "Rot in hell, murderer."

Carmen shuddered from the bang, looked back at the shrinking crowd, the yard between the houses, the grapevine. "I was waiting, Inspector," he said, turning toward the front seat. "You understand?"

The inspector looked at him once in the rearview mirror, then back to the road. Carmen closed his eyes and smelled the fresh-picked grapes sitting on his father's lap. It was a hot summer night in the village and the rich dark soil was cool on Carmen's bare feet. The love bugs flapped their wings above their heads while his father held a single red grape against the light of the moon like a ruby.

"Something very special indeed," the vendor said. "Put the grapes in the mouth of someone breathing their last and they will

get well.''

They were together now with their gifts and the middle boy raised his telescope to look at the king's daughter. When he did he saw people weeping and doctors around her bed. "She's dying," he said.

"Quick," the youngest boy said to the oldest. "Take me there on your carpet."

Once at the castle, the youngest boy knelt by the king's daughter who was now lying still and pale. He put one grape in her mouth and waited, then he placed another inside her mouth and she began to stir, so he placed another and another and soon her face regained color and she opened her eyes.

"Your gift truly works a special wonder," the king said to the boy. And so they were married and lived happily ever after and inherited all the vineyards in the valley.

Obake for Lance

Edith M. Maxwell

Elissa saw Lance's yellow hat weaving toward her above the crowd of Japanese commuters. He slouched up to her on the subway platform, evoking a skinny young Humphrey Bogart. "Hey, good-looking, where you headed?"

"Lance? What are you doing here?"

His hat was pushed back on his brow, and his lips clamped a cigarette in the corner of his mouth. He stretched his arm out to the wall and leaned against it so the two of them were enclosed in a private space, so the hundreds of people who milled behind them seemed far away. His face was near hers—they were both almost six feet tall—and his wide mouth quivered with intensity, as it always did. The skin at his temples was so delicate it showed tiny blue veins; the hair that escaped his hat was blond enough to look white.

"Looking for you."

"Lance!" Elissa's pale cheeks flushed, and she laughed and shook her head. "You're supposed to be working, aren't you? George said he passed you going onto the base as he was leaving it."

"Just went in to swap shifts with Rennie. You know, old Doser'll do anything for me." He inhaled the smoke, then pinched the cigarette between forefinger and thumb to knock the ash off.

"The U.S. Navy lets you trade?" she asked, even though she knew they did. Her boyfriend, George, sometimes traded shifts with Lance or Rennie, although for George it seemed a more serious matter. George was serious about almost everything.

"No problema, sweet cheeks." Lance's face then took on a shadow. "The bosses think they care, but they don't. All they care about is getting promotions and pretending we're keeping the great U.S. of A. safe."

A polite announcement broadcast through the cavernous station and a tidy row of yellow lights near the platform's edge began to blink. "Well, I didn't swap shifts with anybody," Elissa said, ignoring his last remark in light of George's recent promotion. "I have to be teaching in an hour. And here comes my train now."

"Looks like you got company, then," he said, taking her elbow with a gentle move and excusing them through the crowd toward the whispering of the arriving train, saying "*Sumimasen, sumimasen*," with exaggerated courtesy and a forward lowering of his head each time he said it.

The train into Shinjuku from the southwestern suburbs of Tokyo was never empty, but at 4:00 P.M. it was much less crowded than at prime commuting hours. Lance and Elissa even found seats. They squeezed in between a couple of adolescent boys in black school uniforms who snickered to each other and whispered about the foreigners—*gaijin da yo!*—and an old grandmother in traditional kimono with a bulging cloth of goods tied on her back, the green-and-white *furoshiki* knotted in front of her shoulders. Her eyes were closed, she sat kneeling with her feet tucked under her on the seat, and a pair of straw sandals waited on the floor beneath her. In front of her stood two businessmen impeccably dressed in blue suits, talking with intent looks on their faces but never meeting each other's eyes. Always the new and the old confronted each other in Tokyo.

Lance's arm and Elissa's pressed together. Heat spread between them. He was an alien north that pulled her magnet off its accustomed pole and unsettled her.

"So, what's the lesson for today?" Lance asked her. He then casually positioned his arm over the seat behind her, as if he didn't know this brought their bodies even closer. It reminded her of going to the movies in early high school when the boys pretended complete nonchalance to hide their desperate eagerness to touch a girl, any girl. Elissa smiled. She almost caught the eye of a woman sitting across from her, who she knew had been looking at her, but the woman now studied her hands in her lap with great care.

"Oh, you know, we'll just talk. They're engineers, and they know English grammar; it's just sort of painful for them to actually have a conversation," Elissa explained. "I think today we'll discuss what they did on the weekend, what they do on weekends in the winter, what they did on weekends as children, that kind of thing."

"Ah, yes. I went to za bar. I durank-u rahts of sake. I felt-o berry sick." Lance's imitation of her students' accent was perfect. Elissa laughed, a loud pealing sound. She couldn't help it, it just came out of her, but people almost stared. They never looked directly at anyone, but there was now an alteration in nearby expressions that told her they had taken notice. "Yep, that's about it for some of them. I'm hoping we'll branch out into talking about a few other activities, though."

"Like, I scurewed wis my wife-u?"

"Lance! You're terrible." Elissa shifted in the hard fiberglass seat to turn toward him, wondering how the old woman could possibly sleep with her legs under her.

"Do these make it better?" he asked, pulling a small flat box out of the plastic bag he carried. He opened it and offered Elissa a bean cake, a soft triangle of rice flour dough filled with dark sweet bean paste. It was one of her favorite Japanese treats.

"I love *obake*! You like them, too?" She savored the sweet, wishing she weren't so receptive to Lance's attentions.

"What you like, I like, *ma cher*," he said, lowering his voice and leaning in.

"Right." Give me a break, man, she thought. "So anyway, Lance, why did you come looking for me?" Elissa asked. "What's going on?"

"Well, I just wondered if you'd do me a little favor."

□   □   □

Elissa walked with her sack of morning marketing to the small house in Minami Rinkan that she and George shared. It was modest—some might call it almost a shack—compared to its neighbors with their scrubbed-clean windows and tidy postage-stamp gardens, but the rent was cheap. She was saving much of her considerable salary for graduate school.

She noticed a slip of yellow paper sticking out of the red mailbox, and stood in the soft air for a few minutes trying to decipher the characters. It was from the post office—that she could read—but despite weekly Japanese lessons for a year, her *kanji* reading ability was still just beyond rudimentary. Then she remembered that time on the subway a month ago, when Lance had asked if she would receive a package for him from his sister in the States.

"It's too complicated going through military mail," he had said. "She just wanted to send me a birthday present—is it all right that she mailed it to your house instead?"

"You mean she already sent the package?"

"As a matter of fact, she did. I, you know, told her it'd be okay with you."

"But George gets stuff from his mom all the time through the base. What's wrong with the pouch?"

"Just seemed easier this way," Lance had said, jittering a foot perched on his other knee.

Then he had leaned in close again. "And, I'll have an excuse to come and see you."

She had felt his heat. Her body had started to resonate on the wavelength of his concentrated energy. She had wanted to stop the train and pull Lance with her into the nearest dark corner, the closest hotel room, the first secluded spot in the park. "Well, I guess it's okay. I mean, if it's already in the mail." Elissa had shaken her head, trying to clear it of these disturbing vibrations, these wild thoughts. "And just to tell me this you switched shifts and took a train into the city?"

So that's what this must be, Elissa thought. She put away her shopping—a tin of instant coffee, a bag of clementines, a paper-wrapped bundle of fish, a jar of the Korean pickled cabbage called *kimchee*, and a packet of dried, salted octopus slices, the last two being favorite drinking snacks of hers and George's—and walked the six blocks back into town. She passed the homes of commuters and housewives for a few blocks, then entered the concentration of shops, bars, and businesses surrounding the train station.

At the post office she presented her yellow slip, and waited almost fifteen minutes while a series of functionaries checked her name and ID card and went off to look for the package. The summer's day was warming rapidly; the ceiling fans blew the air around without producing much cooling. One rather stern-looking man in the blue lab coat customary of bureaucrats finally handed her a shoebox-sized parcel wrapped in brown paper. The return address was from a Jill Weiss in Gilroy, California.

At home again, she turned the package over once. It didn't rattle or smell, so she set it on the table by the door and reminded herself to have George take it in to Lance; he lived in a barracks room on base. Lance, she thought. She had avoided seeing him since the subway ride. He was dangerous. He had the kind of nervous sexual energy that had drawn her into other relationships that had always ended in disaster. It would be just as well if George delivered the package rather than Lance picking it up. George was serious and safe and barely drew her in at all, but right now, she thought serious was the best thing for her.

Her eyes drifted to the table, and she saw her acceptance letter from the doctoral program at Johns Hopkins. Elissa sighed, realizing she couldn't wait to get back to microbiology in the fall. Teaching English had been an interlude, a way to spend time with George and take a break from academic life; it wasn't a career, and her logical side warned her against letting passion distract her from having one.

Elissa had just sat down on a cushion at the low table with her third-year Japanese textbook to study her own lesson for the week—"Parallel Description, Guessing, and Relational Terms"—when someone knocked at the door. Is that Lance? she wondered, and her heart beat faster.

Elissa opened the door and was starting to say, "*Ohayoo gozaimasu.* Good morning," when she realized two police officers stood in front of her, one a woman.

The latter said, in very clear English, "Is your name Elissa Chase?"

Elissa nodded. She suddenly felt chilled, and her stomach knotted. "What is it? Is it George?"

"No. May we come in?"

Elissa stood rooted to the ground. She stared at them, feeling entirely confused. Her eyebrows came together and she examined their faces as if she could discern why they were there from their visages. The male officer shifted slightly and Elissa saw they were waiting for her.

"Sure. *Doozo*," she said, backing into the room and holding the door for them to move inside. The male officer motioned his partner in first.

Inside, the female officer, whose name tag read Sato, moved to Elissa's side. The man glanced around the room, and then faced them with his elbows out and his hands neatly behind his back.

"We are here to arrest you for the smuggling of drugs into our country."

"What?" Elissa asked, bewildered. She looked down, trying to puzzle this out.

The late morning light showed a bar of dust motes above her book on the table, and the August air felt heavy. She looked back at him and shook her head. "I, I don't . . . I didn't smuggle anything! I don't even use drugs." This last was only partially true, but she had been very careful in Japan, and in fact had baked some hash brownies only once, to make the time pass on the nineteen-hour journey when she had gone back to Boston to obtain her work visa.

She saw Sato-san's eyes move to the package on the table. Oh, Elissa realized. They knew just what was in the package. Despite the heat of the day, she began to shiver.

Rumiko-san, the prim housewife neighbor whom Elissa had tried so hard to get to know, who had actually asked her over for coffee once, saw Sato-san usher Elissa, all long legs and bony knees, into the back seat of the tiny police car. Rumiko knew what every other Japanese knew, that the police solved 98 percent of their cases. They didn't arrest innocent people. Elissa's face reddened with shame.

In her seat on the JAL flight Elissa looked straight ahead. The people on either side of her in the wide-bodied plane kept to their personal space as if she were a leper. They had seen her escorted to her seat by a police officer, had seen him have a word with the flight attendant, had seen the attendant's glance at Elissa and the transfer of documents that indicated her status as a deportee. She supposed she was lucky not to be wearing handcuffs.

Elissa knew she looked a wreck, too. She used to feel that her ivory skin and the brilliant red of her hair offset her height and angular frame; now she had seen herself in the mirror looking desperately pale and plain, with her short curls gone limp and a twitch in the corner of her mouth she could not control. She had never fit in in this land of short, dark-haired people with muscular calves and smooth cheeks, but going home like this was not the finale she had imagined.

Elissa was numb. Two days in a Japanese jail had submerged her confusion into a daze. It was clean, of course, and they treated her with the infinite politeness of those in the right, but it was a jail, nevertheless. She had inwardly raged at Lance to no avail, and finally realized that she was helpless to change this absurd, miserable situation. They let her see George only once. He looked sad, and as confused as she was.

"They won't let me do anything, Elissa. I offered to find a lawyer, but they just say you have to leave."

"Can't anyone on base do anything for me?" She was sure someone in the Navy could pull a string if they wanted to.

George looked away. "Well, since we aren't married and you don't work for them . . ."

"But you, you're their star quartermaster, can't they do something?"

He studied his fine-skinned, broad hands in his lap. It had always annoyed her how fastidious he was with his nails, and now she suddenly hated him for it. And she realized he wasn't going to go to bat for her with the Navy brass because it would stain him with her guilt.

"No, I suppose not," she said bitterly. "Seen Lance lately?"

□   □   □

Elissa's hand shook a little as she lifted her cup of sake; she sat alone at the sushi bar. She had resisted eating at the new restaurant in North Cambridge for several years. She didn't know if she could tolerate reviving the memories of ten years before, but her longing for the tangy aroma of sweet vinegared rice proved too strong to resist one evening. She was driving home from her laboratory job analyzing plant toxins—it was menial work, not the post-graduate research she had planned—when she turned sharply left into the parking lot of Sakura.

She sipped more of the warm drink and watched the fleet hands of the sushi chef. In the Japanese winter, after cajoling middle-aged Japanese men to talk about topics with which they were uncomfortable, she used to buy a glass container of hot sake from a vending machine when she emerged from the Minami Rinkan train station at 9:00 P.M., and sip it as she walked home. Now the strong warm arms of the drink and the flavors of sushi, spare and pure, brought it all back. George and Lance abandoning her. Her disastrous arrival in Boston. The Japanese authorities had alerted the Americans, and somehow word got to Johns Hopkins, who then canceled her fellowship. They had plenty of candidates without records; they saw no need to fund someone who could have trouble getting grants or traveling to professional conferences in Japan. She gave up on the idea of graduate school and saw her dreams turn to dark moods. She took the lab job near where she had grown up.

Several years later she dated for a few months, but one night when Matt had taken her out to an especially nice restaurant, he asked her if she wanted children in her life. Elissa stared at him. I did want children, she thought to herself. I wanted a passel of bright readers and spunky artists. I wanted a big, busy, together kind of family. Elissa broke up with Matt the next week.

She kept studying Japanese by herself at home. Sometimes she didn't retain what was in the lessons very well, and had to go over the material repeatedly. She thought perhaps the several glasses of whiskey she consumed every evening had something to do with it, and often promised herself on the way home from work to have just one, or to make tea instead.

The night before had been one of those times. She had unlocked the door to her studio apartment, which was all she could afford to rent. She stroked her cat, turned up the heat, closed the drapes on the starry January night, turned on the radio, and poured a glass of lime seltzer. She caught sight of her as-yet-unopened calendar on the table. The numerals of the year leapt at her and she thought, It's been a whole decade. A wasted, disastrous, ruined ten years. She slammed water into a pot for pasta, put it on the stove, and started to peel garlic with angry vigor. The half-gallon of Jim Beam sat in its place on the counter broadcasting its silent siren song, and finally Elissa said aloud, "To hell with virtue." The first sip of the amber liquid, chilled by ice, slaked her need as it spread through her throat. It rose up with gentle velvet fingers to cloak her brain with the familiar buzz of oblivion. She took a deep breath and felt, for the time, at peace.

The next evening, instead of studying, she prowled the Internet, which yielded a phone number and an address for a certain Lance Weiss in San Jose, California. Elissa dialed the number. With heart thumping, she heard his recorded voice say, "Dude. I'm out, so let me know who you are. Cool?" She hung up the phone. The following day on her way home from work she stopped by Yoshinoya, the Japanese market on Prospect Street, and walked out with a small box in a plastic bag.

That evening she did not study her lessons. She prepared a syringe with what she had brought home from the lab and carefully injected each of the bean paste sweets, then replaced them in the box. She wrapped it in brown paper and addressed it. She poured another glass of whiskey, turned off the lights, opened the drapes, and watched the snow fall in a soft, slow dance.

☐ ☐ ☐

A week later, Elissa sat at her table and stared at the paper in her hand. She lifted her glass and drained the last drops of bourbon-flavored melted ice. The letters under the banner San Jose *Mercury News* looked blurry now, but when she had printed them out from the Internet, they had been clear: "Local Man Dies of Unknown Causes." The article described the sudden death of a certain suspected drug dealer, one Lance Weiss.

Her doorbell rang, but she stayed seated, although the glass in her hand began to shake. She heard knocking at the door, but did not move. The knocking became more rapid and seemed to be in phase with the beating of her heart. She rose and opened the door to a pale young man in blue.

"You ordered pizza, ma'am?"

"Oh," Elissa said, leaning against the doorjamb and staring at him. "Yes, I suppose I did."

In Your Dreams

John Clark

I like the reminders I get on Friday night. Even though it's been more than twenty years since I came out of the fog one morning, covered in blood, with no clue whose it was, I don't want to forget.

I nod to Ray as I assume the position, hands out at my sides. Legs slightly spread while his partner runs the wand up one leg, past my crotch, then down the other. We all know it's a waste of time, but I'm cool with it. Neither of them wants to lose his job because they let up right when one of the hard-asses upstairs makes an unannounced walk-through.

As I wait for the door to open, I wonder who'll get stuck chairing the meeting tonight. Most of the time it's one of us old-timers, simply because the guys on the inside are still so raw and squirrelly they'd waste fifty minutes just mind-farting before getting around to business. Good thing AA teaches patience and tolerance, because there's a hell of a lot of meetings I'd rather attend on a Friday night than the one in the library at Maine State Prison. Still, I like to remember when life was raw as hell and everything seemed ready to leap out and gnaw on your soul.

Sid, Little Pig, and Buster are standing by the coffee urn. Half a dozen pasty-looking younger guys in fresh denim shirts and jeans are sitting toward the back of the room, trying to look tough and being about as successful as a sneaker full of baby crap.

I'm almost sympathetic.

Buster catches my eye and motions me over. "You busy Monday?"

"No more than usual, why?" I said.

"Got a virus on my machine down at the garage. That damn hotshot body and fender guy I hired right out of tech school thought he was being helpful and ended up crapping the whole hard drive. Think you could look at it?"

"I guess. Let me give you a call first thing Monday, and I'll see how the early afternoon shakes out. Maybe we can grab dinner afterward and hit the step meeting over at the Episcopal Church. Haven't been to that one in months." I grabbed black coffee and took a seat off to the side.

Fortunately, some of the guys from mid-block started trickling in. Most of them had enough time in the program so they could chair a meeting and actually have it run half decently. I looked up from studying my coffee to see a guy we called Lamer picking up the gavel.

After the Serenity Prayer, he gave a brief qualification. I tuned out until I heard the words "drunk dream." I smiled, but in my gut, that black knot of dread was welling up again, dragging me back to July of 1983.

I went over and got a refill, hoping nobody noticed how much my hands were trembling. I was grateful to get back to my seat with only a few wet spots on my shirt.

Lamer was still going on about his dream. "So there I was, back on the outside, seven months of sobriety behind me, wearing a new suit and ready to walk into the cheesiest bar in Simonton. It was like someone else was in control of my body. I'm screaming like a terrified kid inside, but I'm headed straight for the bar, waving the twenty I got on discharge and tellin' the bartender to keep 'em coming until this bugger is flat busted. The next thing I know, I'm back in my cell, nearly pissing my pants it seems so real."

Lamer tries to take a sip of his coffee, but he's shaking even worse than me.

I'm perversely relieved. At least his agitation has everyone's attention, so nobody can see Mr. Old-Timer losing his cool off to the side of the room.

I close my eyes and think, Lamer boy, if you only knew how willing I'd be to trade my nightmare for yours. Dreaming about getting hammered would be a walk in the park for me.

After the meeting, I help clean up before heading back through the security gate. Twenty years of nightmares tends to leave you in no hurry to return to an empty house, especially in the dead of winter.

I accept Little Pig's offer to go out for coffee at Starbucks. Lord knows the last thing my stomach needs is another dose of caffeine, but it will stall the inevitable for an hour or so.

Light snow begins falling outside and we have the place to ourselves. Little Pig orders one of those fancy drinks I don't even try to pronounce and proceeds to dust the heck out of the top with powdered chocolate. I settle for more black coffee and a stale orange muffin.

We sit in comfortable silence, watching as the flakes outside grow bigger and begin to fall faster. That's one nice thing about the fellowship. After a while, us old-timers don't feel a need to say anything around anyone with a few twenty-four hours behind them. It's almost as though we share sobriety by osmosis.

Of course, after a while, if you still hit meetings on any kind of basis, you already know everyone's deepest, darkest secrets . . . almost.

Little Pig tips his cup back and waits until the last drops fall past his two remaining teeth. He smiles. "Damn, that stuff is good." He laughs and rubs his protruding gut. "I'd order another, but I'm having trouble getting my pants on as it is."

As he talks, I admire the tiny tattoos on his cheeks for the hundredth time, wondering idly how I'd look with one of my own. Little Pig's a funny sort. Who'd expect a sober Maori in Maine? Hell, who'd expect a Maori of any kind in Maine, particularly in the depths of winter? I know better, but then I've heard his story. Drunks tend to roll into places by accident. Most die, a few lucky ones don't.

Little Pig was a math professor at a small Catholic college in Christchurch when he discovered he loved vodka more than self-respect. It didn't take long for one kidney, most of his teeth, and all of his self-respect to go south while he went east, coming to in the L.A. county jail.

It took six more years for Little Pig to get the devil back in his cage. Now he drives city buses here in Simonton. There aren't many riders that give him any lip. I know I wouldn't. Between the tattoos, the missing teeth, and the long white scar that runs down the side of his neck, he doesn't need to do much to keep order on his runs.

"Still dancing with the Dark Lady?"

I stopped studying the drying stain in the bottom of the cup and nodded.

"She ever give you a break?" Little Pig's eyes were dark wells that said, Been there, done that. Like me, most of his nights are spent on the razor edge of exhaustion, too tired to stay awake, yet too afraid of what was about to reach out and suck you down if you succumbed.

"About once a month, she might wander off for a couple days. I guess she gets tired of twisting my soul and goes after fresh meat, then, sometime after midnight, she's back in spades, kinda like I'm her drug of choice." I twisted my finger around the handle of the cup, fighting a sudden impulse to hurl it through the thick glass just inches from my seat.

Little Pig studied the snow for a long time, as expecting a

secret flake might reveal the answer to his terror. "Oh yeah. I know that feeling well, I do."

The counter girl caught my eye, tilting her head toward the clock. It was almost midnight and she was anxious to get things cleaned up so she could boogie on home before the snow got real bad. Time goes fast when you're avoiding the Dark Lady.

I nudged Little Pig. "You want a ride home?"

He stood and shrugged on his uniform jacket. "Might as well. You never know when a Yeti might pop out from behind a trash can in a blizzard like this and I'd be dancing in the great circle. Next thing, you'd have to break in a new set of ears to handle all your idle chatter."

The snow seemed to anticipate our departure. No sooner had we exited Starbucks, than the wind picked up and those pillow-like flakes developed teeth and an attitude. "Screw the Yeti," I said, "it feels like air sharks out here. Hop in."

I twisted a knee trying to stay upright as I unlocked my door. Little Pig's head looked like bad polka dots by the time I reached over and let him in.

I waited until there was heat coming through the defroster before we swung out into a street that was ready to present adventures all its own. Good thing Little Pig's apartment was just three blocks away.

"You doing anything special tomorrow?"

I shook my head. "Martha and I were going out for lunch, but this doesn't look very promising." I waved my hand at the flowing whiteness in front of the windshield.

"That lady is something else." Little Pig grinned at me. "I sure wouldn't want to be whining at any meeting she was at. She can chew some serious ass."

Little Pig was right. Martha T. was the only woman I let into my life. Way back, I was running on one night about some poor fool who was going too slowly when I was in a hurry to get to a meeting. After the Lord's Prayer, she leaned over and said, "Do me a favor will ya?"

"Sure, what do you want?"

"From now on, drive your own freakin' car, hotshot."

Martha's death on whining newbies. You get like that after you've seen the first hundred or so go back out. Some are lucky and make it back with a little more humility and a sadder look in their eyes. The rest we usually read about in the police notes or on the obituary page.

You'd have to see Martha to understand why she is able to get away with leaning on other drunks like that. She's almost seventy, her hair color changes weekly, and she has more body piercing than half the mall rats in Simonton. Martha won't take crap from anyone, but by the same token, she's always a phone call away when the Dark Lady pushes me over the edge.

"Do you want a ride to the Sunday morning speaker's meeting?" Little Pig's nod left half an inch of melting snow on the seat as he closed the door before navigating the greasy wooden steps leading up to his two-room efficiency. I backed ever so slowly into the unplowed street.

My place was no fancier, but I had plenty of room. My parents died before I hit bottom. That spared them from seeing the sad and disgusting implosion of the fair-haired boy on whom they'd both pinned so many hopes and dreams. When the day I vaguely remember burying Mom came, I inherited 725 Dark Mountain Road, along with enough cash and securities to keep me spiraling downward for another five years.

I may have gotten sober, but any ability to do basic maintenance or upkeep on the place continues to evade me. I was unemployable for almost two years after I put down the bottle, further eroding any remaining assets. After a while, I simply learned to live with a house that was slowly falling apart, but provided as much security as the Dark Lady would allow.

The memories surrounding twenty years of halting steps back toward humanity filled my mind as I navigated the thickening blanket of snow. I knew the anemic city budget wouldn't allow anyone on the highway maintenance crew out before daylight. Those of us solid citizens who needed to travel tonight were firmly on our own. No matter, I was in no hurry to face what was waiting inside that gloomy Victorian on the bank of Ragged River, so I kept the speedometer at twenty-five.

By the time the Dark Mountain turnoff appeared, the weather had deteriorated to a point where I was giving serious consideration to parking the car and taking my chances with the tow truck brigade I knew would be out looking for victims by sunrise.

Hell, they could tow my car and I would be able to buy another one without making a serious dent in my bank account. Early recovery landed me in a vocational training program where the sober me discovered a knack for computer programming and repair, but I still couldn't bring myself to spring for repairs on the house. Little Pig calls it the insanity of sobriety. I guess he's right.

I looked ahead and realized my thoughts about abandoning the car were academic. While they played out in my head, I had steered it down and around the slick curves leading to my driveway. I was in front of the garage door that never seemed to obey the little black box I kept on the front seat. I shrugged and shut off the engine. Time to embrace the evil one.

The light over the kitchen stove welcomed me into the house. When I first got sober and the Dark Lady invaded my reality, I started keeping that light on twenty-four hours a day. The bulb now seemed like an old friend who always waited up, just to make certain I got home safely. More than once I had come away from a meeting with something on my mind that really needed to get out and that light and I had our own mini-meeting over a cup of stale coffee.

I turned up the heat and washed the dirty dishes, stalling the inevitable for a few more moments.

A sudden splatter on the picture window made me jump. I turned on the patio light and realized the snow was changing over to sleet. Good thing I could call Martha in the morning. If this kept up, I'd be lucky to get plowed out before dinnertime. There was no sense in postponing things any longer. I knew the drill only too well. I finished up in the bathroom, making a mental note that I would soon be needing more toothpaste, and headed down the hallway.

There are five rooms upstairs. Only the bathroom and my bedroom are used. It's the same one I slept in back when the biggest thing I worried about was whether the Lone Ranger would still be okay at the end of the radio broadcast. The Dark Lady doesn't need a room of her own and I haven't had anyone stay over since I got sober, so why bother opening up the other rooms?

If I have any lament in sobriety, it's the loss of relationships. I tried in the early years, even thought I was in love once with another program person, but the dark one is too possessive to ever let me have enough freedom to feel anything for another woman. I used to hate her until I finally accepted that what I felt didn't faze her one bit. I crawled into bed and turned out the light.

The pattern varies little from night to night. I stretch my back and legs before trying to sleep on my side. It never works and before I know it, one arm is hooked under the pillow, while the other is just about brushing the floor. That's the sign she waits for, the one that allows her to drag me kicking and screaming into the velvet hell where she lives. I used to fight, but never won. Now I just hope she has her way with me quickly so I can grab an hour or so of sweat-soaked slumber before sunrise.

It always begins the same way. I'm sitting in Lolly's Grill down by the tracks. It has to be late July, because I got sober just before the first of August. I've been throwing back shots of tequila and chasing them with beer since I staggered into the place about noontime. I can see heat lightning rippling silently through the clouds on the other side of the valley. Its pattern never varies. By now, I've seen them so often that I could stand and direct every single bolt like an orchestra leader.

No matter how much I drink, it doesn't work. I'm sitting there in one of those terrible states of lucidity that alcoholics get near the end of their drinking, where the drunker you get the more reality leans over and bites your sorry ass.

Lolly comes out from the grill and stands in the shadows, hands on his hips. He shakes his head. The two of us go back to grammar school.

Somewhere deep inside me, a tiny spark flickers, wanting to do something to redeem my pathetic carcass in his eyes. A water-wall of despair quickly snuffs it out and I wave my glass toward his shadowy figure.

"Hey, old buddy. You know how it is. I can find the cooler. There won't be anyone else coming around tonight. It's too hot and too damn late. You don't have to baby-sit me. Go on home to Thelma. I'll lock the door and leave enough to cover my tab. Hell, I'll even sack out on the kitchen floor if I'm too hammered to drive home."

Lolly shakes his head again and begins untying his apron. After locking the back door, he turns out all the lights except the one by my table and the one over the cooler. I can hear a sigh that rivals the miniature locomotive down at the amusement park as he heads out the front door.

I stagger over to the cooler and grab a couple more cold ones to pay homage to the half-full tequila bottle on the table.

The heat lightning lessens as a soft rain begins. By now, there's barely enough tequila to cover the pickled creature at the bottom of the bottle and I've made three more trips to the nearly depleted beer cooler. I'm having a one-sided dialogue with the worm about the sad state of America when I hear the faint crunch of gravel under tires and a tiny light bounces across the front of the grill. The light goes out and I hear a thump as someone leans an object against the building.

The front door opens tentatively

I'm mildly irritated at the thought of someone interrupting my binge until I look up and catch the chestnut hair framing deep hazel eyes and the most sensuous mouth I can remember seeing since high school. She's maybe nineteen going on ageless and wearing sweat-stained cutoffs below a t-shirt advertising some band I never heard of. The straps on her backpack are pulling the shirt and highlighting her breasts in the dim light

As I'm taking all this in, parts of my body begin to remind me just how long it has been since I threw any action their way.

I stagger to my feet, attempting a bow, and compromise by doing a weaving stutter step while tipping over the tequila bottle.

She recoils and looks over her shoulder before composing herself. "Can I use the phone? My bike has a flat and I need to find a garage that can fix it if I'm going to make the hostel in Reardon before midnight."

I may be drunk, but my brain slips into overdrive. "Gee honey, I'd be happy to let you use the phone, but the line got hit by lightning and we haven't been able to call out since early afternoon."

She looks at me funny, trying to decide if I'm blowing smoke. "How far to the nearest pay phone?" She starts backing away.

"Lemme see," I blubber. "There's one half a mile down Kimble by the park entrance. I could drive you down there. It's getting pretty wet and you don't want to walk that far in this weather, do you?"

I can see the wheels turning in her head. Walk and risk the unknown devil or ride with the one she just met.

"Okay, but let's hurry, I wanna get back on the road as soon as I can." She begins backing toward the door.

I have only one thing on my mind now. I fumble for my keys and don't even bother turning off the lights or locking the door. This is too good an opportunity to waste. "Sure thing, lady."

I have trouble getting the key in the ignition because I'm already thinking about how I'm going to make my move.

"Hey, turn on your lights or I'm getting out right now!" Her hand is ready to lift the lever and throw the passenger door wide open.

"Oh, okay." I'm frantically trying to figure out where I'm going so I won't be disturbed.

As we reach the curve by the railroad crossing, I turn the wheel sharply and she slides toward me, totally off guard. I let go of the wheel and throw a short quick jab that would have made Ali envious. She folds without a sound.

I'm so befuddled by lust, I've forgotten I live alone. There are no neighbors near my nice big Victorian down by the river. It's perfect for a little one-sided tryst.

I pull up to the sagging garage doors and shut off the engine before staggering around to her side. She's heavier than she looks, but that's partly because she's out like a light.

An irrational warning about fouling my own nest flashes through my head. I open the spare bedroom. Her clothing comes off easily, leaving lush white flesh helpless and ready under the moonlight streaming in the window.

By now, I've abandoned any connection with humanity and all I can think of is ripping my own clothing off and penetrating her deeply enough to discharge all my lust and self-loathing. My diseased mind no longer sees a member of the human race lying on the mattress. She's reverted to a convenient receptacle for my sick and aching need. I arrange her body, enter her and everything fades to black.

Hours later, I awaken in my own bed, drenched in blood, with no memory of what happened after I fell on her.

I've experienced the same routine nearly every night since I walked into my first meeting. The Dark Lady meets me at Lolly's and I drag her home. Seven nights a week, no holidays, no sick days, no vacation, no peace. The worst part is I don't know if it really happened or if the worm in the bottom of that tequila bottle turned on me.

It took me nearly a year to get up my courage and broach the subject with Lolly. He just looked at me like I had an extra head and said, "You wish, buddy." I never brought it up again.

Hell, I even went so far as to read three months' worth of back issues of the Simonton *Tribune* looking for any missing persons' reports in the police log. Nothing. Not even a stray dog was reported during that time, so I gave up and accepted that the Dark Lady was my own personal albatross—a soul-searing reminder of all the moral debris accrued during those years of excess and self-destruction. It became as good an explanation as any.

Saturday came and went leaving three inches of ice, downed power lines and no way to go anywhere. The Dark Lady came early and stayed late. I awoke Sunday morning, so desperate for a meeting that I would have crawled over to Little Pig's and carried him on my back. Fortunately, the ice melted quickly and life got back to normal.

Martha called late Tuesday afternoon.

"Hey, lady," I said, "great to hear your voice. What's up?"

"I have a favor to ask, dear. I'm expanding my horizons. Ellen and I have joined a new club and they're teaching us all sorts of neat stuff. Next week we're going to learn how to preserve pears. I seem to remember you saying that your mother did some canning before she passed away. I'm wondering if there might be some mason jars in your cellar I could use."

I couldn't remember the last time I set foot in my cellar other than to show the furnace guy where to go when he came to clean it. "Sure, why don't you come over tonight and I'll order in Chinese."

We set a 6:00 P.M. date and I went back to the business of sorting invoices.

"Thank you, dear, I'm so tired of my own cooking." Martha cleared away the leftovers and wiped off my kitchen table. I retrieved a flashlight from the utility drawer and we went down the cellar stairs, taking turns brushing aside the musty cobwebs.

I pulled the string and light flickered as we navigated around a rusty bike, lying on a slight mound in the dirt floor. A thought flashed through my mind, wondering where it had come from. I could vaguely remember selling mine for beer money years before.

A long time ago, my mother had asked Dad to build her a small wooden pantry in the back cellar. I had no idea if anything was still stored there, but if I could save Martha a few bucks, I was more than happy to do so.

I pulled the dusty plastic curtain to one side.

"Oh shit! Her eyes, they . . ." Martha turned and vomited before staggering toward the stairs.

As I stared at the gallon jar on the shelf and the rotting bundle of clothing, I knew I'd never wonder whether the Dark Lady was real again.

Asa

Kathleen Valentine

Listen. Those are mockingbirds. They always sing at this time of evening. Their song is my signal to pick Asa's flowers. Tonight I'll pick daisies and bluebonnets. Sundown isn't far off and I try to go see him every evening at sundown. Oh, I do miss now and again—especially if the weather isn't so good. This winter was a long one and some evenings I just don't have the gumption to climb his hill. But he understands. No one ever understood me like Asa.

I was fifteen years old the first time I laid eyes on him. But I knew in that sure-fire, deep-down kind of way that I'd never love nobody else. He took the breath right out of me. Right now, I close my eyes, I can see him just like he was there in the morning sunshine. He was bent forward sawing on a board balanced across two sawhorses, his curly brown hair falling over his forehead and those sinewy-lean muscles in his back and shoulders sparkling with sweat as they moved back and forth, back and forth, back and forth. He had his knee up on that board holding it down so's he could saw it and his tan trousers pulled tight across his hips and thighs. Lord, I didn't know nothing about men then but I knew he made my legs feel like I was wading upriver in ice water. My hands, they itched to stroke those drops of sweat away from that sun-toasted skin. And, other things I felt, I didn't know how to call them.

Asa wasn't what you'd call tall. Taller than me by a head but I always was a runt. His shoulders, oh Lord, it seemed to me they just blocked out the world. And he was so brown—I decided then and there he was made for me.

He was twenty-two and how I loved to look at him! He had come to see my daddy 'cause he'd admired the gunstocks Daddy was known for making. When Asa got a look at the curly maple stock on the 30.06 Daddy was oiling down, his eyes near fell out of his head. Right then Asa had him a mind to have it.

"Can't part with this 'un," my daddy says to him. "This 'un's for my daughter. She's as fair a shot as any man but I reckon I got enough of this maple for one more."

But Asa was the feckless sort and didn't have no money. He was a good-enough carpenter and folks was happy to pay him but he weren't the kind that could hold onto money. My aunt Shoog told Mama that Asa had a taste for wine, women, and song.

But Daddy never could say no to a man what admired his work, so he said he'd make Asa a deal. He said we could do with a new chicken coop and a fence around the yard and that would be just about the same amount of pay as a rifle like mine. Asa liked that idea just fine.

Every morning at the crack of dawn I'd hear his whistling as he come walking up our road. He had this cute, bouncy way of walking and he wore his black hat pulled down low over his eyes. When he grinned his teeth was whiter than Mama's fresh laundered sheets flapping in the summer breezes. Asa whistled a lot while he worked—songs I didn't know. I imagined they were what cowboys whistled to their horses late nights out in the Palo Duro Canyon trying to protect themselves from red wolves or the restless spirits of murdered Apaches. The veins along his forearms were thick and stood out like a map of the Guadalupe River. He had a rich, thick West Texas drawl—not like the nasal twang of the boys here in the hill country. Oh, and how he could look you over!

I'd stand by the kitchen window watching him till Mama came looking for me scolding like an old brood hen.

I told him I was seventeen. Either he believed me or he didn't care. Sure didn't take me long to get his attention though. I knew I was cute and he had that eye—that eye some men have that twinkles when he looks at you so's you can't even pretend you're not thinking what you've been thinking right along.

The first time he kissed me he put his hand up under my skirt and squeezed my bottom. Lord, I nearly fainted right there in the dust. We was in back of my daddy's tool shed on a scorcher of a July afternoon. I can still hear the buzzing of the flies in the quiet and the wet pressure of his dense body pushing against mine. I brought him a cool glass of iced tea and he drank it straight down in one long swallow letting the icy liquid roll down over his chin. Then he backed me up against the toolshed and covered my mouth with his sugary, lemon-flavored one. And his hands . . . they were every place they had no business being. I tried for about half a minute to push him away—didn't fool him one bit. He just laughed at me.

"You're likin' me, aren't you?" he said, his hand sliding down under the waist of my undies.

"You're horrible," I said slapping at him. But he just laughed. He always laughed.

From that moment on I was his—body and soul. He got to know every inch of me that summer but I was no fool. I knew when to stop him. By the time September came he was crazy to marry me. And I was crazy to let him.

My mama and daddy would have liked to kill us both! I was too young, they said, and he was a good-for-nothin'. We didn't care. We were so much in love. Nowadays folks would say we was just in heat. Girls today know everything. All I knew was what Asa taught me but he taught me plenty. Oh, I do remember it all.

Growing up in the Texas hill country when I did you didn't learn much of anything about sex. When you were fixing to be married your mama sat you down and explained your wifely duties to you. My mama said a good wife obliged her husband. She said to just close your eyes and let him have his manly ways and think about when you had babies. She said once he got you with a couple children if you was lucky you'd both be so busy all the time there wouldn't be no more time for that foolishness.

I prayed she was wrong—cause I loved every single thing Asa did to me. Why, my mama would die of shame if she knew the things Asa taught me—but that was after we was married. I made sure of that.

We got married on the autumn equinox when the sky was brittle cool and the smell of fresh-cut hay filled the air. Mama and Daddy didn't have much to say—mostly they was just glad I wasn't showing a baby. They didn't know how smart I'd been.

There was a party and dancing. Mama made half-a-dozen sweet potato pies and Daddy brought out some of his good hard cider. But me and Asa didn't care. We just wanted it to be over so we could go to our little house tucked away in the woods. We just wanted to toss aside the new white and blue bridal quilt on our bed and start our married life.

I thought I knew what loving was all about. I thought our summer of scorching afternoons and steaming hot nights had prepared me for being a married woman. What a silly girl I was not to know how much better it would be. The first time Asa put hisself inside of me I thought my eyes would pop right out of my skull like two hickory nuts roasting in a fire. I got so lost in him I didn't even know there was a world past the walls of our bedroom. Didn't care, neither. I felt like a cake of fresh cream butter melting in the heat of an August afternoon. All I wanted was Asa, every minute of the night and of the day.

I tried to be a good wife. I kept our little house as clean as I could. Sometimes we'd go to Mama and Daddy's for Sunday dinner but we never stayed to gab—not on a lazy, sweet-smelling Sunday afternoon when everything was still and we had other ways to use that time. Sometimes Asa'd take me hunting with him but we never fired a bullet. What we did standing up against them old pin-oak trees would frighten every jackrabbit in the county.

Not that our life together was perfect, mind. He had a temper, that one. We had our rows and I spent more than enough time turned over his knee! I learned there was no point in fighting with him cause he always got his way and I just got me a real sore bottom. But I never stopped being crazy for him. He'd go off to work and all day long I'd lay in bed feeling his hands and his body all over me. I'd stand by the kitchen door when I knowed he was coming home for dinner. I'd get my first glimpse of his hat coming up over the rise and I'd go flying to him. Most nights dinner just sat there getting cold.

Four years went by and we didn't have no babies, I don't know why. In a secret little part of me I expect I was glad cause babies need a lot of care-taking and I was scared by what Mama had said—that once we had babies we'd be too busy for all our loving. Mama and Aunt Shoog fretted about it all the time, too.

"Are you doing right by him?" Mama would ask me.

"What do you mean, Mama?" She scared me when she talked that way. "I'm a good wife." I told her. "I have his dinner ready when he gets home and if he has to go back out and do more work at night I always wait up so's he can have some love when he comes back—no matter how late it gets."

I didn't tell her I gave him sugar morning, noon, and night. But she and Aunt Shoog kept fretting. I heard them talking it over whenever they thought I wasn't near enough to hear.

"I don't know what's the matter with that girl of mine,"

Mama would say, "she must not be doing her wifely duties is all I can think. If she don't get him a baby pretty soon . . ." She shook her head. "It's too easy for a man to wander off if he don't have a family to keep him home."

"Don't go blamin' her now," Aunt Shoog said. "It's more a case of that busy bee scatterin' his pollen too far and wide."

"Don't talk nonsense, Shoog. That don't make sense, bees don't make pollen."

"Maybe not," Shoog said lighting herself a pipe, "but that don't mean he ain't the problem."

"My girl says she waits up for him when he works late," Mama said in that low worrisome voice of hers.

Shoog snorted. "What kind of nails do you reckon he's drivin' that late at night, sister?"

Sometimes Mama's silences was scarier than the words she had to say. "I knowed he wasn't husband material but you can't tell my girl nothing."

My stomach knotted up something horrible at her words. Shoog took a long draw on her pipe. "Maybe you best be glad she don't have no youngsters to worry for."

I don't know if we would have got babies eventually. I still get queasy inside when I think about our last morning together. He always looked so sweet in the day's first light, cuddling up with me all sleepy and tender. He loved me for a long time and I kept pulling him back. It looked like snow outside and I didn't want him leaving me but he wanted to go hunting. He'd loaded shells the night before and I packed his rucksack. He told me to stay in bed and wait for him. He said it would keep him warm out there in the woods knowing I was at home, curled up in bed waiting for him to come back to me. He kissed me before he left—bit my lip and my belly button.

That was the last time he touched me.

It was mid-afternoon when the knocking started. I didn't

want to get up. I wanted to do as I was told, stay in bed and wait for him. But the knocking wouldn't go away.

He was dead, they said. A terrible accident, a stray bullet. Another hunter found him. My daddy was with them and when I started screaming he hugged me to him harder than he ever had in my life.

I don't recall a long time after that. I kept chewing at the bite he left on my lip as though by keeping it raw I could keep him with me. Daddy took me back to stay with him and Mama but I just stayed all day in bed trying to die. Trying to get closer to my Asa. When the snow came I'd walk out in it in my nightie until Daddy come after me and carried me back kicking and screaming.

I hated my own body. I hated its miserable aching for him. I'd fill the tub in the wash-shed with water so hot it scalded my skin raw and soaked in it until I was half-conscious. When spring came I'd walk six miles to the Guadalupe and lie in the icy water turning numb. Mama and Daddy feared I had taken leave of my senses. And they were right. Suffering like that is nothing a human woman should have to bear. Maybe that's why God let Asa come back to me.

Late one night as I tossed and turned, wretched with longing, he lay down beside me. I felt him. I felt his body slip down alongside mine. I closed my eyes and breathed him in—the smell of him, the warmth coming from his sweet body filled my senses and I did what I always did. I let go of everything and let him have me.

Slowly life became tolerable again. I could bear the days knowing that at night I could lay down and wrap myself up in Asa.

Time goes by so quickly when you are in love. Nothing else matters. I kept him all to myself—no one else needed to know about Asa and me. I knew I couldn't let on that he'd come back.

Except for my nightly trips to put flowers on his grave I suppose folks thought I had gotten over him. What fools! There's no getting over a man like Asa. Other men tried to come between us—some had the nerve to talk to me about marrying them. It threw me into hissies at first but then I let it go—they couldn't know about me and Asa—how close we were. How close we still are. Sixty years is nothing when you have Asa to come home to.

I know folks say I'm a crazy old lady—ditsy as a titmouse. They see me passing by with my arms full of flowers and they whisper to each other. Pathetic old fools. I look at the husbands of the women who used to be my friends and the ones that aren't dead are old and feeble. I fail to understand how a woman could climb into bed with one of those weak, wrinkled old farts. Makes my stomach turn thinking of them climbing over me. My lover is young and handsome and virile. He fills my nights with unimaginable bliss. My Asa never changes.

My knees crack as I kneel to place flowers on his grave.

"I'm coming to you soon, Asa," I tell him. And I know it won't be long until we really are together. God has forgiven me. The power of my love is so strong it wipes away the thing I did to keep Asa mine. I've been punished long enough. God let me know that when he sent Asa back to me. Mama was wrong—I knew how to keep him mine. My bullet put his body in this grave but I know he's not here at all. He's at home—stretched out naked in my bed. Waiting for me to come home and sink into his heat.

Daddy's Girl

Kate Flora

Sam was pouring coffee when her mother wandered into the room, her shirt misbuttoned, pajama pants held up by a safety pin. "Did you hear anything strange last night?" The shaky, too-loud voice shattered the kitchen's morning quiet.

Sam stared down at the pot, trying to inject certainty into her voice. "Nope. Nothing." A lie. She'd heard some very disturbing things last night, things she was trying to put out of her mind. She didn't have the energy for any more trouble.

Unless there was too much homework or she didn't feel safe leaving her mother alone, Sam sneaked out a lot, going up the hill to her favorite spot. Sam didn't think her mother knew. She'd tried to be very quiet. Sometimes she snooped around at the end of the road, where everyone went parking. It was spooky and dangerous but Sam had a mission. She was looking for a damaged gray car.

"You're sure?"

Sam shook her head. "Why?"

Mom stared at the coffee pot, the pale skin around her eyes crinkled. "You shouldn't be drinking that stuff at your age, you know, you'll . . ."

"Stunt my growth, right? I'm fifteen, Mom. I think I'm pretty much grown. So, what's happened?"

Saturdays, Sam slept in. Cocooned in her blankets, she could pretend nothing had changed, but she had a vague memory of the phone ringing, of the sharp, excited rise of her mother's voice. She tried to read her mom's ravaged face, but Mom had turned away and was staring out the window. Her mother's hair needed washing and she'd gotten so thin the paint-smudged clothes hung like empty sacks.

Outside, the trees marched up the hill, brilliant with autumn color. On the bare slope above, blueberry bushes had turned a rich purple-red. It was a hard season to be sad in but Mom moved through it casting a ten-foot shadow, her sorrow too big for her body to contain. Now she shook her head and tried to focus on Sam. "It's nothing you should worry about."

Parents were absurd, thinking they could insulate their kids from worry, acting like anyone under eighteen was deaf, dumb, and impervious to the undercurrents in adult conversation. Today, her mother was treating her like a child. Yesterday she'd announced a blinding headache, ordered Sam to handle the bills, and drifted away. Sam knew her father expected her to care for her mother. Sam was tough like her father's people. She was trying, but the dramatic spikes of her mother's emotions were exhausting.

"Oh, God. Just go ahead and tell me. I'm not a baby." Sam pressed her fist against the jittery feeling in her stomach.

But Mom had disappeared inside her head. Talking to her now would be like banging on a locked door. She wore one of Dad's old shirts, twisting the shirttails between her fingers like rosary beads. Nicky's mom was coming at eleven to drive them to soccer. There was no time to try and learn the big secret.

"I've got to get ready for the game." Mom didn't react. Sam was having a brilliant soccer season, but her mother had no clue. Sam unplugged the coffee, went upstairs and pulled on her uniform.

Her mother's voice followed her out. "Sam? Wait. You can't

leave." Sam didn't slow or look back. She'd do a lot for her mother, but she wasn't giving up soccer.

Nicky couldn't wait to blurt out the news. "Did you hear what happened? Ellie Newman went out last night and she didn't come home. She's totally disappeared."

Sam didn't want to hear this, didn't want to associate it with last night's "no, don'ts," and "stop, pleases." The ugly gurgle and silence. They could just be sex, couldn't they?

"Probably went to a friend's house," she said. "That's what always happens. Everyone gets in an uproar and then the missing person turns up. You know, like when Tommy Doherty went missing. Turned out he'd gone hunting with his dumb-ass uncle and they hadn't thought to tell his parents, and that senior girl, Donna something. She was lost at the Mall."

These days, Sam wasn't in the mood for bad news or even bad speculation. It was too easy to believe bad things happened. Nicky's eyes were wide. "No way. Not this time. Her parents called all her friends and, like, nobody's seen her." Then Nicky delivered the clincher. "She went out on a date and never came home. Nobody knows who she was out with, either."

"I'm sure she's fine," Nicky's mother said.

"Maybe she ran away," Sam said. "It happens."

"No way she's gonna run away. Not with the cheerleading competition coming up. I heard she spends five hours a week working on her thighs, just so she'll look good in her uniform."

Despite all the times their mothers had pushed them together over the years, Sam didn't like Ellie Newman much. Ellie was snooty. Boy-crazy. And dumb. She dressed like trash and treated unpopular girls like dirt. Sam was smart, athletic, and decidedly unpopular. Not that she cared. "Girl needs to get a life."

As soon as the words were out, she regretted them. She knew too well having a life wasn't always a matter of choice. "So what about that Camden-Rockport team? You hear anything?"

But Nicky wouldn't be distracted. "Listen to this. She told her mom she was going out with Dave Solo, but when Mrs. Newman called there, Mrs. Solo said it was impossible because Dave has guitar lessons over in Gunther on Friday nights. I'll bet she's, like, dead or something." Nicky's face reddened. She started fiddling with the zippers on her pack.

"How's your mother doing, Sam?" Nicky's mother asked.

Like talking about how her mother was handling her father's death was a better subject than a high-school girl gone missing. Sam used to think grown-ups knew how to do things right.

"She's okay. You know. It hasn't been very long." Sam's throat was tight. She stared up through the bright trees at the blue sky. The world shouldn't be so goddamned beautiful when everything sucked like this. When people were so damned stupid.

She stared down at her legs, puckered with cold between blue satin shorts and high blue socks. The blue veins under pale skin reminded her of her father's temple when she found him there in the road, illuminated by the eerie white-gold of her flashlight. His skin so white beneath his vibrant red hair, his body twisted and grotesque.

□   □   □

"Hit and run," the cop had said, as if that explained anything. As if "hit and run" had anything to do with her capable father or her dreamy mother or the way life just pulled down a black curtain that night and shut out everything bright. Goddamnit, they lived on a deadend road! There was no traffic except the occasional tourist driving up to see the view or couples going parking.

But the cops had learned nothing. Nothing! In the beginning, they'd tried. One nice guy, Jack Kelly, had come pretty often to ask questions and see how she and her mother were doing. But after her mother had pitched a screaming fit and thrown a frying pan at him, he'd stopped coming. Someone ran down her father crossing the road from the house to the mailbox, and drove off, and that was the end of it.

But not for Sam. She'd wanted to scream and cry, tear her hair, break things and generally behave badly, but her mother occupied that territory. All the sniffling, sad-eyed aunts and shuffling, inept, uncomfortable uncles had acted like it was her job to be the grown-up. Someone had to be and Sam, with her father's looks and outdoorsy nature, was a better candidate than the dark and volatile Delores. Sam had made grocery lists, done laundry, seen that her mother ate, showered, and didn't act so odd some well-meaning neighbor called the welfare, sucking it up until her insides ached like she'd drunk poison.

When she couldn't stand it anymore, she'd grab a jacket and flashlight and run up the hill as fast as she could go until she got to The Rock. The great hunk of granite sat all alone in the middle of the blueberry fields, dumped there by a glacier. "Samantha's Rock." Her father had helped her climb it back when she was tiny. Then she'd clambered up, flapped her arms, and crowed with glee. Now she perched on top and just thought about things, feeling closer to her dad. Sometimes she stood up and screamed.

She'd told The Rock all about her miserable goddamned life and how she was going to find the person who'd killed her father and get revenge. And she'd buried her face in the scratchy sleeve of her father's jacket and cried because it was so damned pathetic for a fifteen-year-old girl to imagine she was going to find someone the police couldn't.

Pathetic or not, Sam was working on the case. She kept her ears open for gossip and rumor. The cops had found glass from a shattered headlight and some flecks of dark gray paint. Nights when she could, she'd stealthily circled the area where everyone went parking, searching for a damaged car.

On Wednesday she'd skipped class and sneaked into the high-school parking lot. She was making her way down the rows, looking for a broken light or scratched paint, when behind her someone cleared his throat, scaring the hell out of her. Sam had whirled around and found Mr. Hendrie, the shop teacher, standing there. He looked kind of weird and nervous. Mr. Hendrie had curly brown hair and a boyish face and silly girls were always getting crushes on him.

"Samantha . . . uh . . . Mattheson, isn't it? Aren't you supposed to be in class?" She didn't like the way he looked at her.

"I needed some air." She'd placed her palm against her abdomen, signaling female troubles. "I wasn't feeling well." Men of Mr. Hendrie's generation—her father's generation—usually got embarrassed if a girl did that.

He gave her a funny look, a narrowing of his eyes and a slight smirk, like he knew what she was up to. Then he cocked his head and faked sympathy. "I know things haven't been easy for you lately. Still, young lady, I think you'd better get back inside— school hours and all. If you're not well, you can go to the nurse." He was looking at her chest. Sam willed herself not to blush. A challenge and a half for a pale-skinned redhead.

What was he doing out here anyway? He ought to go back inside. She had work to do. She'd only made it down one and a half rows. Then she noticed the unlit cigarette drooping in his hand. Teachers weren't supposed to smoke. She forced a smile and trotted obediently away, feeling the stain of his eyes on her. On the way, she passed Ellie Newman.

Later, waiting for the bus, she'd had the eerie feeling she was being watched. Looking around, she'd spotted Mr. Hendrie in the shadow of some bushes. Creep.

The next day, she'd gotten her mom to drive her, saying she needed to be there early. Combed the whole lot and found nothing.

□   □   □

They were early for soccer. A bunch of high-school boys were out on the field, kicking a ball around. Sam looked longingly at their parked cars, wanting to check them out, but she didn't want Nicky to know. She slipped her barrette off, set her bag down beside Nicky's, and then felt her hair. "Oops. I think my barrette must have fallen out in the car."

"Here, dear." Nicky's mom handed her the car keys. Nicky was already telling some other girls about Ellie Newman's disappearance. Sam clenched her fists, closing her mind against last night's words and sounds. She couldn't be worrying about Ellie Newman. She had a job to do.

Sam started inspecting cars, checking nervously over her shoulder from time to time. She didn't find anything. Carrying out the charade, she unlocked the Volvo and peered inside, then backed out and slammed the door. It still wasn't game time, so she decided to do a few more cars. Three cars down, she bumped right into it—a rusty old gray beater with one fender that was less rusty and didn't quite match.

Excitement and fear surged like a pulse. This might be something. She looked around quickly to see if anyone was watching, then bent and scraped a fingernail against a rusty spot. A bit of paint flaked off. She needed to save it, maybe give it to Jack Kelly. Flakes of paint and the license plate number. But she couldn't just stick it in her pocket and expect it to be there at the end of a soccer game. Not the way she played.

She walked back to the Volvo. Nicky's mother was one of those incredibly organized people with a perfectly clean car. Luckily, part of her organization included a little note pad stuck to the dashboard. Sam grabbed a piece of paper and the pencil, hurried back to the gray car, jotted down its license number, then folded the paper into a small envelope and dropped in some paint.

"Hey!" A loud, unfriendly male voice. "What the fuck did you do to my car?"

Sam shoved the paper into her pocket and stood up. He was

about twenty feet away, charging toward her, looking dramatically angry. David Solo. Captain of Varsity soccer. Heart throb
extraordinaire. Rock-star handsome with his cultivated three-day
stubble and gold-streaked hair. The big jerk. She couldn't believe
this piece of crap was his car.

She rose, waggling one foot. "I was tying my shoe. You got
a problem with that?" She shook her head and thumped the car
on the hood above the new fender. "As for this, if *this* is your car
. . . " She narrowed her eyes. "You were what? Afraid I'd hurt it?"

"Like hell. You were—"

"Were what?" He might be the king of attitude, but Sam was-
n't giving an inch.

"Sam! Come on! Hurry," Nicky called. "We're warming up."

"Gotta go." Sam dodged around him and jogged off, weak-
kneed and sick at nearly getting caught. When she glanced back,
his stare was ugly. She slipped the paint chips into her bag, tied
back her hair, and ran onto the field.

For the next hour, she channeled that adrenaline surge into
soccer. On the field, she could be tough. Ruthless. In charge.
Soccer was the only thing in her life that was any good. Shoulder-
to-shoulder with the opposition, the ball just beyond their feet,
she could transform her sadness and anger into competition. She
might look pale and fragile, but it was a disguise.

Afterward, Nicky's mother bought them pizza, going on too
long about how the game was getting too rough. A regular mother. Sam wished. Well, to hell with what she wished. Life was
what it was.

When she got home, a Sheriff's Department car was idling in
her driveway. Was there news? Had something happened to her
mother? Had someone finally called the welfare? Sam climbed
stiffly out of the Volvo and limped up the drive.

Jack Kelly lowered the window. "Afternoon, Sam." He gave
her one of those barely perceptible cop nods, then jerked his chin

toward the house. "Your mother won't let me in."

"She's having a bad day."

"She's had a lot of those," he said. "It's time she pulled herself together. I need to talk with her." His eyes swept over her. "Soccer today?"

"Yeah." Like what? She always wore blue satin shorts, limped like an old gimp, and had grass-stained bruises on her knees?

"You win?" She nodded. "You look kinda beat-up."

"Right," she agreed. "It was fun."

Kelly grinned as he swung his door open and got out. "You're something else, Sam." He was a big man with a weathered face and a wonderfully calm manner. For a second, she wanted to lean against him, maybe cry a little, and tell him what she'd heard, how crazy and confused she felt.

She swung her gym bag onto her shoulder. "Come on in, then. This about Ellie Newman?"

"It is."

She liked it that he didn't play games. She was sick and a half of being condescended to. Hearing people ask her mother, how's Sam doing, Delores? Like her mother had a clue. "What makes you think Mom might know something?"

He shrugged. "If she's not sleeping nights, you know, she might have heard something. Noticed something."

"You think it might have happened here?" Sam felt a chill so deep her bones hurt.

She opened the door and led him inside, dumping her bag in the hall and heading into the kitchen. She glanced quickly around. The house didn't look too bad. "You want coffee?"

"Coffee would be great."

She put coffee and water in the coffeemaker and pushed the button. "I'll go find her." Maybe she would tell him, when he was done with her mom. Tell him and give him the paint chips.

Her mother was in bed, still in her ratty outfit, a washcloth over her eyes. Sam raised the shades. "Rise and shine, Mom, we've got company."

"That asshole Kelly? Tell him to take a hike."

Before the accident, her mother never talked like this. Sam and her father had teased her for being so damned ladylike. "He wants to ask some questions about Ellie Newman. Just talk to him for a few minutes and he'll go away."

"I've got a headache."

The level of the bourbon was down considerably, so the headache wasn't surprising. "Just a few minutes, Mom."

"I can't." Her mother put an arm over her eyes.

"A girl is missing," Sam said. "If you can't help, tell him that. But at least make the effort." Her mother turned away. "Stop being so goddamned self-centered. You're not the only person in the world something bad has happened to, you know!" Sam whirled and ran from the room, slamming the door behind her.

Kelly read her face and shook his head. "She won't come out, huh?" He shoved his chair back. "Guess I'll have to go to the mountain."

"The mountain? What are you—" But Sam was talking to his back. She chugged two Advil and followed him into the bedroom.

Kelly had dumped her mother's discarded clothes off a chair and set it beside the bed. He was saying, "and, as you can imagine, the Newmans are pretty hysterical about all this. Ellie's their only child. I know you're usually awake in the night. Did you hear anything last night? Any cars at all?"

"Go away."

"Delores," Kelly's voice was gentle, matter-of-fact, not accusing, "Cindy Newman is your friend. She's in real trouble and needs everyone's help right now. I'm asking you to put aside your own problems and think if you can help her." He shifted in the chair and waited, patient as anything.

Finally, Sam's mother drew her arm away from her face and pushed herself up on the pillow. Her face was creased. Her skin yellow. The circles under her eyes made her look old. Before this happened, she'd been a pretty woman. "I heard a car go up around eleven-thirty. I didn't hear it come back down. That's all I can tell you."

"Noisy engine? Quiet? Did you notice anything unusual about it?"

"No." Her eyes wandered to the window, following passing clouds. "I don't know why you're bothering me, Jack. It's Sam you should ask. She's the one up there wandering at all hours of the night."

"Mom!"

"It's true, isn't it?" Her mother sighed. "You go up to that damned rock your father loved so much. It scares me out of my mind having you out there at night, but I don't expect I could stop you if I tried."

You could have tried, Sam thought. Talked to me. Asked me about it, instead of lying around like a lump of lead.

"Think that coffee's ready, Sam?" Kelly asked.

"She shouldn't be drinking coffee."

"Sam's fifteen, Delores. It's not coffee drinking you should be worried about. It's how thin she is. How hard she drives herself. Who's being the grown-up around here?"

How the hell did he know all that?

Sam's mom gave Kelly a poisonous look. "My daughter thinks that if she sits on that goddamned rock she'll be closer to Malcolm." She pushed back a clump of dirty hair. "Sam thinks she's so tough, looking after her crazy mother. Carrying on like some teenage saint. Then, when she thinks no one's noticing, she's out there howling like a banshee. Half the town must hear it."

She manufactured a bright smile. "We're just two crazy women, Jack, but if anything happened up here last night, Sam would know. It's like I told that Solo boy when he called. Anyone wants to know about last night, they should ask Sam."

"David Solo called here?" Kelly turned to Sam, his genial face jammed with worry, snapping out his words. "Sam, were you . . ."

She knew he meant well, but she couldn't talk right now. Furious and gut-sick, Sam bolted for the door, snatching a jacket off the hook as she ran. Kelly clomped after her, calling, but she never paused. Her mother had told David Solo she'd been out on the mountain last night. A woman who couldn't be bothered to help the police or raise her daughter was sharing their private business with a stranger? A stranger with a gray car and a mismatched new fender?

Sam knew every inch of the woods. If she didn't want to be found, she wouldn't be. She ran until her side hurt, then threw herself down on a bed of ferns, staring up at the scudding clouds. The leathery leaves pricked her bare legs. It was chilly and already starting to get dark, but anywhere was better than home. Right now she hated her mother. Just hated her.

Gradually, the ferns sprang back up around her, blocking the wind. Playing soccer hard had made her tired. She huddled under the jacket and closed her eyes and drifted. She woke because people were talking loudly. She opened her mouth to complain, then realized where she was. Raising her head slightly, she saw two shadowy figures tromping through the trees.

She held her breath and listened. A man spoke. Another answered. It might be hunters or cops looking for her, but she wasn't going to wave her arms and yell, "Yoohoo," until she'd scoped them out. Dave Solo knew she came out here.

The path they were following would pass right by her. She kept her head down, listening. A voice, startlingly near, said,

"This is taking fucking forever. I thought you knew your way around up here."

"Hey, I was bringing girls up here before you were a gleam in your pappy's eye."

"And killing them?"

"That was an accident."

An older man and a younger one. Very close now. Sam muffled her breath with her sleeve.

"How do you kill someone by accident?"

"Look, it just happened, okay? We can discuss this later. I just want to dump her and get the hell out. This place gives me the creeps."

"Despite all the fond memories? So, is Ellie your first dead one? She was so dumb. Thought it was the coolest thing in the world to tell her folks she was going out with me when all I'm doin' is takin' her to meet you."

"Yeah, well. I help you, you help me."

She could practically hear the shrug in his voice. Carefully, Sam raised her head. They were carrying something. Or someone. Her stomach twisted.

"Was Mathieson *your* first dead one, Solo?"

"Oh, fuck you, Teach. It's like you said. An accident. I'm tryin' to see how fast I can get from zero to sixty and the old fart just comes wandering out in front of me."

"We're just a couple accident-prone fellas. Look on the bright side. At least you got to work on your auto-body skills."

"In the privacy and security of your garage."

"Didn't want to see my best student, never mind the school's best forward, go to jail. And your parents would have been so cross."

They were joking about it. Joking! Sam battled her squirming stomach, hand pressed over her mouth.

"Speaking of Mathieson, his girl was snooping around the

school parking lot the other day. Still looking for the car that hit her father." Hendrie's tone was snide.

"Yeah, well, she was hangin' around my car this morning. First time I've driven it since. And her mother says she was out on the mountain last night." Solo sounded worried. "That's too much coincidence for me. We've got to do somethin' about her."

No way, Sam thought. She was going to do something about *them*. She wanted to burst out of the bushes and confront them, but while she might be impulsive, she tried not to be stupid. She lowered her head and listened.

"Yeah, she's a bright little thing. Kinda had me worried, too. But it's taken care of," Hendrie said. "Her mother's been drinking a lot lately, and drunks, you know, are notoriously careless about fire."

I'll show you a bright little thing, asshole. Sam waited until they'd moved up the trail, then hurried back downhill. Through the window, she saw her mother sprawled on the couch, asleep. So much for a guilty mother waiting anxiously for her child's return. The door was locked. She used the spare key and went straight to the phone.

The dispatcher said Kelly was out and offered his voice mail, but Sam held her ground. "This is Samantha Mathieson. I have important information about Ellie Newman, that girl who's missing, and I will only speak with Jack Kelly." He grudgingly asked for a number Kelly could call back.

Sam's legs collapsed. She sat on the cold tile floor with the phone in her lap, waiting. When he called, all her resolve to be calm deserted her. "It's David Solo and Mr. Hendrie, the shop teacher," she blurted. "They're up on the mountain now, doing something with Ellie's body. Then they're going to come back down here and, and burn my house."

"Calm down, Sam. You're going too fast for me. Let's start over, how do you—"

The receiver in her shaking hand chattered against her ear. Two men—one of them her father's killer—were coming after her and her mom, and he wanted her to be calm? "Just get here." She slammed down the phone.

Sam knew what her father would say. "Look after your mother, she's not tough like us." Sam coaxed her mother upright and led her, half-asleep and reeking of bourbon, to the car. Sam was too young for a license but her dad had let her drive sometimes. It was scarier at night, but she managed to steer the car a wobbly half-mile down the road and park it in their neighbor's driveway. She tucked the blanket she'd brought around her sleeping mother and ran home.

Her side hurt. She was thirsty. But the killers were coming for sure and she couldn't be sure the cops were. She had to get ready. She tried to imagine what her father would do, then hauled out his shotgun and loaded it with birdshot. They might be killers but she wasn't. She pulled on a dark hooded sweatshirt and pants, turned off the lights, and went outside to wait.

They made enough noise coming down the hill to wake the dead, stumbling around the yard and fiddling with their tools. When they fumbled out jars of gasoline and bent over unscrewing the lids, Sam braced the gun, aimed at their backsides, and fired. The explosion, screams, and general commotion brought a swarm of cops running around the house.

Sam sat on the slope, half-deaf from the noise, watching, until a calm voice called, "That you, Sam? You okay?" Jack Kelly started toward her.

"I'm armed and dangerous," she said.

"I noticed. Are you okay?"

"I will be."

"Good girl." He held out his hand and she gave him the gun. He transferred it to his other hand, then pulled her to her feet.

"You know that poem about James Morrison?"

"Took great care of his mother, though he was only three?"

"That's the one. And you did, too. The Parkers have taken her home for the night. Now, any chance you could help us locate Ellie Newman?"

"I've got a pretty good idea."

It was midnight when they finally got the body out of the old well. Sam was tired and a half but she couldn't imagine going home to bed after all this. She sat on the old stone foundation, leaning against Kelly's shoulder, wrapped in his creaking leather jacket, while police swarmed around under the lights.

"Officer Kelly?"

"Jack."

"Jack. Tell me the truth. Will the child welfare people take me because of what happened tonight? Because Mom was drunk and I shot a gun and drove without a license?"

"That's what you've been worried about?"

She nodded.

Even in the strange light he looked sad. "Your mom's gonna be okay, Sam. And you? You're a goddamned hero. The wel-fare'd be afraid of you."

Sam rested her head against his shoulder again. It was sad about Ellie Newman. Sam wished she'd liked Ellie more. No one deserved what had happened to her. At some point it would prob-ably hit Sam and she'd feel really awful. But right now, she felt good. She'd caught the man who'd killed her father. She'd saved her mother and her house. And she'd shot both of those assholes in the ass. She closed her eyes. This was all pretty exciting, and Mathiesons were tough, but right now, she was just plain tired.

Mental Hygiene

Roberta A. Isleib

If only Dr. Rebecca Butterman had been in session when the detective beeped her, she could have avoided witnessing Lawrence Merriweather's mutilated remains. The other events of the day—a tricky Rorschach inkblot interpretation, Mr. Oliver revealing his infidelity to his wife for the first time during their joint therapy hour, and then the scornful invectives of a sullen teenager—all this felt painless in comparison to Merriweather's corpse. The greasy remnants of the grilled cheese sandwich she'd wolfed down for lunch began a slow rise from stomach to throat.

"Sorry about that, Rebecca." Detective Caroline Rumson laughed softly and guided her past the technicians who buzzed around the body. "I forget that you shrinks only have strong stomachs for mental carnage. I need you to get on this ASAP. There's going to be a lot of pressure to close the dental clinic if we can't make an arrest right away. I think we can wrap it up quickly— apparently Dr. DeNardia has a history of mental instability. They even sent him to have psychological testing done last year."

Dr. Butterman took a series of deep, centering yoga breaths, a technique she often recommended to nervous patients. She was beginning to see first-hand just how little the breathing touched a case of serious stomach-wrenching anxiety.

"What the hell was sticking out of that man's throat?"

"Betty Ann, the receptionist, called it a zerfing chisel. They use it for scaling plaque off teeth. Like I told you on the phone, the victim is Lawrence Merriweather—he's one of Dr. DeNardia's patients. Maybe you know him—he researches, well, best say he used to research, some kind of brain biochemistry." Rumson cocked her head in curiosity.

"This hospital has a staff of five hundred, plus god-knows-how-many adjunct faculty. It's the second-largest facility in Connecticut. I don't know every egghead in the place, for crying out loud." Dr. Butterman sometimes suspected that the detective resented relying on a psychological consultant—unconsciously, of course. But as a result, she enjoyed getting the upper hand in their relationship—by whatever subtle means it took to get there. "What do you need me for?"

"First, locate DeNardia's records in the psychology clinic and give me a summary of what you people found. Maybe he should have been banned from seeing patients at all."

There it was again—*you people*, as though psychologists in their generic entirety were responsible for the ill-fated attack by zerfing chisel. Sooner or later, she and Caroline were going to have to have it out.

"Did he sign a release?"

The detective nodded.

"What else?"

"I'd like you to sit in on the interviews this afternoon. Can you clear your calendar?"

The first interview was with Frank DeNardia himself. Dr. Butterman had located his testing file in the clinic. Last year's psychological evaluation had been scheduled after a complaint was lodged by one of his patients. He'd undergone a thorough battery of testing—interview, intelligence test, complete personality profile. When the results came back, the dentist was remanded for weekly psychotherapy and assigned to the clinical director. Now Dr. Butterman started to understand the urgency of her involvement in this case. It would look particularly bad if the head of the Yale University Mental Hygiene department had one of his clients arrested for a brutal murder.

"You were evaluated at the psychology clinic last summer." Detective Rumson addressed the dentist in her brusque, television-cop voice. "Why?"

"I was having thoughts about wanting to harm my patients," said Dr. DeNardia simply. "I mentioned it to several of them. My receptionist told me later I shouldn't say such things in front of other people. So I suppose one of them complained." The dentist leaned forward and placed his elbows on his knees. "But I didn't hurt Mr. Merriweather. He'd done a good job with his cleaning the last six months. And I've been going to my counseling sessions every week. Just ask my therapist." Then he smiled, revealing a set of perfectly straight, eggshell-white teeth.

Dr. Butterman was certain she could locate the appropriate descriptive code for his mental state in the *Diagnostic and Statistical Manual of Mental Disorders.* But let's face it, this guy was a fruitcake. Speaking as though one's dental hygiene would naturally be related to whether one should be a murder victim. But did the dentist commit the murder? She was not convinced.

"Why do you suppose you had feelings of wanting to hurt your own patients?" she asked.

He shrugged. "My doctor and I have been working on understanding that." He tugged on his earlobe. "They do make me mad, just lying there like beached whales and whining about how what I'm doing hurts them. But I don't have the whole answer yet."

Butterman waited until the detective had ushered the dentist from the room, then pulled out the psychological testing file a second time. She located the Rorschach Miniature Inkblots in Color scoring sheet. The page, which contained a mini-replica of each of the ten Rorschach cards, was covered with scribbled notes and arrows. Dr. DeNardia had described aggressive action scenes when presented with most of the stimulus cards, especially those in color. The test administrator made the obvious interpretation that the dentist had hostile and angry impulses that he found difficult to control. No surprise—he'd admitted as much in the interview. The test report also noted that he had an arsenal of potential coping resources that worked well when he could muster them. But how much progress had been made in shoring up those resources? She'd have to speak to the clinical director later.

Detective Rumson stalked back into the office, a small gray-haired woman in tow. Dr. Butterman shuffled the test results back into their manila folder. "This is Betty Ann Romano," said Rumson. "She's the receptionist for Dr. DeNardia and two other dentists in the clinic."

"The others had the morning off," squeaked Betty Ann. "Oh my lordy, lord. I can't believe this is happening."

"Who else was in the office this morning?"

Betty Ann gripped her short curls with both fists and furrowed the skin above her eyebrows into Shar-pei folds. "There was Mr. Roden. He comes in almost every month demanding whitening gel syringes. I'd suggest you take a long, hard look at that man. He's crazy."

"Excuse me," said Dr. Butterman. "What are whitening gel syringes?"

"The stuff they use to bleach teeth," explained Betty Ann. "Usually it only takes two of the syringes to do the job, then maybe a touch-up every six months or so. We recommend it to almost all of our patients." She ventured a small, but very white smile. "But Mr. Roden can't get enough. Susan slipped him some extras, but Dr. DeNardia finally put his foot down this morning and said, 'No more!' That man was so angry when he left."

"But why kill Lawrence Merriweather?" asked the detective.

Betty Ann began to cry. "It couldn't have been Dr. DeNardia. He's talked about hurting patients, but I can't believe he'd ever do it. I've answered his phone calls and scheduled his appointments for twenty years."

"Who else was around the office this morning?" asked Rumson.

"Just me and Susan."

"Susan?"

"The dental hygienist. She's worked with us for fifteen years. She was helping me with the filing this morning. We were talking about gardening. I prefer wildflowers but she goes for the more formal, English style. The roses are pretty and all, but the chemicals she has to use to keep them pretty." She began to weep again. "I don't know. People walk up and down this hallway all day long. The security in this hospital is dreadful. Someone could have slipped in from outside and stabbed Mr. Merriweather and we'd never have known it."

The detective led the sodden Betty Ann out of the room and returned with Susan Olmsted, the hygienist. As they took their seats, Rumson's cell phone shrilled. "Dammit," she said. "I have to take this. Go ahead and start—I'll be back shortly."

Susan settled into the chair across from Dr. Butterman and gazed around the room. Finally her eyes rested on Frank DeNardia's test file. Just the edge of the inkblot score sheet poked out from the folder.

"Oh how pretty!" she exclaimed. Before the psychologist could protest, Susan eased the Miniature Inkblot scoring sheet out from the file and held it close to her face. "I don't care for the black ones, but these colors are beautiful—up against that white, white background. You could frame this—it's just that pretty."

"Tell me what you noticed at the clinic this morning," Dr. Butterman prompted, reaching to retrieve the score sheet. It was extremely irregular to have an employee looking at her boss's psychological test materials.

"It was a busy day, and in between patients, I helped Betty Ann with the filing." She frowned and made a clucking noise. "She tends to get behind and then you can never find a chart when you need it. With the way insurance companies operate these days, you have to stay on top of things."

"How did Dr. DeNardia seem to you today?"

Susan thought this over carefully. "He was a little on edge when he came in. I don't think he's been sleeping well. He forgets things. He puts instruments back in the wrong place. It's not at all like him."

"Were you aware that he had been having thoughts about harming his patients?" asked Dr. Butterman as the detective reentered the room.

"Oh that," said Susan with a dismissive wave. "He'd never follow through. You know how upset you can get if things aren't going right. Sometimes he just says things he doesn't mean."

"Tell us about Lawrence Merriweather," the detective demanded.

"He does a good job taking care of his teeth between visits." Then she hesitated.

"What else?"

"That's all I can think of. Very little plaque, no receding gums, he almost never bleeds during a cleaning."

"What's he like?"

"He seems like a nice enough man—a little boring. He always wants to talk history and biography." She scrunched her face with distaste. "Me? I love mysteries."

"And Mr. Roden?"

Susan smiled, her teeth even whiter than her coworker's. "I warned him not to come in when Dr. DeNardia was here." She dropped her voice to a whisper. "Dr. D believes too much of the whitening gel can harm the enamel. I think he's too conservative, but he *is* the dentist."

"Thank you for your time," said Dr. Butterman.

"Please wait outside with the others," said the detective.

Susan gathered her lab coat around her shoulders and walked briskly from the room.

"Well, Doctor?" Rumson demanded. "What do you think?"

"You start," the psychologist countered.

"Murder by zerfing chisel. I would not rate that as a well-planned methodology."

Dr. Butterman laughed. "More like someone got pissed, grabbed the first instrument available, and struck." She paused, her chin resting on her fist. "On the other hand, was it really a random choice? What did you say they use it for?"

"Plaque," said the detective. "Scaling scum." Both women laughed. "Let's go with random then. Next, who was pissed at Lawrence Merriweather?"

"Sounds to me like you better get some of your people gathering background data," said Dr. Butterman. "Possibly one of the dental employees knew the man in some personal context that they aren't disclosing."

"Duh. I hired you for psychological insights here, not tips on basic police procedure."

Dr. Butterman rubbed her eyes and sighed. "Try this out. We're looking for someone who may appear in control, but underneath the emotions are ready to boil over. Which is exactly what DeNardia's test profile suggested."

"It would be a matter of the right trigger," Rumson agreed.

"I have a hunch about the teeth bleaching. It's a long shot, but if I were you, I'd bring them all back in here and push a little more on the whitening system. Maybe someone's ready to crack."

"I think it may be you, dear," said the detective. Then she

shrugged and went to the door. "Dr. DeNardia? Susan? Betty Ann? Could we see all of you in here, please?"

Dr. Butterman stashed the psychological test folder under the blotter on the desk. "We'd like to hear more about your teeth-whitening program."

All three broke into demonstrative alabaster grins.

"We offer it to all our patients," said the dentist. "Susan is an expert at talking them into trying it."

"And they look so much better when they've worn it for a few weeks," added Betty Ann. "I wouldn't be surprised if Susan was responsible for some major improvements in their lives." Susan just beamed.

"How does it work?"

Susan produced a chart from the pocket of her white lab coat and held it out toward the two women. A row of single teeth ranging in color from cigarettes-and-coffee yellow to stark white marched along the sheet. "We make an impression of the upper and lower teeth. Then we use this color chart to determine where the patient starts and how light they wish to go."

"What about Mr. Merriweather?" asked Dr. Butterman. The smiles evaporated.

"We've tried," said the dentist with a shrug.

"He just wasn't interested?" asked the detective.

"Oh, he claimed he was interested," said Susan. "Four years ago he bought the whole system. We had the personalized dental trays made for him and everything. But then he refused to try it."

"What was the problem?" asked Dr. Butterman.

"Every visit there was a different explanation," said Betty Ann. "First he claimed he was a problem sleeper."

"This time, he had read the patient information about the possibility of heightened sensitivity during the bleaching process." Susan spat the words out. "He insisted it would give him neuralgia."

"You'd had enough," observed Dr. Butterman.

"Have I been a good boy?" Susan sneered. "He asked that every time he came in." Her face twisted with rage. "I couldn't listen to any more excuses. He'd been a bad, bad boy."

Dr. DeNardia and Betty Ann rose slowly from their seats and backed toward the door.

"Would you two kindly wait outside?" asked the detective. "You have the right to remain silent," she told the dental hygienist.

□   □   □

Detective Rumson banged her draft beer down on the sticky counter. "What finally tipped you off?"

"The inkblots," said Dr. Butterman. "She picked up the Rorschach score sheet before I could get it away from her. I've never seen such a strong reaction to color. And her responses were not mitigated by form. Only the most histrionic patients react this way, and it's usually in the service of warding off some very ugly impulses underneath."

"So now you're diagnosing murder based on a suspect's reaction to someone else's inkblot test?" The detective sounded incredulous.

"It worked, didn't it?" Dr. Butterman fingered the tooth color chart that lay on the bar, then held it up next to her friend's face. "You might want to consider this bleaching treatment yourself. Right now I'd say you fall somewhere between numbers four and five."

Rumson batted the card to the floor and called for the check.

New Derby, New Year's Eve

Barbara Ross

Young Officer Schnabel drove slowly eastbound on Route 9, alert for any motorist who might have skidded in the rapidly accumulating snow. Despite the holiday, at eight-thirty in the evening traffic was light, as if New Derby's citizens had taken stock of the weather and sensibly got where they were going, or even more wisely, stayed home.

Schnabel glanced out his passenger window as he passed the bright lights of Hunan Palace. Its parking lot was mobbed with cars, snow piling on their roof tops. At the front door, a woman in a fur coat laughed with her escort. Her coat fell open as she moved, revealing a tantalizing glimpse of something short, red, and sequined.

Half a mile before the edge of town, Schnabel pulled his car into a parking lot. It was his favorite lay-by, the perfect place to sit and watch for speeders, or, on this night above all others, for tell-tale signs the driver had had one too many. The lot surrounded a little plaza housing three businesses; a sub shop, dry-cleaners, and laundromat. The sub shop and dry-cleaners were shut tight, but lights blazed from the laundromat windows.

Schnabel made a wide arc with his patrol car, driving carefully in the snow, until the car was perpendicular to the road, hood forward, in case he had to pull out and give chase. The laundromat was behind him, clearly visible through his rear window, which was just beginning to collect a fine coat of wet snow.

Schnabel turned and saw a solitary figure sitting in one of the plastic molded chairs along the side wall of the laundromat. The man sat, profile to him, turning the pages of the Boston *Herald* while his laundry tumbled in the big stainless steel dryer by the front door. As Schnabel watched, something pink streaked by the dryer's window—once, twice, three times.

By shifting in his seat, Schnabel could see the man's car, parked toward the back of the tiny lot. Snow obscured the roof and hood, but Schnabel recognized the lines of an old bomber station wagon, the kind his parents once had for transporting six children on vacation. Not many like it on the road these days.

Schnabel sat and watched the road, turning every so often to glance at the solitary man. The poor guy. He looked to be in his late twenties, about Schnabel's own age, and he sat alone, doing his laundry, on the one night of the year when everyone should be with friends. That's where Schnabel planned to be as soon as he got off shift at midnight, with his old pals and new girlfriend.

Schnabel turned the key in the ignition. He couldn't stand the way the man made him feel. He'd find another place to lie and wait, perhaps his second-favorite hidey-hole, closer to the Center. Any place would do, really, just some place where the lonely creature in the laundromat wouldn't haunt him.

Ruth Murphy's legs ached from standing and it wasn't yet nine o'clock. The older generation had cocktail party calves, the ability to stand and chat for hours. Like the related ability to stand with a drink in one hand, a plate of food in the other, and somehow eat the food, it was a generation-skipping thing that had leapt over Ruth's forty-something cohort.

"You're looking pensive." The hostess, Anna Abbot, materialized beside Ruth. At eighty-two, Mrs. Abbott looked like she could stand all night and do a rhumba on the ceiling to close out the evening,

"Pensive? Am I?" Ruth laughed.

"Don't deny, don't deny. And I know what you're pensive about." Mrs. Abbott leaned forward confidentially. "It's the first New Year's Eve since your confirmation as Police Chief, and the first snowstorm of the winter to boot. You think you should be at headquarters commanding your troops."

Ruth smiled. Not only was she thinking about work, she was *at* work. Her promotion to Chief made attendance at Mrs. Abbott's annual New Year's Eve gathering of New Derby's movers and shakers mandatory. Much as she adored the old lady, Ruth would much rather have been home, warm by the fireplace, playing Scrabble with the kids.

The thought of the kids and the demise of the family New Year's Eve gave Ruth a pang. Sarah, ever-popular, was off with friends at a sleepover. But James, at fifteen, was too old to be sent to a cousin's, too young to drive off to his own amusements. The picture of James sitting home alone in their old Victorian house, its facade dotted with dark windows, made Ruth's heart ache.

"Shame on you," Mrs. Abbott admonished.

"Huh?"

"Don't think about your job. If your force is as good as you think it is, everything will be just fine. Now, go off and have some fun, like your charming husband."

Ruth followed Anna Abbott's gaze to a corner of the huge living room where Marty Murphy, deep in conversation with two women, was, indeed, pouring on the Boston-Irish-lawyer charm.

Ruth glanced at her glass of ginger ale with distaste. She was the designated driver, and as New Derby's Police Chief, had to practice zero tolerance. Ah well, nothing to do but mix and mingle.

☐ ☐ ☐

Frank Maloney stood at his post by the gaping doorway that separated Target from the rest of the mall. It was deserted as far as the eye could see. The combination of the holiday and snow had discouraged even the hardiest of shoppers. Stupid, really, to be open so late on New Year's Eve.

Without anyone to watch, the time dragged. If not for the people-watching, the security guard job would've bored him stiff. No use complaining, though. It got him out of the house in his retirement. With Irene dead, he'd have gone mental staring at the four walls.

Frank raised a hand and returned the wave of the lone checker standing in the great rows of check-out counters. "Boring night, huh, Frank?" she called. She was Hispanic, so it sounded like, "Boreen nightte, uh, Frink?" Lovely sounding, really. She was a cute little thing. One of the things he enjoyed about the job was the chance to be around so many young people.

Frank thought about Damon Platen, the boy he was filling in for tonight. In exchange for the chance to party New Year's Eve and sleep it off all New Year's Day, Damon had taken five shifts for Frank, including Christmas Eve, so Frank could travel to Atlanta to meet his first grandchild.

A movement by the doorway caught Frank's eye. A little girl, barely walking, toddled out of the store into the mall. She was wearing a too-big Christmas dress, bright red velvet with a white crinoline pinafore sewed to it. The Target price tag was still hanging down the back. The child had no shoes on. Frank shuddered to think about her bare feet on the cold stone floor, though she did look as if walking barefoot were a struggle for her. Shoes would have sunk her, surely.

Frank was preparing to give chase when he saw the mother following. She stepped out into the mall with an exaggerated casualness, coat folded in her arms, her shoulders hunched forward, eyes trained at the ground. She was painfully thin-bodied and limp-haired, with dark circles under her eyes and almost translucent skin. If she was any more than sixteen, he'd eat his shirt.

As Frank watched, the pair made their way into the mall, the toddler in the red dress walking like a drunken sailor, the mother close behind, looking for all the world like she needed a good meal. When they turned the corner, moving up the wheelchair ramp into the main part of the mall with no sign of coming back or paying for the dress, Frank left his post and followed.

□ □ □

Officer Schnabel was relieved when he finally got to his second-favorite lay-by. It had taken much longer than he'd expected. When he'd come up to the light at the legal U-turn on Route 9, he'd seen a car slide into a snowbank on the other side of the road. Schnabel had come around and parked behind it, his blue bubble-light flashing. He tried to help the poor guy out. When he couldn't, he called a tow truck, and waited, directing traffic until it came and went.

By the time he left the scene, Schnabel was chilled to the bone. The wet snow had wicked down the back of this neck and up his pants legs, despite the heavy orange raincoat, boots, and cap. He'd gone to Dunkin' Donuts to get a hot chocolate and a bagel, and finally crossed back to the eastbound side and pulled into his spot, where he sat with the heater blasting.

He'd just settled in when a car with all its lights off sped by on the other side of the road, going way too fast for the conditions. Schnabel cursed, activated his lights and siren, and started to give chase, but the car was barreling toward Derby Center. By the time Schnabel made the U-turn around the concrete island in the middle of the road, it would be long gone.

With a start, Schnabel remembered where he'd last seen that car.

He radioed the description ahead, so someone else could catch it, then raced out of the parking lot and sped eastward.

Something told him he'd better get back to the laundromat.

◻   ◻   ◻

James Murphy was in a state of panic. He didn't know how things had gotten so out of hand. As soon as Mom and Dad left, the guys had arrived, as pre-arranged, for a parentless night of poker. It had seemed like a great idea at the time. But then, Marco Fernandez, the total idiot, had told Felicity Feldman about the party. Felicity had four friends sleeping over, and wouldn't that be perfect? Five boys and five girls. James had protested, but the others overruled him. What could go wrong? These were the same girl-buddies they'd known since grade school. So Felicity and her overnight guests had sneaked down her back stairs and out the kitchen door, while her parents entertained guests in the living room.

All of this would have been fine, but one of the girls in Felicity's group was in love with a guy on the football team. She called him as soon as she got to James's house, saying the coast was clear, to come over and bring his friends.

Since then, the news had spread all over town, and groups of kids, some of whom James had never even seen before, were arriving every minute. People had brought cases and cases of beer, but they were long gone, as was the warm Sam Adams Dad kept in the butler's pantry. Now the kids had started on the big bottles of whiskey and rye kept in the cabinet over the stove for when his grandparents and great aunts and uncles dropped in. James prayed they wouldn't find his father's wine hidden in the cellar.

The house was a disaster. Dad's stereo was blaring. James looked out at his driveway, clogged with cars, and into the street beyond, where all manner of vehicles lined the roadway in spite of the snow emergency parking ban. Luckily, the neighbors all seemed to be out at parties of their own.

Still, James was very, very worried.

□   □   □

Billy Sharp realized his mistake and turned on his headlights just after the cop peeled off in the other direction. He was grateful the cop was gone, yet sorry at the same time. When it looked like the cop might chase him, Billy's heart pounded and his palms sweat in a very satisfying way.

Billy had about died when the squad car had pulled into the laundromat parking lot. He'd already finished hacking his way through the laundromat wall into the dry-cleaners and made several careful trips into the shop, crawling on his belly to avoid the motion detectors, opening the big fur storage boxes and crawling out with one plush coat at a time. There were seven coats in all, not bad for a time of year when most people had their furs at home. Billy imagined the owners, down in Florida or off on cruises. He imagined how angry they would be when they came back and found their coats gone. Their anger made him happy.

When the cop had arrived, Billy, thinking quickly, picked up a Boston *Herald* someone had left behind, threw a rag into one of the big dryers where the cop could see it whirling, plugged two quarters in, and waited. Sure enough, the cop took off. Billy finished the job, loading the furs into the station wagon, placing them carefully way in the back around the baby seat. He knew just where to fence those furs.

Billy had to get rid of the car. The old wagon had a distinct look about it and the cop must have called in his plates. He pulled off Route 9 and meandered through the side streets. Up ahead was a big house, lights blazing in every window. The driveway and street were choked with cars, a wild party going on. Billy smiled. Perfect. He pulled the wagon to the side of the road where it would soon be covered in snow and headed up to the house.

All in all, a good night's work. Perhaps it hadn't been necessary to toss the lighted match into the cart full of shirts at the dry cleaners, but he'd done that for his own pleasure.

□ □ □

Frank Maloney stirred cream into his coffee. They were sitting in Friendly's, the girl and her sweet child across from him. The girl was crying. "Mister, I was going to bring the dress back. I swear I was."

Frank had followed them to the very center of the mall, where mother and daughter had disappeared into the one-dollar photo booth. He heard the girl cooing, "Smile, Holly, smile." The light had flashed four times.

When they stepped out, he grabbed them. "What do you think you're doing?"

The girl looked at him, looked at his security badge, and burst into noisy sobs. He steered her into Friendly's and sat her and the child in a booth. Crying all the while, she resisted his offer to pay for a meal. So he'd ordered two cups of coffee, two slices of pie, and a dish of vanilla ice cream for the baby. And what a beautiful child. Blonde like her mother with curly locks and wide blue eyes. The red velvet dress brought out the roses in her cheeks.

"I would have brought the dress back." The mom was still sobbing. "I just wanted a picture. To remember. It's her first Christmas. She was born on New Year's Day last year. I wanted a picture with Santa. I put the dress on layaway and paid a little at a time on it since Halloween. But then," she hesitated, "the money got used for something else. It didn't matter, anyway. Pictures with Santa cost $12.50 and where was I going to get that kind of money?" She looked up at Frank to make sure he understood. "So, I thought if I came after Christmas, when the dress was back on the rack, I could take it and get a picture of Holly in it. And when she's older, she can look at it and know her Mommy loved her enough to put her in a pretty Christmas dress and get her picture taken."

The girl began to cry again and while Frank watched, Holly reached over and patted her mother gently on the back.

Frank thought about his new grandson in Atlanta, just three months old, lying in his mother's lap in his green velvet Christmas romper. Frank thought about the gifts for the baby piled under the Christmas tree, from all his aunts and uncles, Frank's own children and their spouses. Never had a child been more wanted or loved.

The Santa's Village set up was still in the middle of the mall, waiting for the workmen to dismantle it next week.

"Let's go," Frank said.

The girl looked panic-stricken. "Where?"

"Back to the store."

At Target, Frank picked out film and a camera, the same kind he had at home. He'd return it tomorrow. They got a Santa suit, 50 percent off in Seasonal, black boots from Outdoors, and a pillow from Bedding. Frank felt no guilt about leaving his post. There was no one else around.

The young mother, who had mumbled that her name was Penny, got into the spirit of it, laughing as he held the pillows to his chest. The baby sat in the shopping cart and giggled.

"To Santa's Village," Frank said, leading the way. "If we're going to do this, let's do it properly."

□ □ □

Ruth hung up the phone. She'd checked in at headquarters despite Mrs. Abbott's blandishments. Lieutenant Lawry, the officer in charge, assured her everything was fine. There'd been a burglary and a bit of a fire at the dry cleaners on the city line. Could have been quite a conflagration, but due to some quick thinking by Officer Schnabel, the building had been saved.

"What did they take?" Ruth asked.

"Fur coats."

"Some kind of animal rights thing?"

"Nah, a punk. Schnabel has a great description. We'll get him."

Other than that, Public Works was doing a good job with the snow. All the roads were passable. Most people would stay wherever they were until after midnight, anyway. She should stay at the party and have fun, Lawry said.

What Ruth really wanted was to go home. She'd done all her duty chats. Her legs ached. Her face ached from smiling and she was stone-cold sober. But it would be unaccountably rude to leave before the midnight toast.

She wished she could call James. The thought of him all alone broke her heart. But he'd really hate her checking up. She'd wait and call him after midnight, using Happy New Year wishes as her excuse.

Billy Sharp was beside himself. The party guests were younger than he'd expected. High schoolers, he figured, the same age as his woman. It was hard for him at twenty-nine to blend into the woodwork.

And, there wasn't a drop to drink in the house, though there must have been at one time, judging by the state of the downstairs lavatory. Food was in short supply, too. The refrigerator door hung open, its interior denuded except for a few odd jars of mustard and salad dressing.

From the living room came the sounds of an escalating altercation. Evidently, someone wanted to drive home and someone else thought he was too drunk. Others joined in with opinions and there were shoving sounds followed by the crash of furniture and the tinkle of breaking glass.

Billy heard the sound of sirens in the distance. He wanted to leave, but his car was too hot. He settled in to wait it out.

Schnabel smiled to himself as he drove back to headquarters. He felt stupid for having missed the burglary in the first place, but happy he'd gotten back to the dry cleaners in time to prevent a worse fire. Without accelerant, it had taken awhile for the shirts to get really going, but the Fire Chief had said if they'd arrived later, the whole place would have gone up.

More than anything, Schnabel was feeling grateful to Lieutenant Lawry, who had relieved him at the fire scene in plenty of time to get his report written and be out to party with his girl at midnight. Lieutenant Lawry had a soft spot for the uniforms who worked holidays.

Schnabel was almost to headquarters when his radio squawked. Change of plan. Some kind of wild party and altercation at a house in Derby Center. There were two cars already there, but they were requesting back up. Lawry himself was going over for some reason.

Schnabel radioed he was in the area and requested the address. "What?" he said, not trusting his ears. "Can you give that to me again?"

□   □   □

Ruth's reaction was the same as any parent's if they approached their house and saw the street blocked by four patrol cars with their blue lights blazing. Sheer terror.

She and Marty abandoned their car a block away and ran to the house. Lieutenant Lawry met them on the porch. "Everyone's fine" were the first words out of this mouth.

Instantly, Ruth's terror turned to rage. "What the hell is going on here?" she demanded.

"Just a little party that got out of hand," Lawry reassured. "We're calling parents now. Anyone whose parents can't be reached will get a ride home in a squad car. Any vehicle that isn't driven away we'll tow to the municipal lot. Everything is fine. It'll take a little time to sort it out is all."

"Thank you, Lieutenant." Ruth felt enormously grateful. She stood on her porch at a loss for further words, looking off into the distance. Her neighbors' windows were dark, no cars in the driveways. "Who called it in, anyway?" she asked.

"I did." A doleful James stepped out from behind Lawry. "I didn't know what else to do."

"Hey! You! Stop right there!"

Ruth turned to see Schnabel take off across the snowy lawn, chasing someone who'd just run out the side door of her house.

"Stop 'im!" Schnabel yelled. "He's my laundromat guy!"

□   □   □

Frank Maloney helped the night manager close up. They turned off the lights, locked the doors, and set the alarms. Frank walked the perimeter, inside, outside, and mallside. His car, covered with snow, was the last one left in the parking lot.

When he drove around to the front of the building, they were still there—Penny and the baby named Holly for the season of her birth. The snow had stopped and the temperature was falling rapidly. Little Holly didn't even have a snowsuit. Penny had wrapped her in a blanket and zipped her in her own parka like a papoose.

Frank slowed his car and rolled down the window.

"He was supposed to come for me." Penny was clearly worried. "He was supposed to meet me right here. I was a little late, you know, because of the photo. Maybe he got pissed and drove away."

"C'mon," Frank said. "I'll give you a ride home."

Penny shook her head. "If he's mad, I don't want to go home."

Frank thought about his Cape Cod style house on the dead-end street with the two big bedrooms on the second floor in addition to his own room on the first. He and Irene had bought it specifically because it was so great for children. There were no children in it now, and no Irene. Sometimes he thought the sound of his own puttering would drive him crazy.

"Get in," he said. And then, when she looked uncertain, more gently, "I won't hurt you. I have an idea."

Penny stepped off the curb and got into the car. Holly was asleep against her chest and they drove in silence through the snowy streets past the big houses twinkling with Christmas lights and party guests in the windows and all the snowed-in cars.

If Penny noticed, when they passed a certain house in Derby Center, the familiar silhouette of an old station wagon being pulled out of the snow by a police department wrecker, she never mentioned it to Frank.

Perdition

Carol Perry

Ethan was dead when I found him. He must have had a heart attack or a stroke or something. I didn't see any wounds or blood. I suppose I should have left him there and gone for help.

It was the end of a long August day and, in New Hampshire, that means relentless heat and humidity. Purdy, my beautiful Border Collie, and I had been swimming down at the cow pond. I'd raced her into the cold, murky oasis, fully clothed, to save my flesh from being roasted clean through. It was Heaven and I could tell Purdy loved it as much as I did. She paddled out to the middle and back, which for a twelve-year-old farm dog is a magnificent feat.

The time zipped by while we splashed and bobbed, tracking clouds and floating aimlessly. Before I knew it, the winking sun hid behind the top branches of the last oak left standing out in midfield.

"Come on, Purdy," I called, trudging up the bank and rubbing muddied feet in the grass. "I still have to pick Rommel's stall." I squeezed my thick ponytail, sending a cascade of brown water down my back.

Purdy struggled to stand and shake herself again. I took off running, and Purdy took up the challenge. We raced to the barn and up the steep incline, which actually put us on the third level of the barn.

I'd purposely left the stall picking till last, knowing Ethan would be finished in the barn by then. Ethan worked for us— handyman, field worker, grain thrasher, whatever. He was a loudmouth drunk and when he wasn't aggravating somebody in town, he was here on the farm stalking me.

I hated him.

Half my life, seven of my fourteen years, had been spent try- ing to avoid him.

"Marilyn Monroe, that's who you look like," he'd say, wait- ing with his toothy grin as though he expected me to break into giggles of delight. If I broke into anything, it'd be a swift kick to his groin. I knew it wasn't my face he was staring at. If I sent him my head in a carton, I doubt he'd know whose it was.

"Hey there, Gal, you sure are a long, cool drink" was anoth- er one of his favorites as he watched me lug a milk pail down to the house. Sometimes, he'd just push his baseball cap back on his greasy brown head, lean his gangly self against the tractor or the hay bailer and look me up and down, not saying a thing. I can't count the times I quit the barn and left a job half finished because of him.

Rico, his sidekick, wasn't bad. Sometimes, I noticed him peering at me from behind a hen roost or from across the back- yard, but he kept his distance. He was grimy and he reeked from lack of soap and water, but at least he never spoke to me.

When I told Pa about Ethan, he asked me if he ever touched me. Even though Ethan's brains were in his overalls, he knew where to draw the line. "No, Pa, he never touched me," I said.

"Looking don't hurt nothing," Pa said. "Leave it be. Ethan is a good worker and that's not easy to find these days." He said that if Ethan ever did touch me, that'd be different. He said that if he ever tried to touch me, then he'd get rid of him. He also told me not to tell Ma.

Purdy won the race to the barn in a close finish. I draped

myself against the empty stall to catch my breath. A race with Purdy was still a losing proposition but I never quit trying. Someday, I thought, she's going to have an off day, and I wanted that winning feeling.

When I let go of the wall, finally breathing normally and able to stand upright, I looked around for Purdy. That's when I saw Ethan laying over by the silo opening, his nose buried in loose hay and spilled grain.

Let him lay there, I thought. I'm not going near him. Seven years of being scared and furious had done me in. If he wanted to lay there in that dry, scratchy stuff and suffocate, it was fine with me.

Purdy, after sniffing Ethan's limp body and nudging at his head, turned and looked square at me as if to say, "How about a little help over here?"

Oh, for God's sake, I thought, and grabbing the water hose, I filled the galvanized milk bucket. Fine, I decided, I'll empty a bucket of cold water over him and run.

"Out of the way, Purdy," I mumbled and aimed the trajectory straight at Ethan's face.

"Oooee!" I couldn't help squealing out with pleasure. I doused him good.

Ethan didn't move. Not even when I kicked him in the rump. Then, suddenly, his head rolled to the side and his jaw swung open. His glazed eyeballs, staring straight at me from his ashen face, sent a shiver through my spine.

"He's dead, Purdy," I whispered. "I think he's actually dead." I sat down on the hay bale near Rommel's stall to think. There was no reason to run for help, he was dead, and I didn't want to mess up the possibilities of the moment. The opportunity.

Ethan was gone, but it had been much too easy. He was finally out of my life, yes, but I wanted more. I sat there staring at the useless carcass thinking how unfair it was that he just up and died like that. No suffering, no discomfort. I didn't even have the pleasure of hearing Pa giving him what for, of seeing him run off the farm, of telling him he can't treat no daughter of his like he did and to never come back here.

And there was Ma. I wanted her eyes opened up about Ethan and the way he'd treated me all this time. She'd know, too, about how Pa had protected him. I wanted to see her give Pa a good piece of her mind for letting someone treat her little girl like that.

Sitting there in the quiet of the barn with Purdy dozing beside me, I knew what I really wanted was not revenge on Ethan; I wanted revenge on Ma and Pa.

I'd like to see Ma and Pa upset. I'd like to see them put out, annoyed, backed into a corner. I'd like to know whether they had it in them to stand up for me. That was another thing I'd never get to see.

This was not fair. Ethan didn't even know he was dead. He simply and quietly left the farm without one bit of suffering; without one bit of my being saved by Pa; without Ma standing up against Pa for letting it go on. No, it was not fair. I wanted justice.

It wasn't too late, I decided. Something could be made of Ethan's going. I jumped up so quickly Purdy jumped up too and barked. "It's okay, Purdy," I said. "Come on. Ethan isn't going to get away this easy."

Reaching into Rommel's stall, I grabbed the pitchfork and ran over to Ethan's body. Sliding the tines under his back, I rolled him until his arm hung over the lip of the silo. Then, with one last roll, I watched him plunge in a free fall, sending up a cloud of dust as he landed in the soft, dry store of grain.

Peeking over the silo's edge, I saw a hand and the heel of his shoe barely visible in the shadows of the long, dusty cylinder. Soon, when the fall harvest was in, more grain would slide down the chute and sometime next summer, with the silo cleaned out and readied for a new crop, there wouldn't be enough left of Ethan to examine. They'd identify him, but with no evidence of foul play, it would be a simple case of a fool falling into the silo. Happens every once in a while. Especially to the alcohol inclined.

Meanwhile, there'd be some excitement around here, everybody trying to figure out what happened to Ethan, investigators showing up, probably reporters and photographers, too. "Ethan off on a toot?" Pa'd wonder. "He's disappeared," Ma'd say. "Anybody see him go? Any messages from him? Who saw him last?" reporters and inspectors'd ask.

There wouldn't be any reason for me to get involved. Everybody knew full well that I stayed away from the creep. I wouldn't know where he was. I wouldn't have one iota of a clue. And the fact that I didn't care wouldn't surprise anybody either. I didn't know and I didn't care. He's gone and I hope he never comes back, that's what I'll say, and nobody ought to be surprised.

In the meantime, they'll have fall and winter to work it out. Why would he just jump up and leave, they'll wonder. Was it foul play? Maybe somebody killed him. Did he finally pick the wrong man to fight? Did somebody do him in? Things'll liven up around here, a mystery to get us through the winter. Pa and Ma would be agitated as hell.

And me? I could finally relax. I could go to the barn without planning my chores around him. I could just come and go. Free.

□   □   □

At some point after the dust had settled, I began to wonder about that foul-play question and whether somebody really did kill Ethan. More and more, as time went by, it seemed like a real possibility. He was sure easy to hate.

It could've been somebody on the farm, I thought, somebody I knew. Somebody who might've even been in the barn that day when I found Ethan, dead, on the floor next to the silo door.

One morning, I'd just reached the barn, deep in thought and pondering all those possibilities, when I was stopped dead in my tracks by a sound, a strange cackly grunt. Startled, I lifted my head seconds before slamming right into Rico, who was standing at the open door, his hands on his hips and his feet firmly planted in the packed dirt. The smell of his tobacco chaw and his dung-caked boots hit me straight on and curled my stomach.

Before he spoke, he spat to the side and wiped his sleeve across his chin. "Well, Missy," his voice was deep and clear, "with Ethan chewin' grain for all eternity down in that silo, looks like you and me are gonna be real good friends from now on."

My heart stopped and I felt the blood drain from my face. Purdy, crouching low against my leg, her tail between her legs, whimpered long and low.

The Intruder

Ruth M. McCarty

"Damn it." Mandy Perkins held the elegant crystal glass up to the window. The sunshine highlighted the chip she'd felt with her fingers. Mandy had spent the morning rewashing the glasses and china she'd used at the party she and her husband, Jake, had hosted the night before. Her guests had insisted on helping, and Jake had insisted she let them, even though he knew she'd have to wash everything again. It had taken all her self-control not to get up in the middle of the night to wash the dishware after he had insisted they go to bed.

She carefully wrapped the chipped glass in several sheets of newspaper and threw it in the trash. Now she had an uneven number of glasses! She'd have to buy a replacement as soon as possible.

As she polished the chrome faucet on her kitchen sink, she looked out at the autumn colors in the woods behind her house. She loved the subdivision. Their house sat back in the woods, barely visible from the street and secluded from the neighbors. Sometimes at night, though, when she was home alone, she missed the city, and wished her neighbors' houses were closer.

A loud rustling sound from above startled her. She cocked her head and listened. Jake had just left to buy a Sunday paper, so Mandy knew it couldn't have been him making the noise. Ever since they'd moved into the house, she'd heard strange noises at odd times. She'd mentioned the noises to the builder, but he'd just smiled. "You're in the country now," he'd said. "You'll have lots of intruders. It's probably field mice. Just put some traps in the cellar and the attic."

Mandy made a mental note to tell Jake about the latest noise when he returned. Maybe now they could go buy some of those politically correct traps and catch whatever was making the noise.

With the kitchen back in order, Mandy brewed a cup of tea and took it out to the deck to relax in the autumn sun. She'd no sooner sat down than she noticed the door to the shed was ajar. She put down her cup, crossed the lawn, and peered in. Annoyed at the leaves and dirt all over the wooden floor, she grabbed a broom and swept the mess into a pile, and then into a plastic bag, which she promptly put in the trash barrel. She shut the door tight before returning to her tea.

When Jake returned, he settled into his recliner and turned on the television to watch the football game. Mandy read the Sunday paper, then spent the afternoon sewing valances for the spare bedroom, the sound from above long forgotten.

□   □   □

Mandy stood at the counter the next morning when Jake came downstairs for breakfast. "Jake, do you want me to make you a sandwich, too?"

"No, I'll just come home for lunch and use up some of the leftovers from the party. That seafood casserole Libby brought last night was so good, I'm surprised there's any left."

Jake worked about five miles from their house, at an architectural firm. He'd heard about the subdivision from his boss, John Sullivan, who'd been one of the first to build there. "It's a great piece of property," he'd said, "except for the few older houses on the street heading up to it. The builder's buying them out one at a time, though, so he can tear them down and put up new ones. It's a great place to raise a family." Sullivan had been right. All the older houses except one had sold, and the subdivision had filled with young families.

"Well, just make sure you don't eat the chicken," Mandy said as Jake grabbed his car keys off the rack by the garage door. "I'm planning to use it for dinner tonight."

"Okay, honey," Jake said and brushed his lips on hers on his way out the door.

Mandy looked at the clock. She'd have to leave soon, but first she polished the granite countertop with a soft rag, straightened the kitchen chairs, and made sure all the burners on the stove were turned to the off position. Then she unplugged the coffee pot, her last ritual before leaving for her job at the mall. She'd be on her feet until five tonight and looked forward to just heating up leftovers when she returned home.

□ □ □

Although daylight savings time wouldn't end for a couple of weeks, the dense cloud cover had darkened the autumn sky. From the street, Mandy could barely make out the outline of the house. She drove up the wet, leaf-covered driveway and pressed her garage door opener. She and Jake had talked about putting up one of those automatic sensor lights, but it was just one more item they'd added to their punch list. At least a light came on inside the garage as she pulled in.

Mandy hung up her coat, traded her heels for comfortable slippers, and turned on lights as she walked to the kitchen. She noticed right away that the chairs were slightly out of place and a few crumbs littered the countertop.

Oh, Jake, she thought. He never got the chairs right, and no matter how many times she told him to use Windex and paper towels to wipe up the counter, he never did. He'd just smile at her when she complained. She knew she was being a little nutsy about it, but she loved this house and wanted it to look perfect.

Just like in the magazines.

Mandy set the table for supper. She'd bought the dishes with her employee discount and loved the way everything matched. She only needed to heat up the chicken and take out the tossed salad when Jake came home. Maybe she'd warm up some of the casserole too, that is, if Jake hadn't finished it at lunch.

She flipped through a home-decorating magazine until she heard the garage door open. She waited until Jake came into the kitchen, then put her arms around his neck and gave him a kiss. "If I knew that was waiting for me, I would have come home sooner." Jake smiled at her. "How about a glass of wine? I could use one after the day I had."

"Sounds good to me. I'll start dinner while you get it."

Mandy opened the refrigerator and pulled out the salad and a bottle of Italian dressing. She moved the chocolate éclairs left from the party and then pulled out the dish with the chicken. What the hell? There was only one breast left. "Jake," she hollered, "I told you not to eat the chicken I was saving for dinner."

Jake turned from the built-in bar with two glasses of wine in his hands. "Not guilty," he said. "I didn't get a chance to come home for lunch. I had a sandwich delivered."

"Very funny. There were two chicken legs and one breast on this plate this morning and now there's only the breast left."

Jake laughed. "Honey, I swear, I didn't eat it. I really didn't come home."

"But who ate the chicken?"

"You must have thought you had more than you did."

"No, I distinctly remember what was left after the party. I knew I wouldn't have to make a big dinner tonight."

Jake handed Mandy a glass of wine. "Maybe one of the guests took it out of the fridge when you were cleaning up. It was delicious."

"Well, maybe, but I'm positive there were three pieces there yesterday."

"It's no big deal. There must be something else we can throw together."

Mandy shrugged. "I guess. But, Jake, the chairs were messed up, and there were crumbs on the counter when I got home."

"Mandy, you probably forgot to push the chairs in after breakfast, and maybe you didn't wipe up after you made your sandwich. Who cares, anyway? The clean-house police?"

"I care."

Jake pulled Mandy into his arms. "Come on, let's go try that new Italian restaurant downtown."

They passed the old Reynolds house as they drove into town. The screen door sat at an angle because the top hinge had been broken for months. Three sides of the house had been painted mustard yellow several years earlier; the fourth had never been touched. Junk cars littered the yard.

"Damn, you'd think they'd paint that last section." Jake said. He swore about one thing or another every time they passed the house.

"Tommy Reynolds seems like a hard worker," Mandy said, trying to keep Jake in a good mood. Knowing how he felt about the Reynolds family, she'd been surprised when Jake had hired one of their many kids to help with the yard work. She'd watched Jake and the boy out the window on Saturday afternoon as she prepared the finger foods for the party that night. The temperature had reached fifty-eight degrees, a wonderful Indian summer day, and they both looked warm. Jake surprised her when he brought a glass of lemonade to the boy. He'd even brought out a towel so the kid could wipe his face. Mandy had bit her tongue when she'd noticed it was one of the brand new towels she'd bought especially for the party. She didn't remember washing it, though.

"Yeah, I guess he did work pretty hard. Let's hope he keeps it up," Jake interrupted her thoughts. "Oh, by the way, I gave him the code to the alarm system."

"You what?"

"Not the master, the one we can change when he's done helping with the yard work. I knew you wouldn't want him pissing in the bushes."

"Jake," Mandy said. He was right, but she didn't know which was worse, Tommy Reynolds urinating behind a tree or into her sparking clean toilet.

□ □ □

Mandy invited Libby over for a cup of tea on Wednesday, the only day Mandy got out at noon. As a real estate broker, Libby had a flexible schedule. Mandy still had Libby's casserole dish and was itching to give it back, so her countertop would be back to normal.

"Your party is the talk of the neighborhood," Libby said. "Especially your tiramisu."

Mandy smiled. She really liked Libby. Libby had a glow about her, always perfect from head to painted toenail and seemed so sophisticated compared to Mandy's other friends. A shame she was such a young widow.

As Mandy poured boiling water into Libby's cup, she heard a loud bang.

"What was that!" Libby jumped in her seat.

"It sounded like it came from the attic."

"I don't think so," Libby said. "It sounded to me like it came from outside."

"I don't know, Lib. I've been hearing a lot of strange noises, and they seem to be coming from up there." Mandy pointed to the ceiling above.

Libby got up and walked to the sliding glass door, then turned to Mandy and laughed. "Well, it looks like your flowerpot is the culprit."

Mandy crossed to the door and there on the deck, one of the new chrysanthemums she'd bought for the party had fallen and spilled dark soil on the pressure-treated wood.

"That's weird," Mandy said. "I could have sworn the noise came from the attic. Strange things have been happening lately."

"Like what?"

"Well, maybe I'm making too much of it, but on Monday, I planned to heat up the leftover chicken. I thought there were three pieces left, but there was only one. Of course, Jake said someone from the party must have eaten them . . . but . . . I guess he was right."

"Mandy, you did a great job, but there were a lot of people here. Maybe you just miscounted."

"Yeah, I guess, but . . .well . . . it's really creeping me out."

"Oh, before I forget. I saw one of those Reynolds boys crossing through your yard. It looked like he was heading for the woods."

"It must've been Tommy. Jake hired him to do some yard work."

Libby cringed. "I'd be careful if I were you. Those kids are trash."

□ □ □

After Libby left, Mandy thought about her warning. She'd have to tell Jake when he got home. She'd make him fire the boy and change the alarm code. She opened the sliding doors, and clutching a dustpan and brush, headed to the spilled plant. As she crouched to sweep it up, Tommy Reynolds stood up from beyond the railings and wiped the sweat from his forehead with the bottom of his t-shirt, exposing a six-pack abdomen.

"You scared the hell out of me," Mandy said. She felt her cheeks get warm as he defiantly looked at her, starting at her breasts, before reaching her eyes.

He mumbled sorry, then took off his shirt, threw it over the railing, and went back to pulling weeds from the autumn garden.

For the first time in her life, Mandy left a mess to clean up later.

□ □ □

Jake called at four to tell Mandy he'd be working late and hoped to be home around nine. Mandy figured he and the other guys would probably go out for pizza and beer after working late, so she opened a can of soup for her dinner. After cleaning up the kitchen, she went into the great room and turned on the Home and Garden channel, her favorite station. Lost in the "House Hunters" show, she nearly jumped out of her skin when the ceiling shook from a loud thud from above. Her heart felt like it was running out the door on its own. She reached for the fireplace poker and headed across the room, then yelled up the stairs, "Who's there?" She heard a creaking sound. "I'm calling the police!"

She dialed 911, then called Jake's cell phone, but got his voice mail instead. After what seemed like an eternity, two police officers, guns drawn, came rushing up the deck with Jake right behind them.

"Mandy, honey, are you all right?"

"There's someone up there!"

"Stay here," a blond baby-faced officer said. He and his partner headed up the stairs to the attic. After a few minutes, the officer called them up and aimed his flashlight beam into a dark corner in the back of the attic. "Looks like someone's been living here. The window's unlocked and there's an impression in the grass below that looks like a ladder."

"I keep a ladder in the shed," Jake said.

Mandy looked at the sleeping bags; one lay open on the floor and the other folded as if for a pillow. A paper plate and a beer-sized glass were on a cardboard moving box. When Mandy got closer, she put her hand to her mouth. "Oh, no. Chicken bones. My God, Jake, someone's been here all this time!"

"Al, get some bags out of the car so we can run a print on the glass," the officer said, then pointed to a pile of clothes on the floor. "Is that one of your t-shirts?" he asked Jake.

Jake shook his head. "No, not mine."

"Al, bag the clothes, too."

"Wait a minute," Mandy said. "Tommy Reynolds had on a shirt just like that this afternoon, and that looks like the one he wore on Saturday."

"Tommy Reynolds?" the baby-faced officer glanced over at his partner. "I'm sure we have his fingerprints on file. We'll check them against the ones on the cup."

"Jake, he has the alarm code!"

Jake looked at the officers. "It's a temporary one. I'll change it right away."

After the police left, Jake put his arm around Mandy. "Don't worry, honey. The police will get to the bottom of this. I'll bring the sleeping bags to the cleaners in the morning. And don't worry about this mess. I'll clean it for you. Now, come downstairs."

Jake changed the code before they went to bed. He fell asleep immediately and began to snore as if nothing had happened. Mandy, on the other hand, couldn't sleep. She felt sick at the thought that Tommy Reynolds had been living in their house. She knew what she had to do. She had to get up and scrub the mess.

Mandy dumped half a bottle of Lysol cleaner into a bucket of hot water and carried it to the attic. She got down on her knees and with gloved hands scrubbed the wood with a disposable cloth. The medicinal scent of the Lysol calmed her nerves. She moved the box that the plate and glass had sat on and was startled to find the missing towel in a heap behind it. She crept downstairs, got a plastic bag and a new pair of disposable gloves, crept back upstairs, then packed the towel to take to the police.

☐ ☐ ☐

When Mandy woke the next morning, Jake had already left for work. She hadn't had time to tell him about the towel. She called her boss, told her she'd be late, then headed to the police station to drop off the towel.

Later that afternoon, the older officer named Al stopped at the mall to see Mandy. "I just wanted to fill you in on what's going on. The fingerprints on the cup do belong to Tommy Reynolds. We stopped at his house this morning and spoke with his mother. She swears he sleeps at home every night, and that she had washed his t-shirt on Sunday night. She said she hung it on the line and it was missing the next morning when she went to get it. She figured the wind blew it away."

"What did Tommy say?"

"He wasn't home. We'll talk to him later tonight."

"Did you get the towel I left at the station? Jake let Tommy use it on Saturday. You know how hot it was that day." Mandy shook her head. "Jake brought him a drink, too."

The officer nodded. "Well, if you think of anything else . . ."

"Okay." Mandy said, then she remembered something. "Oh, wait. The other day Libby Johnson was over for tea, and we heard a crash. It turned out to be one of my flowerpots, but Tommy Reynolds was outside working on my garden. Libby tried to warn me about the Reynolds family. She said she saw Tommy cross my yard and go into the woods. Maybe he's into some cult-type of thing."

"Well, like I said, we're going to talk to him tonight. His mother said he'd be home around five."

Mandy stopped at Libby's on the way home and filled her in on what happened the night before. "Thank God you're all right," Libby said. "Those kids give me the creeps." The phone rang and Libby picked up on the second ring. "Sorry, I can't talk right now. I've got company." Then after a pause she said, "Yes. Uh-huh. I'll see you later."

"Sorry about that. One of my agents. He had some questions about one of the houses we have listed."

"You could have taken the call. I have to get going any way. I want to get home and lock up before it gets too dark."

"Well, be careful."

Mandy drove into the garage and watched in the rearview mirror to make sure no one ran in before it closed. She felt safer now that Jake had changed the code. If Tommy tried to get in the alarm would go off and the police would be there in a flash. Taking a deep breath, Mandy felt a little better. She took off her heels, put on her slippers, and headed to the kitchen to start supper. As she reached into the refrigerator to take out the carrots, she heard footsteps from behind. She only had a second to see the intruder in the perfectly polished, chrome toaster, before a single blow to the back of her head sent her flying to the floor.

□ □ □

Jake Perkins answered his cell phone on the third ring. "Mr. Perkins, you need to come home right away. There's been an accident."

Jake drove into the yard, slammed his SUV into park, and ran to the back of the house. Red blood was spattered over Mandy's clean kitchen. "What's happened?" Jake gasped, turning a sickly shade of white. "Where's Mandy?"

"Mr. Perkins, did you change the code on your alarm system?"

"Yes. I did last night. Please tell me, Is Mandy all right?"

"Why did you come to the back door and not the front?"

"Wh-what are you talking about? I figured Mandy would be in the kitchen. That Reynolds kid . . . he didn't break in, did he?"

"No, Mr. Perkins, he didn't break in. He looked through the window, saw your wife lying on the floor, opened the door with the key from under the mat, and set off the alarm. He didn't bother to turn it off, though. He just ran to the phone and dialed 911."

Jake Perkins closed his eyes. "My wife, is she dead?"

"No, Mr. Perkins. Tommy Reynolds saved her life. If he had come five minutes later she would have bled out."

Libby Johnson came running up the back deck. "Jake, what happened? I saw the police cars fly by my house."

"Libby," Jake warned. "Go home, you don't need to see this."

"Oh, my God! Look at all that blood. Tommy Reynolds must have killed her. I saw him on my way up here, running into the woods."

"Shut up, Libby." Jake said.

"That's funny, Libby," Officer Al said. "My nephew, Tommy Reynolds, is sitting in the other room with my partner." He turned to Jake, "Tommy told us how he thought you were pretty weird to be wearing gloves on the hottest day in October when you handed him that glass of lemonade, and he couldn't figure out why his t-shirt disappeared. Guess we all could figure that out now. It was the perfect setup. Almost. Oh, and by the way, the hospital just called. Your wife's going to live. Thanks to Tommy. Looks like you two better lawyer up."

Widow's Peak

S.A. Daynard

"Some scenic vista," he grumbled. "Hardly worth the trek."

"Not out there," she said, "down there."

"Where?"

"Over the edge. An outcropping that looks like a man. Move a little closer . . . closer . . . closer."

"I don't see a man down there."

She gave a shove, took a look, and shrugged. "I do."

Contributors' Notes

Skye Alexander is the author of numerous metaphysical books including *10-Minute Feng Shui, 10-Minute Clutter Control, 10-Minute Magic Spells, 10-Minute Tarot, 10-Minute Crystal Ball, The Care and Feeding of Your Chi, Magickal Astrology*, and *Planets in Signs*. Her first mystery novel, *Hidden Agenda*, won the Kiss of Death Award from the mystery division of the Romance Writers of America in 1998 for the year's best book of romantic suspense. Her stories have appeared in several anthologies including *Undertow, AstroMysteries, The Larcom Review*, and *Mystery in Mind*, and been translated into German, Portuguese, and Korean. More of the amorous adventures of Max McCoy are included in her novel "Confessions of an Aging American Playboy," which she hopes will be published soon. She lives in Gloucester, MA.

Elizabeth Armstrong lives in Newton, MA, with her family. Raised in the Midwest, she graduated with a BS in Nursing from the University of Iowa. After working as a nurse for six years, she attended law school at the University of North Carolina at Chapel Hill, where she received a J.D. with Honors, was articles editor for the *Law Review*, and won the Joyner Award for legal writing. Following a clerkship with the North Carolina Supreme Court, Elizabeth worked as an assistant district attorney for Durham County. Her work has been published in legal journals, *The Bishop's House Review*, and *The Independent Weekly*.

Catherine Cairns lives and writes in Massachusetts. Her work has appeared in *Women's World*, Kate Harper Greeting Cards, and *New England Writers' Network*. Her essay "Consensus" won the *Writer's Digest* Chronicle Contest (March 2004). A member of Sisters in Crime and Mystery Writers of America, she loves history and murder mysteries and has combined them in her first mystery novel, now in search of an agent. Her web site is www.catherinecairns.com.

Kevin Carey lives in Beverly, MA, where he edits film and video, coaches basketball, and often writes at the Atomic Café. He has recently received an MFA in Creative Writing from Fairleigh Dickinson University in New Jersey.

John R. Clark is the Library Systems Specialist for the Maine State Library. He began writing for local newspapers and library publications in the mid 1980s. He writes fantasy and dark fiction and is currently working on a series about Berek Metcalf, a Maine farm boy who discovers his magic abilities when drawn to an alternate world. John is a regular contributor to the Maine literary magazine *Wolf Moon Press* and is internet editor for *Behavioral and Social Sciences Librarian*. He lives in Hartland, ME.

S. A. Daynard lives in New Hampshire. She is a member of the New England Chapter of Sisters in Crime and Mystery Writers of America. Her short stories have been published in *The Threshold!, Shiver, The Bohemian Chronicle*, and *Undertow: Crime Stories by New England Writers*.

Clayton Emery is an umpteen-generations Yankee, Navy brat, and aging hippie who grew up playing Robin Hood in the forests of New England. He's been a blacksmith, dishwasher, school teacher in Australia, carpenter, zookeeper, farmhand, land surveyor, volunteer firefighter, and award-winning technical writer. Clayton lives in New Hampshire with Susan, his doctor wife, spends his time restoring a 1790 house and gardens, and following the adventures of his son Hunter in the Coast Guard.

Kate Flora, Maine native, is the author of six books in the Thea Kozak series featuring tall, tough, chip-on-her shoulder consultant Kozak and her state trooper significant other, Andre Lemieux. She recently completed "Stalking Death," the seventh book in the series. As Katharine Clark, she is the author of the suspense novel, *Steal Away*. A lapsed attorney and full-time writer, Flora teaches writing for the Brown Learning Community, Grub Street, and the Maine Writers and Publisher's Alliance. She is a past international president of Sisters in Crime. With two other authors, she has formed Level Best Books, a publishing cooperative. Their first book, *Undertow*, an anthology of New England Crime stories, was published in November, 2003. She is currently working a true crime story about a murder in Portland, Maine. Her website is: www.kateflora.com.

Judith Green is a sixth-generation resident of a village in the Western Mountains region of Maine (although her credentials were tarnished by education out of state), and she is delighted that generations number seven and eight live nearby. She is the director of Adult Education for an eleven-town area, and writes high interest/low level stories for adult new readers, with twenty-five volumes in print. She is currently working on a novel featuring Margery Easton.

Roberta Isleib, New Jersey born clinical psychologist, took up writing about golf psychology to justify the time spent maintaining a whopping handicap. Her debut novel, *Six Strokes Under*, was nominated for an Agatha and an Anthony. *A Buried Lie* was released in 2003 and Putt to Death in 2004. *Fairway to Heaven* will follow in spring 2005. Roberta lives with her family in Madison, CT. Her website is http://www.robertaisleib.com

Toni L. P. Kelner, in addition to being an avid mystery reader, is a fan of science fiction and the television show *Buffy the Vampire Slayer*. All three of these interests show up in the story "Security Blanket." Kelner has published over a dozen short stories, and her short fiction has been nominated for the Agatha, the Anthony, and the Macavity awards. Kelner is also a mystery novelist, and has written eight books in the Laura Fleming mystery series. *Wed and Buried*, the latest, was released in paperback in July 2004.

Janice Law is a teacher and novelist. She has written the Edgar nominated Anna Peters series of mystery novels and regularly publishes short stories in *Ellery Queen* and *Alfred Hitchcock Mystery Magazines*. Her most recent publications are the contemporary novels, *The Night Bus, The Lost Diaries of Iris Weed*, nominated for the Connecticut Center for the Book Fiction Prize in 2003, and *Voices*. She teaches part time at the University of Connecticut.

Edith Maxwell is the author of linguistic treatises, award-winning technical manuals, and fiction, including short stories that have appeared in *The Larcom Review* and the *North Shore Weekly*. She has also written a book of memoirs about life in a West African country, "A Year in Ouagadougou." She is a fourth-generation Californian who has lived in Massachusetts for twenty-two years and has spent several years abroad in Japan, Brazil, Mali, and Burkina Faso. Her first mystery novel is in progress.

Ruth M. McCarty is a member of Sisters in Crime and Mystery

Writers of America. Her short story "Not My Son" appeared in *Undertow: Crime Stories by New England Writers*, an anthology by Level Best Books. She received honorable mention in the *Alfred Hitchcock Mystery Magazine*, September 2001 issue, for the March 2001 Mysterious Photograph Contest.

Michael Milliken can't escape New England. He was born in Maine, where he currently resides outside of Portland, and educated in Connecticut at Yale University. He later received a Masters in Fiction Writing from the University of New Hampshire. This publication is his first.

Susan Oleksiw, a co-founder of Level Best Books, is the author of the Mellingham series featuring Chief of Police Joe Silva; the most recent title in the series is *Friends and Enemies* (Worldwide, 2003). Her short stories featuring Hindu American photographer Anita Ray have appeared in *Alfred Hitchcock Mystery Magazine* and elsewhere. A consulting editor for the *Oxford Companion to Crime and Mystery Writing* (OUP, 1999), she is also the editor of a series of reader's guides to crime fiction published by Macmillan/GK Hall. She was also a co-founder and editor of *The Larcom Review*.

Carol Perry is a member of Sisters in Crime and the International Woman's Writer's Network. She has been published in the New England Writer's Network magazine and won its Humorous Short Story Award in 2001. She has been published in *Tapestries*, an anthology, and won honorable mentions in *ByLine Magazine*. After a long career in education, she now dedicates her time to writing, often calling upon her rural Massachusetts upbringing for inspiration. She is working on her first mystery novel and has written a book of historical fiction.

Barbara Ross is a Boston-based writer and former editor of

SheDunnit! the newsletter of the New England Chapter of Sisters in Crime. Many of the characters in this story are featured in her just completed mystery "An Ambitious Woman," for which she is seeking representation. Her current project, "Receptivity, Inc.," draws on her experience as co-founder and chief operating officer of a successful internet company.

Kathleen Valentine is a professional graphic artist and web designer. She has written about art for publications such as *American Art Review* and authored the exhibition catalog *Legacy: The Artist Families of the North Shore* for the prestigious North Shore Arts Association. Her many inspirational columns for the Gloucester *Daily Times* are on-line at www.parlezmoi-press.com. She is currently at work on her second novel.

Riptide
Crime Stories by New England Writers

edited by
Skye Alexander, Kate Flora,
& Susan Oleksiw

Please send me _____ copies @ $14 per copy _____

postage & handling ($2 per book) _____

Total $_____

_____ check (payable to Level Best Books)

_____ credit card

Name on card _____

Card No. _____

Expiration date _____

Send book(s) to:

Name _____

Address _____

City/Town _____